HellBound

Dria Andersen

Copyright © 2020 Dria Andersen

All rights reserved.

ISBN: 978-1-7321126-7-4

Dedication

To my husband who is my sounding board, my cheerleader, my critique partner, and all the things I needed to finish this project. I appreciate every hour, every word of input and most of all, your unwavering support.

To my family who had to deal with the random meltdowns and moments of frustration. Thank you for your patience.

To my sister Tina, who reads everything I write and gives me honest feedback and encouragement, thank you mucho mucho. I appreciate your continued support and cheerleading!

Also, to my Auntie Cathy who, probably unbeknownst to her, first fueled my love for reading. It's her bookshelf I raided for all things romance.

Thank you to every fan who continues to stick with me while I tell the stories playing in my head. I appreciate each and every one of you.

Author's Note

It's hard to know what to write in the author's note, so most of the time I skip it. But, in this case, I'm just so overwhelmed with having finally finished this series. I started it in 2010 with just an idea that I thought was maybe too fantasy to be paranormal and would be hard to sell, but I really wanted to tell the story. It took me six years to get down the story I wanted, with the characters and creatures that I thought would make a compelling story. They all started from a random list of gods I'd found from an online post. All I wanted when I started the series was to build a world of otherworldly creatures that were Black. I felt like, at the time, there were not a lot of fantasy-based love stories with Black characters.

Now, ten years later, I am finished with the Tegan brothers and the Haven series and am super proud of myself. There were a handful of years in there that I didn't think I'd be able to finish it. This isn't the end of the world of Demi, I have a few stories planned and I'm sure the Tegan brothers will pop up in some of the other stories, but this is the last of their stories. I hope you guys have liked the world that I built and I'm truly thankful for those of you who have stuck with me through the whole thing.

Table of Contents

Prologue

The god Azra stared at the wall, his mind clouded with grief and he hated to say it…fear. His chamber was empty, not even furniture conjured in the stone room. It stood empty, the twenty-foot white walls seemingly endless. It matched the static of his thoughts and suited his mood. Even the chair in which he sat was white, there was no color in the room save him. Which made the burst of light moments later that much brighter when his brother flashed into the room.

"I was just thinking how awesome guests would be at this time," Azra said dryly.

Rugaba growled and stood in front of him. His six-foot-seven body looming over Azra's sitting position. Azra blinked lazily and sighed before gazing up into his brother's face.

"A daughter, Azra?"

Pain stabbed through him and instead of answering, Azra tightened his hands into fists, turning his gaze back to that blank wall. In his mind, he brought up the image of his daughter's mother. Deena's wide and shapely hips, her full lips, but mostly her dark eyes. He'd been first ensnared by the innocent curiosity in her eyes. Her curly hair had been pushed back with a printed scarf, leaving those large eyes to dominate her face, and pull him in.

"Why have you kept this from me?" His brother's voice pushed away the image.

"Her mother kept her from me!" He snapped, resentful that he'd been pulled from his brooding by his brother.

Rugaba studied him as their gazes crashed together. "I could have looked out for her, Azra."

He scoffed. "And let you see my child when I couldn't." He hated to admit to the petty feeling.

"You left her up there with those…those…you left her with humans, to fend for herself."

"Because you think I would leave my daughter to those wolves if I had any other choices." Azra shook his head.

"She has a Kokoro soul," Rugaba stated, his anger lighting his eyes.

Azra shrugged, because what could he say to that? He would not apologize for giving his daughter one of the stronger souls accessible to a human, or rather part human. His daughter was a demi-god. No simple human soul would do.

"You knew where she was, this whole time. You questioned why I helped Oya, knowing you used one of the souls for your daughter."

"Careful of your tone in my realm, brother," Azra warned, irritated by the truth that hit a little too close to home at the moment.

Rugaba growled and took a step closer. "How did you get her to do it?"

Aah, so it was jealousy angering his brother at this moment. Rugaba and Oya was a relationship long dead, and something his brother was still not over. Azra debated telling his brother a lie, but he could never be called tactful.

"She stole from me, Rue. A favored was owed."

Rugaba paced away, his anger sending a prism of color dancing against the white walls of Azra's chamber. He whipped back to his brother.

"Your daughter doesn't know you."

Pain lanced through him and his voice abandoned him. He crossed his arms over his chest.

"Why would you give her such a strong soul and leave her to the humans to raise?"

"Her birth was an accident, but I will not apologize for my daughter's existence." Azra ground out between his clenched teeth.

"You've always been careful," Rue said thoughtfully. "I wonder what's so different about this human."

He turned his head, his anger, and grief still fresh.

"I sent her to the Meadows."

The Meadows, a peaceful place on Alafia, one reserved for souls to rest. It was where she'd belonged, and Azra was happy she'd been granted it. Deena had been all innocence and light until he'd come into her life. He stood and turned his back on his brother, hiding his emotion.

"You didn't have to do that, I thank you." He finally managed.

"She worshiped me, despite being tossed aside by her Esin, she was still faithful. I take care of what's mine."

Azra whipped around, it was on the tip of his tongue to deny that she was ever his brother's. But what could he say? Deena had never really belonged to him. Though she'd given her heart to him, it was to Rugaba she prayed when she needed help. He swallowed his anger.

His brother watched him, his eyes curious, empathetic. "What of the girl?"

Azra cleared his throat. "I sent your man to retrieve her. She'll be safe at Haven shortly."

He left out the part about it being one of many favors Fallon had done for him.

Rugaba let out a relieved breath. "I trust you to do what's right with regards to your daughter."

"I would end—"

"Guard your words, Azra!" Rue snapped, interrupting him.

Azra swallowed his anger, knowing Rugaba was right. Anything from his mouth would come to pass, and what he'd nearly said…he shuddered.

A bright light flashed and an angry Oya stepped from it. The beautiful goddess was in her traditional burgundy robes, them flaring behind her as wind swept through his once still chamber.

"So many visitors," Azra murmured.

"I despise you." Oya snapped.

"And yet, this is your second time visiting me in such a short time." He taunted.

She growled.

Rugaba stepped between the two of them. "What's happening?"

"The activity around my temple has picked up." She spat.

Azra looked between his brother and Oya, a sinking sense of doom besetting him.

"Why are you here, Oya?" Rue asked.

"Something has set the Ajo off, they are hunting in groups, that's unprecedented, and there are Demi with them."

Rugaba gave Azra a confused look. "And what has that to do with my brother?"

Azra swallowed a curse, already knowing what she would say. Grief for Deena swamped him anew, along with the certainty that all his chickens were finally coming home to roost.

She growled. "The beacon."

"Which beacon?" Rugaba looked between the two of them.

"The one that allows someone to find any soul in any part of the underworld." Oya hissed.

Rugaba gave Azra a sharp look. "Brother, you wouldn't."

"I needed a way for my daughter to visit me."

Deena would never have been able to travel to Azreal, but his daughter, his flesh and blood, could. He wanted a way for her to find him safely on her first visit if he were so lucky. Despite the danger the Earth was now facing, he still couldn't find an ounce of regret for it.

Rugaba sighed and rubbed a hand down his face. "From the top, if you please."

Oya growled and started pacing. "Fuck the top, from now, now! My tribe is in danger from this."

"I sent a soldier from the Amanda to retrieve it. Once it's at Haven, Leonalph can bring it back to me." He sat back in the lone chair in the room.

Oya crossed her arms over her chest. "You gave the beacon to a human for safekeeping."

He narrowed his eyes, not liking her tone. "My daughter's mother, yes. But my daughter is now in possession of it."

"So another human has the beacon?" Rugaba reiterated.

"One with a Kokoro soul no less," Oya grumbled.

"Azra, even for you that's reckless." Rue sighed.

"She is Demi," he first corrected. "I've had people watching her," he said stubbornly. There were no shortage of Demi ready to make a deal with 'the devil'. There had always been someone looking out for his daughter.

"She was never in any danger."

Oya scoffed, "you clearly haven't been keeping tabs on that girl. She dives headlong into danger."

Azra growled. "I have kept her safe."

Oya shrugged, she couldn't deny him that. No matter the scrapes his daughter got in, he saved her.

Rugaba looked between them. "You were both hiding this from me."

"You're the god of fate, brother, who's to say you wouldn't have made her life worse." Azra pointed out. It was one of the reasons Rugaba didn't interact with humans, outside of the Primal Source's decree.

Rugaba inclined his head conceding his point. "Back to the matter at hand. So, to recap, Azra stupidly gave a human the beacon, giving the Demi a way to find Ofeeree, once of course, they find Oya's temple and crossed into this realm," his brother ticked off with his fingers. He turned to Oya, "and the three souls needed to unlock his prison are out in the world. Do I have the right of it?"

Said in such a succinct way, Azra realized how fucked they were. "The Amanda will do their job. You trust them right?"

At this point, he could only put his faith in the Tegan brothers. It was on them to save the Earth. The three of them shared a worried look.

Chapter 1

Asa's nose twitched at the smell of stale coffee that rose from the kitchen. She didn't want to be here long. At least no longer than needed. The landlord had been reluctant to let her in, but she'd threatened to call the police. He only gave her a few minutes and she could tell he'd already gone through and taken some of what she was sure Herman considered 'valuables'. She didn't care. There were a few items of her mother's she wanted but then the asshole's relatives could have the rest.

She shuddered as she passed the couch where he'd spent so much of her youth. The apartment was different, but that couch…it was memory-laden, and none of them good. Asa could still picture him there, hunkered down in the seat cushions, a beer in one hand, and the other hand free to slap her at a moment's notice.

She hated him.

And though it gave her a moment's guilt, Asa was glad Herman was dead. Her mother's husband, she didn't deign to call him her stepfather, had died three weeks ago. Suicide, the authorities had said. Too bad he hadn't done the world a favor and jumped off the roof prior to killing Deena. She shook her head and got back to the task at hand. He'd been awaiting trial for her mother's death. How he'd gotten out of jail in the first place was a mystery to everyone involved in the case. It didn't matter to her, he was dead, and she couldn't care less about the state's idea of justice.

She swallowed her bile as she walked into the sparse bedroom that the monster had once shared with her mother and had lived in alone up until three months ago when he'd beaten Deena to death. She wanted to cry, she wanted to rage, but instead, she choked it down and walked to the small closet where some of her mother's clothes still hung.

She'd tried over the past year to come and retrieve her mother's things, but Herman had not let her come get anything, threatening her life if she so much as stepped foot near his apartment building. Rage had darkened his face, spittle leaving his mouth as he railed and blamed Asa for Deena leaving. She'd finally got through to her mother, had finally convinced Deena to leave the bastard and Herman hadn't taken it well. Unknown to her, he'd spent the last year looking for her mother. Until he'd finally found her…and killed her. Despite Asa's best efforts, a tear escaped.

She knelt at the door of the closet and reached back around some boxes Herman kept to disguise what he'd taken for ransom from her mother. Her hand gripped another cardboard box and she pulled it from the dark. She couldn't say how she knew where it was, or why this particular box was it, but as always, her instincts led to treasure. Some more valuable than others.

This more valuable than anything.

More tears collected and spilled over as she traced the picture of her as a small girl, wrapped in her mother's arms taped down to the top of the box. She didn't dare open it and let the memories out. There would be time for that later. A more appropriate place to grieve. She hugged the small box close and stood, giving a cursory glance around to the place that looked like it had never seen the other side of a cleaning product. She didn't feel sorry for Herman and what he'd become without her mother at his beck and call. She hoped he was currently rotting in hell.

Asa left the apartment and flipped a bird to the landlord on the way to the small compact she'd bought for her mother to get around. Deena hadn't wanted to take it, claimed she could catch the bus everywhere she needed to go. Asa sighed. Deena was so stubborn. And secretive. She'd found that out once she started handling the details of her mother's estate. Deena had been well cared for. And it wasn't just the money Asa sent back monthly to her. There had been money from an unknown benefactor. She'd not known that until a few days ago when she'd met with the bank manager.

Bank manager.

It blew her mind. She thought her mother poor. Assumed Deena had struggled mightily to send her through college. What other reason had they lived in the shithole with that crazy bastard for so long if not for that? Deena had had money, but she'd let that asshole steal it and use it to drink and be lazy on the couch. Asa had always found her mother confusing, even more so in her death. She'd found a note from Herman telling Deena that she could finally come and get her stuff. It had been what lured Deena out of hiding and had allowed that monster access. She glanced over at the unassuming box and drummed her fingers on the steering wheel.

What the hell was so important that her mother would meet with Herman?

She looked up as a horn behind her blew. She raised a hand, waved, and took off. She peered into the side mirror as the hairs on the back of her neck stood up. It was a sixth sense she'd honed in her job. Treasure hunting—what was labeled 'asset retrieval' on her taxes— was not for the faint of heart. There was always someone out to get what she'd uncovered, not to mention clients that may or may not have been on the right side of the law. She had her own set of enemies. She took a bunch of nonsense turns to flush out the person following her. On her fourth right turn, she spotted a car following her. The car itself was nondescript. A medium silver sedan, something that wouldn't have otherwise stood out as different. Except, Asa was always hyperaware of what went on around her. They probably hadn't counted on that. She squinted and counted two people in the car. For some reason, though alarmed, she wasn't overly worried. She sped and turned some corners and lost them. She pulled onto her mother's street.

Son of bitch.

The car that had been following her was parked near Deena's house. A man waved from the driver's seat and she narrowed her eyes. She'd underestimated them. Who the hell were they and what did they want with her? Most importantly, no one but her assistant knew where she was, so how did they find her? She parked in the driveway and got out of the car, looking back at them. When they didn't move, she entered the house and hit the deadbolt. She went to the living room window, moving aside the heavy brocade curtains, and peered out to the street.

The man was standing across the street, leaned against his car. He was tall and bulky, his all-black clothes and menacing demeanor, giving her security vibes. Who did he work for, then? He waved at her again. He held up a small note and pointed to her front porch. She closed the curtain and debated what to do. A few moments later, his heavy footfalls sounded on the front porch and she tensed. His steps retreated and the house went silent.

Was it a potential client? It wasn't the first time someone had hunted her down, probably wouldn't be the last. She was good at her job, and word of mouth moved swiftly in the small circle she inhabited. She fixed herself some lunch, eating at the kitchen counter amid the moving boxes until curiosity finally got to her. She peeked out the window and the man's car was gone. She looked out the peephole. Not seeing anything, she grabbed the bat by the front door and opened it. There was a note taped to the front door. She snatched it, looked around, and closed the door. She put down the bat and unfolded the note. It was an address of a local cafe and the words:

Just one meeting.

She looked to the bottom of the note and it had *Fallon Tegan* and a phone number; that was it. She folded the note and tapped it against her chin. So a job then. She sighed and set the note on the table by the door. She didn't know that she was ready to start back with work. She needed to pack up the rest of her mother's things and figure out what she wanted to do with the house. Asa looked around at the half furnished house, still littered with unopened and unpacked boxes. The wood floors and high ceilings had been a selling point for Asa, while her mother had gushed over the front porch. In the many places they'd lived, they'd never had one.

Aside from the fancy blackout curtains and a few pieces of furniture here and there, Deena had been in the house a year, and nothing was put into place. Each time Asa had visited she'd been the one to buy furniture. The overstuffed couch facing the fireplace, the queen-sized bed in the guest room where Asa slept…all of it had been bought by her. Deena had been content that her kitchen was stocked and her bedroom was comfortable. Had her mother known how little time she'd had? She looked at the note again. She could put off dealing with her mother's things. Taking another job would push it off for a few more months. Maybe that was the best thing to do.

Chapter 2

On most days Xavier could go through the song and dance of forced niceness.

Today, though...

He sighed. Today would be pushing the very limits of his patience. He adjusted in the leather chair at his desk and swallowed the streak of curse words bubbling up. He was operating on about three hours of sleep. His dreams or lack thereof had him restless. For the past year, he'd been having erotic dreams, which, in and of themselves had not been bad, but waking up with a raging hard-on and not being able to satisfy it was taking its toll. Even taking matters into his own hand only worked half the time. For the last two months though, the dreams had been missing, and he was having a hard time sleeping without them. He'd found himself waking up once an hour trying to chase the dreams.

This morning he'd given up on sleep and had been in his office since the early dawn. He hadn't even bothered to get dressed, opting for the all black uniform of the Amanda. The cargo pants, polo, and black boots were ingrained in his head, thus the easiest thing to manifest on his tired body. The only light in the room was coming from the holographic screens of his comms station. The high tech computer had three screens he toggled through as he worked. He pinched the bridge of his nose with one hand and flipped through the screens with the other. There was a treaty dispute, a brewing coup, and all manner of thefts that needed his attention before the plethora of Demi complaints and requests in his emails could even be glanced at.

The light in his assistant's office flicked on, and the scent of her perfume drifted into his office. The next smell to hit him was that of coffee. He squinted at the clock on the other side of his desk, his eyes as tired as his body. It was barely seven a.m.

"Why?" Adia asked as she slapped the button on the wall that controlled the lights in his office.

Xavier hissed as light flooded the room. "I work better in the dark."

"Lies." She set a large mug of coffee in front of him. "You have several items on your agenda today." She narrowed her eyes, her gaze tracing his face. "From the looks of it, we're not getting nice Marshal this morning."

"Fuck nice," He murmured, after taking the first sip from his cup.

Adia was a young Benu, beautiful in the human skin she'd chosen to cover her first form. Her large wings were tucked and hidden with the magic all demigods used when on Earth. Caramel skin, dark brown eyes, and a messy plethora of red curly hair surrounded her face, the high cheekbones standing out. She'd run from her home and Liliana had rescued her. He sighed. There was no telling how many rescued people Liliana had working up and through Haven. He didn't actually mind because his sister-in-law was good at what she did. She read people like no one he knew. He'd had no cause to complain since Adia had started eight months ago as his executive assistant. She didn't flinch at his outbursts of temper, she didn't so much as blink when dignitaries came into his office or on his communication line demanding time from him.

The Benu thought a lot of themselves, and despite his new assistant being a runaway, her attitude was every inch a Benu noble. She didn't think he knew her background but he did. She was running from her Ileri, her betrothed, and even as he knew, he kept her secret. She was very young, he could understand her reluctance in settling down with two mates who would be demanding.

Adia sighed. "Your first appointment is already on the way here. He called to make sure you hadn't canceled again."

"Screen whoever it is and send them away if you can."

She rolled her eyes but left to do his bidding. He closed his eyes and savored the caffeine flowing through his tired body. Using his magic, he dimmed the lights a notch, still unable to take the glare. He looked around at his new office, happy for the move. It was a bigger room and had the added benefit of the outer office in which Adia occupied. She sat between him and the annoyances that came with running the Amanda. He appreciated that more than anything. He'd moved his favorite paintings down, as well as the leather sofa he'd slept many nights in, but everything else in the office was new. The fancy oak desk he sat behind, as well as the chairs in front and behind said desk. Liliana, his sister in law, had covered the stone floor with a lush carpet under his desk, and though he'd never tell her, he did enjoy sinking his bare feet into it on the late nights he worked.

Finishing his coffee, he went back to the treaty dispute he was working on. It was annoying, the two realms were fighting over something that even the oldest person on the realm couldn't remember. Adia's face popped up on his office communicator. He growled at her interruption.

"What?"

"You need to take this appointment."

"You couldn't get rid of them?"

She gave a sheepish look off to her left before glaring back at him. "He is here earlier than his appointed time, but he says it's that important."

"What does he want?" He toggled through his screens, a breath from just hanging up on his assistant. He didn't have the spoons to deal with appointments and the work on his desk. "Just send him down to Liliana. She's back at her desk and can handle help reqs now."

She sighed but said nothing. He stopped working and gave her his attention.

"It's not a help req, it's a safety issue."

He closed the hologram of Adia and called his sister in law. Liliana's image popped up immediately, her chipper smile grating on his already strained nerves. She too was in her human skin. Radiant light brown skin and long, curly hair made her green eyes stand out. Her skin tone was complemented by some kind of green blouse she wore with a vee deep enough to show off the curves she'd received and kept from the birth of her first child.

"Good morning, Marshal."

"Get down here." He ordered.

She smiled sweetly but raised a finely arched eyebrow.

He sighed. "I'm sorry. Please."

"Be there in a sec." Her image blinked out and left his office in silence.

He went back to his work, pushing the whole thing from his mind. At least, he tried to work. His mind went back to his mystery woman and his missing dreams. Why had the dreams stopped? For the past year, he'd been having dreams about the beautiful woman, her lavender eyes haunting him. They had started innocent enough, the two of them just talking. He'd found an outlet in her, telling her about his day and the troubles with his job. The dreams had taken an erotic turn before stopping altogether. He missed them, and her.

"Xavier."

He growled and looked up, startled out of his thoughts. Liliana stood in front of him. "What?"

"You're going to want to hear this." She escorted an older looking male into the office and sat him down in the chair in front of his desk.

He closed the screens on his comms station, blanking out the computer altogether. Liliana sat on the corner of his desk.

The male cleared his throat, fidgeting with the cable knit sweater he wore over a t-shirt and slacks. He looked put together, not necessarily wealthy, but nothing about his demeanor said that he went without. Xavier did observe the healthy pallor of the male's human skin that told him either the man had a lot of power or spent a lot of time under the power of Earth's sun. It wasn't unusual for some Demi to settle on Adro, opting to live on the realm and in their human skin. Still…Xavier was always suspicious of those who chose to do so. It often meant giving up the use of the Demi's stronger powers in an effort to better blend in with the humans.

The Demi as a rule coveted power and did not willingly give it up.

Xavier looked down at his schedule, noting Patrick's name and where he lived. He'd have Fallon do a cursory check of the area to make sure nothing unlawful was going on.

"I've been trying to get on your schedule for a couple of months. I decided to drive down from Tennessee in the hopes you'd see me."

Xavier blinked at him, not saying a word.

Liliana waved her hand, "go on."

Patrick re-started his story. "There was an older woman, human, who moved onto our block about a year ago."

"Gods above, Lily." Xavier snapped.

"Patience, Grouchy." She said with a smile.

He sat back in his chair. "Pick up the pace of this story, or just skip to the end if you please."

Liliana rolled her eyes. "Go on, Patrick."

"She died a few months ago, and then all of a sudden the neighborhood got another raise in power."

Xavier frowned. "Another?"

"The human had some kind of power; we initially dismissed it as Divine power. But a little after she died it changed, was bigger."

"Why do I care about human power?"

"Just finish the story, Patrick." Liliana cut in.

Patrick shrugged. "We weren't able to figure out what kind of power the old woman had, but then her daughter moved in and—"

"Who is we?"

"I'm a part of the neighborhood association, we look after the safety of our neighborhood."

So there was more than one Demi gathered. He would definitely send Fallon there to do an inspection. Xavier rubbed his temples. "Lily, this could be handled by Fallon or someone in the security office. Why do I have to hear this?" He turned to Patrick. "I'll send someone out there to investigate the source of the power. Has anyone in the neighborhood been harmed?"

Patrick shook his head, panic in his eyes.

"Then get out of my office."

Patrick scrambled out.

Liliana crossed her arms over her chest. "That was rude, Xavier."

"Lily, I don't have time for this kind of stuff, why do you think I was so quick to send files down to you. I don't want to handle this type of petty shit."

She put her hands on her hips. "What he neglected to tell you in his haste out of the door, is that the power was not just human power, but god powers he felt."

"What?"

She gave him a smug smile. "Do I have your attention now?"

"Why did I have to hear it from him?"

Xavier glared at his sister in law. Liliana was drawing out this male's visit if only to fuck with him. He knew, and she knew, hence the smirk she wore on her face.

"It would've taken you ten seconds to say that. I didn't need a back story." He grumbled.

"You're impossible, and I don't know why Adia has lasted longer than the other assistants I've sent to you."

He shrugged. "She gets me."

Lily snorted.

He ignored her and dialed Fallon on his communicator, but then cursed. His brother was away. He ended the transmission and called his youngest brother instead. Leo strolled in before the call connected. Xavier frowned at the sweatpants and sleeveless sweatshirt his brother wore. He was in his third form, the mix that showed both his Cagyn and Eshu heritage. His long multi-colored black hair was tied at the top of his head into a bun, the copper power lines from their Cagyn heritage, lit with power, and running up and down Leo's exposed muscled arms.

"Why are you out of uniform?"

"Hello, my love," Leo murmured, leaning over Liliana to nibble at her lips. He turned to his brother when they were done. "I'm training this morning, why, what's up?"

Xavier pulled out the file on Patrick Adia had given him, and then pulled up the Oras for the Demi neighborhood where Patrick lived, ignoring his brother's question. The Oras they used to surveil the Earth realm were nearly identical to the satellites humans used, except that the magic they used made them more accurate, and all-encompassing. The only other people with access to them, outside of him and his brothers were maybe two other shift commanders. Xavier frowned and moved through the Ora screens.

Leo sat in the chair Patrick had vacated and stretched his legs out, flipping through the file. He didn't repeat his question, used to Xavier's moods.

"The address is wrong." He murmured, flipping through the datebook Adia made him keep on his desk. Any time someone asked to see him, they were required to submit all their information, including their current address if they were staying on Earth.

He found the address and matched it to the one in the file, then went back to his comms station and typed in the address. The Oras went black and came back up with images of areas nowhere near the address. He pulled up the map overlay and swiped to put it over the images. The address Patrick had given was a dark spot, no imaging.

He turned his gaze to Liliana. "When did the male say the power moved into the neighborhood?"

"When the old woman died?" she answered.

Xavier growled.

Leo snickered. "You're so mean, X. You gotta relax."

"How long ago?"

Liliana tapped her temples. "If only we had someone who could answer that."

He gave his sister in law a droll look. He stabbed the call button on his desk. "Adia, call that male back into my—"

The door opened and Patrick walked back in, wringing his hands.

Xavier smiled, "See, she gets me. I don't know why you sent down those other six, they were terrible assistants."

Liliana rolled her eyes. "No, you were mean as hell and drove them out of your office crying. You're terrible to work for. Lucky for you I found a Benu who wanted the job."

The Benu were usually ill-suited to work for others, their haughty manner kept them from any job they deemed menial. It worked perfectly for his assistant, in that she never took shit from any of the number of self-important people he dealt with daily. He waved away Liliana's concern and turned back to the male.

"How long did you say since the power showed up?"

"I, a few weeks?"

"Be specific," he barked and the guy flinched.

Liliana sighed.

"Umm, two, maybe three." Patrick stuttered.

"Which is it?"

"I…" Patrick looked to Liliana.

Xavier snapped his finger to get Patrick to focus on him. "Two or three, man?"

"Two, at least two."

"You're dismissed." Xavier waved him off.

The male looked to Liliana again.

"Perhaps, we should just hear the whole story before we send him out," Leo inputted.

"Adia," Xavier barked into the intercom.

She came in, unhurried, her face placid. He handed her the files. "This will take a little while, get the rep for the Mina on my calendar sometime today."

Something was going on, and the fastest way to find out was to ask the Mina. They were a precognitive race and he had contacts on their realm that were useful.

"Yes, Marshal." She walked out, giving Patrick a sympathetic smile.

Xavier stared at the male. What trouble was he dumping into his lap? "I don't want the whole story. What about the power troubles you?"

"Well, you know how some Demi are. With a power that obvious in our neighborhood, there are going to be some unsavory characters showing up to find out what it is." Patrick said nervously.

He swallowed another growl and cut his eyes at his sister-in-law. The situation could have most definitely been handled by their security office. Though, he would admit to being curious about the blank spot over the neighborhood.

"What kind of neighborhood is it? Why are you worried about other Demi showing up?"

Patrick squirmed in his seat and cleared his throat. "We're…that is to say, we, the Demi who live there do not have a lot of magic, to begin with. We enjoy the simple life of the humans."

Leo scoffed and shook his head.

Patrick flinched at the sound.

Xavier eyed him and wondered what the man was hiding. "Tell me about the daughter."

"She's powerful. Seriously powerful, which is odd because I was there when she bought the house for her mother. I've seen her when she came to visit the human. There wasn't anything like the power surrounding her now." Patrick swallowed.

Xavier shared a look with his brother. Leo raised his eyebrows in interest. Fuck. Xavier sighed.

"And you think there are god powers?"

"I know it," Patrick said, his voice stronger than it had been moments before.

"And explain to me, how you know that?" Leo's voice was low, menacing.

Patrick started visibly sweating. "We've done nothing to invite a visit from Death's Messenger," he whispered.

"I'll be the judge of that," Xavier injected. He released his pheromones and watched as the male visibly calmed, his breathing slowing until he was in a near trance. He leaned forward and caught Patrick's gaze. "Tell me how you're so sure the female has god powers?"

"One of the residents is a Mina, he knows and has assured us of it. Either way, we think it's in the best interest of all involved for the Amanda to investigate." Patrick stammered out, his voice flat and monotone.

Xavier sat back and crossed his hands over his chest. He pulled back his magic and waited until the glazed look in Patrick's eyes cleared. The male shook his head and looked around.

"You're dismissed. I'll send someone to check it out."

Patrick scrambled out of the chair, tripping over his feet as he rushed from Xavier's office. He turned to his brother.

"I want the daughter here. Lily, find a Kira discreet enough to examine her when she gets here."

Leo and Liliana both stood. "On it," Leo said before escorting his wife out.

Xavier went back to the Oras and put the address in one final time. He cursed finding the same blank spot. He prayed he wasn't sending his brother into an ambush.

Chapter 3

The quiet of the house pressed around Asa and her chest tightened. Tingling started at the base of her skull and moved down her spine, her breathing becoming choppier with each inhale. She was having a panic attack. She moved from the door and rested her head on the fireplace mantle, sliding the box she'd put there earlier to the side to lay her skin against the cool wood. She counted and forced her breathing to slow. She reached sixty before the tingles stopped, rounding up to one hundred before her heart rate settled back under control.

Better, she straightened and glanced at the small box she'd slid aside. Curious, she pocketed the note and pulled out the knife she always carried. She sliced the blade through the tape keeping it closed. She cocked her head as she moved the cardboard flaps and stared at the jewelry box inside. She'd never seen it. She tried to open it but saw the small keyhole. She rushed over to her purse and pulled out the envelope that had been in her mother's safe deposit box. Along with some jewelry, and a book full of contact numbers Asa would need to go through later, a small key had been in there.

She went back to the jewelry box and inserted the key, opening it. There was an envelope with her name on it. She set it aside. She wasn't ready to read more words from her mother. Perhaps tomorrow or in another month. She pulled the delicate gold chain from the box, gasping at the large gold coin dangling from it. What was it? The swirling mesmerized her and she stared for long moments. She opened the clasp and put it around her neck. The coin settled in the valley of her breast, warm against her skin. Goosebumps chased down her skin and she shuddered. She held it against her chest, her throat getting tight. There was a smaller chest inside there, but it wouldn't budge when she tried to open it. There were words burned into the top in a language she couldn't place and she'd studied ancient languages in school. What the hell was it? She turned the small wooden box over and saw neither latch nor keyhole. She set it aside to look at later.

She looked over at the envelope.

Tears slid down her face and she lowered her body to the floor. She closed her eyes and took a shuddering breath and wished the man from her nightly fantasies was there. She would give anything to be enfolded in his arms, have him tell her that it would all be okay. She swiped her face, happy she hadn't bothered with makeup that morning. Normally she wore a full face, she loved makeup, but this morning, she hadn't been able to summon the energy. She thought of her dream man. She didn't have a name for him. Mr. X, she'd taken to calling him. For nearly a year, she'd been having nightly dreams with him as the star. Some of the dreams had left her wet and panting in the morning, but they got her through the lonely days when she traveled. She lowered her head to her raised knees. She would love to have anyone with her now, to help with the grief. It had always been her mother and her and now she had no one.

Guilt pushed her to open Deena's note. She pulled it out of the envelope and opened it. The fine hairs along her arms and neck raised as she spied Deena's handwriting.

'My little treasure hunter, I hate that you're having to read this note instead of the answers I should have been brave enough to give you. I know your curiosity and can imagine the questions burning in your mind. In order to get the answers, you'll have to visit what's called Haven. I'm almost afraid to send you to the Divine community and the Esin where I grew up for fear of what they'd do to you. But all the same, the numbers in the address book I left you will reach them. There, you can answer the many questions you have after my death. I know by now you wonder about the life I led, and there's no telling the mess I left behind. The first number in that book is a person, probably the only person in the world who may know enough of my story to hopefully give

you closure. To find out about your father, though, Haven would be your best opportunity. I'm sorry I never gave you answers to your many questions about him. Shame and cowardice are to blame, but I understand if you're angry with me about it. I hope that you can find the answers in my death I was too scared to give you while I lived. Show them the necklace, and hopefully, your father will answer the call. I love you so much my Asa.

-Mom'

Haven? Asa pulled her bottom lip between her teeth and frowned. She traveled a lot for her job and encountered a lot of stories, myths as some of them turned out to be. Over the years, vague stories about places that operated as havens for the supernatural had crossed her radar. Could her mother be talking about the same place? She shook her head. The stories she'd heard were in the myth column as far as she'd been able to ascertain. Vampires and creatures not heard of outside of folktales were always a part of the stories about the havens, so she'd never really given it any serious thought. Her assistant on the other hand…Chandra collected stories about those havens.

Asa pulled the necklace out from under her shirt and stared at it. The male on the coin looked handsome and almost familiar to her. She gripped it in her hand and felt her body heat. Her mother was right in that she had questions, what would getting the answers cost her? She needed to think, but grief had her in a stranglehold, clouding her mind. She couldn't make any decisions surrounded by the tragedy of her mother's death. She needed a distraction.

She considered the note from the man on the porch as she looked around at all the unopened boxes. She could take this last case and then come back and deal with all her mother's stuff. The house was paid for and not going anywhere. She'd call her assistant and have her arrange for someone to watch the place while she took the job. Feeling her anxiety lighten, Asa pulled out her cell phone and pushed herself up from the floor. Chandra answered on the first ring.

"How you doing?"

Asa sighed, "Fine, honestly. But…there's a guy,"

Chandra sucked her teeth. "You took another job?"

"Not yet, I haven't," Asa said defensively. "I need you to look him up."

"Asa you're supposed to be there dealing with your mother's things, coping with death in a healthy manner."

"Everyone copes differently."

"You're stalling," Chandra accused.

"Am not."

Silence fell between them.

"What's his name?"

Asa let out the breath she was holding, grabbing the card from the floor beside her. "Fallon Tegan."

"I'll see what I can find. How did he find you? I haven't seen any calls or emails from anyone by that name through our usual channels."

That was a good question, actually. "I don't know. He showed up at mom's house."

Chandra growled. "You're determined to get killed or sold off into some kind of human trafficking."

"Chandra," Asa chided. "You watch too much t.v."

Chandra scoffed. "How? I have two kids and you are constantly calling me all hours of the night to get you out of shit. When do I have time to watch t.v?"

Asa chuckled, "touché. Where are the kids, by the way, it's quiet over there."

"Scott took them out because I was near to strangling them. Spring break is the worst."

Asa laughed, "I thought you were taking them to Orlando? That's why you're off this week, right?"

"And yet, I am taking calls from you." She reminded her best friend.

"My bad," Asa said unrepentantly.

"We're leaving tomorrow, I had to get my chair repaired today."

"How did that go?"

"I had them add NOS to my wheelchair, so I'm going to be speeding through the amusement park like an asshole." She said dryly, tapping on the keys of her computer.

Asa snickered. "You're ridiculous."

"I don't see anything alarming on the interwebs at the moment. I'll keep looking and email you when I'm done. When are you meeting him to find out what the job is?"

"I didn't agree to meet him."

"Oooh, look at you, growing up and shit."

"But if you don't find anything, I'm going to call him and meet tomorrow."

"Oh brother." Chandra sighed. "All right, I'll see what I can dig up. Be careful, Asa."

"I always am, and if not, I have you."

"That's not a healthy life philosophy."

"If I die, you'll be a millionaire."

"That is so morbid Asa, besides, I don't need your money, my husband got a good job."

They laughed together at their running joke. Every time Chandra got her out of a scrape with customs, or some foreign government or another, the woman joked that she would quit because she didn't need the money. Asa would be lost if Chandra made good on her threat, the woman did everything for her.

"I'll text you a pic of this note and the location of the meeting once I arrange it." Asa looked around the empty house. Her eyes fell to her mother's note. "There is something else," she muttered.

"What you got?"

Asa sighed, knowing the can of worms she was about to open. She and Chandra regularly argued about the existence of the havens, so she prepared herself for her friend's smugness.

"My mother left me a note. In it, she mentions that to find answers about my father, I need to visit someplace called Haven."

A thick moment of silence fell between them. Even the sound of Chandra's typing had paused.

"I.freaking.knew it!" Chandra screeched in Asa's ear. "Didn't I tell you they existed?"

"Calm down, Chandra. For all you know, mom is talking about a halfway house or some kind of town." Asa rolled her eyes as Chandra ignored her, and continued to celebrate on her end.

"Girl, just admit it. I was right, and now, instead of taking this job with the potential murderer, you should join me on my quest to find an actual haven."

Asa groaned. "I have neither address nor even the smallest clue of where this Haven my mother speaks of is, so no, I will not turn down a paying job."

Chandra sucked her teeth. "Ms. Deena didn't leave an address?"

"Nothing."

A sigh, before a reluctant, "well damn. That does take the wind out of my sails."

"Exactly. The note gave me next to no new information, so for now, I'm putting it aside." Asa took a deep breath and ran her hand across her face. She had to put it aside because she was in no place to deal with all of Deena's secrets.

"Fine, but that's not going to stop me from looking, just so you know," Chandra muttered.

"Has my skepticism ever stopped you before?"

"True that. You think since she didn't give an address the haven was close?" Chandra started typing furiously. "I've never heard any stories about one being in Tennessee, but let me look through my notes."

Asa growled. "I'm not doing this with you, goodbye."

She disconnected the call and shook her head. Chandra was on the hunt, and now Asa would have to hear about the mythological havens for the next who knew how many days. Still, work was on the horizon, and so she could breathe easier. There would be another time to deal with emotional shit. All the tension from the day dropped from her body and all at once she was exhausted. It was a little early to be going to bed, but she wanted the escape of her dreams and Mr. X.

Asa sighed as she looked around the luxurious hotel room. She ran her hands down the long silk nightgown she wore and smiled. He hadn't yet arrived. She walked around and lit the candles laid out around the room and tried to quell her anticipation. She should be used to the dreams by now, but every time she had them, excitement filled her. As she lit the last candle, her body started to hum, her sign that he'd arrived.

Her Mr. X.

She turned and her heart jumped at the sight of him. He wore a loose gray top with matching pants, the material soft and thin, and good lord, showing her everything he had to offer in his pants. Her hands itched to touch him. How long had it been since she'd last had the dream? His eyes were dark with lust, the outer ring glowing gray, his full and sensual mouth turning up into a welcome smile. His skin was dark chestnut, smooth and unlined so she could never guess his age. His hair was wavy and reached his shoulders, surrounding a face chiseled and serious. Dark slashing brows, a prominent nose, and a small cleft in his chin gave him a dangerous aura. She shivered in need.

"I've missed you, *elewa*." He said, stepping forward.

She rushed to him and sighed as he enfolded her into his chest. "It's been a tough couple of months."

His fingers slid into her hair, holding her to him. "I have you now," he said softly and Asa couldn't stop the tears that tracked down her cheek.

He pulled back and lifted her chin with his finger. "What's happened, *elewa*?"

"My mother died, and I've been having a hard time dealing with everything."

Talking to him had always been easy. They traded stories of the day and sometimes work. Perhaps she should find it odd, the details of his life her mind conjured, but she'd never really given it any thought.

He kissed her softly and then lifted her, carrying her to the bed. He laid her across the soft mattress and leaned over her. She wiped her face and drew him to her.

"I lit candles for us, not for me to cry."

"I'm here for whatever you need, love."

"Anything?" she whispered, pulling him down.

He closed the distance between them and peppered soft kisses across her face before devouring her mouth. His hands roamed her body and she sighed, opening her legs to him. He crawled over the top of her and settled between her thighs, his heavy weight comforting.

She pulled back and traced his face. "I need you."

He growled and nuzzled into her neck. "Anytime, *elewa*." He bit down on her shoulder and her back arched.

Why couldn't he be real, why couldn't she have him in her life? He growled and licked a trail up her neck, nipping on her ear.

"Are you here with me now, my love?" He asked, seeming to read her mind.

"Yes," she whispered.

He pulled back and stared into her eyes and she didn't know what he looked for, but she made sure her eyes reflected every bit of her feelings for him. He smiled and her heart broke, longing nearly throwing her from the dream. She gripped his waist tight, praying to hold on for as long as she could. He chuckled and slid down her body, nuzzling his face against the silk against her stomach. She moaned as he lifted the fabric slowly, his warm hand heating her skin.

He lifted the gown to her waist and a hungry growl rattled his chest as he stared at her sex. "Do you know how long I've wanted to taste you?"

Her body heated, her sex flooding with moisture. He growled again and licked across her sex. She closed her eyes and threw her head back as he devoured her. His licks hungry, his teeth nipping at her center. Her heart was pounding in her chest, electricity singing through her blood. He slid a finger into her and her eyes shot open, her sex clenching. It was the first time he'd done so in her dreams.

"X," she whispered, as he made it two fingers, sliding in and out of her.

His tongue slid across her folds, and she couldn't stop the orgasm that barreled down over her. He sucked on her until her legs shook. She pulled at his shoulders.

"I want you inside," she demanded.

She wanted to feel him if the dream allowed for it because it never had before. He slid up her body and she gripped his erection, panting in need. His eyes were a copper color now as he watched her.

"I want to feed from you," he growled.

She didn't know what that meant. "Whatever you need," she whispered.

The smile he gave her was all ravenous need and her sex clenched in desperation to have him inside. He gripped her waist and guided his dick to her entrance.

"Yes, or no, *elewa*."

"Yes!"

He plunged inside and she let out a rough exhalation in relief. To feel him for the first time. She lifted her hips as he pulled out, not wanting to release him.

He chuckled and scraped his teeth across her neck, "greedy little thing," he whispered.

He drove back into her and Asa arched her back to take as much of him as she could. He worked her, his hips moving faster, his hands holding down her waist as he pistoned in and out of her body. His heated whispers bathed her neck among his scattered kisses and bites. Her legs tightened, her sex clenching hard as her orgasm seemed to fill her body.

"Nearly there, love," he panted.

His hand left her hip and went to her clitoris strumming that button until the dam broke and sensation flooded her body.

"That's it, *elewa*, open your mouth," he said, gritting his teeth, holding back his orgasm.

She did as he asked and he moved to kiss her, but instead, hovered right at her mouth, their breaths mingling. His eyes glowed and Asa felt a wave of heat starting from her toes, rising quickly over her skin.

"There it is, *mi ife*."

She closed her eyes as another orgasm swept her. X shouted and she felt the heated pulse of him as he came. She opened her eyes to watch and light surrounded both his body and hers. His face was a mask of bliss as he hovered over her mouth. He finally closed the distance, his hips still pumping as he kept their orgasm going. She sucked on his tongue, nipped at his bottom lip, grinding her hips into his until her body shuddered. He pulled back and drove into her one last time, pulling her tightly to him, as his body tensed again. Finally, he relaxed, his weight dropping to her fully.

She hummed in satisfaction and ran her hands across his back. "That was a first," she murmured.

He laughed. "Fuck, woman, how am I supposed to get any work done tomorrow?" He kissed along her neck. "This is all I'll be able to think about."

She smiled wistfully wishing that was true. They lay cuddled like that, neither saying a word for a while.

"I'm crushing you," he said after a few minutes.

"I love your weight." She protested as he rolled over and pulled her on top of him.

"Fuck, I'm tired, *elewa*."

She kissed his chin and nuzzled into his neck. "Sleep, my love."

He tightened his grip. "I don't want this to end," he whispered.

She lay her head on his chest and sighed. She knew how he felt.

Chapter 4

"No," Xavier growled, swiping at the toys dancing in the air around his shoulders. A chortle was Kell's response to his uncle's command. Still, the toys landed on the carpeted floor with a soft thump.

"I don't know why you're fighting it, omo." Xavier murmured, pacing the small nursery.

Kell babbled, his tiny hand stroking across Xavier's short hair. He gave his nephew what he wanted and allowed his magic to drop enough for his hair to grow out. The whorls along his arms came next, the amber light pulsing along with his heartbeat. Xavier moved to the rocking chair in the corner of the room and sat. He arranged his nephew into his favorite position tucked in the crook of his arm. Sighing, Kell traced the lifted lines on Xavier's arms, hypnotized by the light. He released relaxing pheromones and started the chair. It only took moments of the rocking motion for his nephew's eyes to start drooping.

Xavier stared down at the baby, marveling as he always did at the fact that Kell had him so thoroughly wrapped around his tiny fingers. Xavier visited his nephew often, the kid's presence relaxing him in a way that was so rare for him.

"I'm not sure how you manage that," Liliana whispered, leaning against the door jamb.

Xavier looked up at his sister in law and smiled. He stood and laid the sleeping infant into the playpen his mother kept in her office. He rubbed the silky black hair on the top of Kell's hair, his heart aching.

"It's just pheromones." Xavier stretched.

"And yet, his father, with those same pheromones can't get him to take a nap during the day," Liliana grumbled.

"Have you seen the two of them in here playing? Leo ain't even trying to get that kid to sleep." Xavier shook his head and stepped around Liliana, dropping a kiss to the top of her head.

"Going back to the office?"

"Yep. Has Leo contacted you?"

"Not yet, he left last night."

He nodded and thanked her, leaving her office. He strode through the hallways quickly, his eyes taking in everything, checking for problems. The balm of his visit with Kell shed with his every footstep. Adia smiled as he came into the door.

"You and Kell must have had a good day, you're back earlier than planned," She commented, standing.

He grunted and continued to his office. Adia followed behind him, her head down, her hands swiping across the screen of her tablet.

"I carved you out an hour with Kell, and then some time to eat. You're done a little earlier than usual, so you'll have a longer lunch."

He sighed in appreciation at the tray of food on his desk. "You're the best thing to happen to me, Adia."

She rolled her eyes. "You got about forty-five minutes before your schedule starts back."

He nodded, waving her away. She chuckled and walked out. Before he could get good into his food, he heard a familiar growl from the outer office. Rolling his eyes he waited. Ranolph entered his office and plopped down in the chair in front of Xavier's desk without invitation. His father's power, even after centuries, surrounded him. As the former Amanda Marshal, he'd wielded it like a sharpened sword, deadly and with precision. Retirement had done nothing to diminish that.

Ranolph had not been Marshal in going on two hundred years, and yet, he sat before Xavier his suit immaculate, the black on black understated but still intimidating.

"Leo still won't let me see the child." His father's accent was thick, despite his centuries back and forth to Adro.

"Baba, what would you have me do?" Xavier dipped his bread into sauce and pushed it into his mouth.

"Why won't he talk to me? Surely he understands why I did what I did."

"Clearly he does not," Xavier muttered dryly, continuing to eat. "You can't order your way out of this." He looked up when no reply came from his father and snorted. "Even now I see the machinations going on in your head, baba. What are you planning?"

"He will be king, Xavier, he needs training," Ranolph grumbled.

"He's not even a year old yet, dad."

"But you're not arguing that he needs training."

He shrugged. That was not the *gotcha* Ranolph thought it was. Xavier was an advocate of doing whatever needed to be done to keep his family strong. He was like his father in that. It came with seeing every facet of the Demi world, its worst and its best. As head of the Amanda, he saw it all.

"Baba," X sighed. His father was nagging the wrong person.

"Fallon won't talk to him for me."

He snorted before sipping at his juice. "You went to Fallon? Even after you gave him so much shit about coddling Leo." He nearly smiled at the stones on his father.

Ranolph crossed his arms across his chest.

"Have you apologized to Iya?" He asked suddenly.

"Sharine is…"

Xavier held his hand up. "Don't, the answer is obviously no. Perhaps you should look for absolution there instead of harassing your children."

Ranolph growled. "Are you doing okay?"

He smiled at the subject change. "I'm fine, baba."

His father narrowed his eyes and studied Xavier's face. "I don't like it when you lie to me, omo mio."

"It is what it is, dad, I'll work it out." He leaned back in his chair, finished with his lunch.

"Do you need help?"

"Not help, necessarily. Have you ever heard of a god or goddess settling among humans?"

Ranolph frowned. "From humans perhaps, but they see everything supernatural as a sign from the gods. What has happened?"

Xavier thought over his words carefully. He always went to his father for advice. Ranolph was the only other person who understood what his job entailed and all the stress that went with it.

"I had a Demi in here yesterday worried about god powers in their neighborhood."

"Just the powers?" Ranolph hummed. "I imagine a Demi could tell the difference which means it could be an artifact of some kind."

Xavier cocked his head. He hadn't thought of that. "It would explain his worry."

His father nodded. "Yeah, if there is an artifact in his neighborhood with god powers, then there are going to be creatures that come looking for it."

Xavier cursed and prayed Leo reached it before someone else did.

"I'll put some feelers out for you."

"I got it handled so far."

Ranolph eyed him. "Anything else?"

He shook his head. He hadn't yet told his father about the Kokoro souls, and now he highly suspected this mess in Tennessee had to do with it. "Not at the moment." He said instead.

Ranolph watched him carefully, his scent changing as he released his pheromones. Xavier relaxed under his father's magic but kept his resolve in place.

"It's fine, baba." He whispered.

"I'm proud of what you've done with the Havens. Have I told you that?"

Shock had him silent. Xavier could only shake his head.

His father stood to leave. "Well, I am. You have a storm brewing on your hands, but I've taught you well, and am not worried. You and the dignity and pride with which you serve this post is a legacy I have always hoped for and have been proud to watch unfold."

Xavier was unsure what to say to that, so he stayed silent.

"Come to me if you need help, omo. I don't want all this…unrest in the family to leave you stranded." Ranolph speared him with a serious look before leaving the office.

He wiped a hand over his face. He needed to get back to work. He'd done next to nothing this morning. His dream last night… he sighed. It was hotter than any of the others he'd had about his dream woman. All day his dick had been hard and his mind had been everywhere but on his work. He needed to focus, but his beast bucked against his human skin. Somehow, when he woke this morning, his beast was sated as though it had actually fed. And now, it wanted to scour the world for a female that could very well not even exist. He'd had to wrestle with his power, instinct nearly driving him out the front door of Haven. Responsibility held him though. His father couldn't have timed his visit better. It served to remind Xavier of what his duty was. Growling, he set his lunch dishes to the side and pulled up his computer. He needed to get some work done.

###

She was stupid.

Asa clutched the necklace and took a deep breath, that one thought circling her brain. She'd called the number and arranged to meet with the guy last night, and now she sat in her car realizing how stupid the whole thing was. When asked how he knew where to find her, he'd said he knew her father which…She had been tempted by many things from people wanting something from her over the years.

This was not that.

It felt bigger, and her gut never lied. She thought about the note from her mother. What were the odds that her mother would mention her father and then this stranger would as well? For a man who'd had nothing to do with her for damn near forty years, it was strange that he would pop up now. She pulled down the mirror and adjusted her makeup, happy with her beat. She ran a finger over her newly threaded brows, a happy little sigh. It had been months since she'd taken time off and pampered herself, and while painful, she couldn't argue the result. She growled. Okay, she was full on stalling at this point. She was there, outside of the café.

Might as well go in.

Asa slapped up the mirror, adjusted the collar of the white dress shirt she wore over her wide-legged Ankara print pants. She stepped out of the car in three-inch heels, feeling confident, her utmost girly. Habit had her sending a quick text to Chandra, even though she knew her assistant was traveling. She opened the café door, it was lunch but there weren't a lot of patrons. The two she'd come to see would've stood out regardless of the number of people there.

Fallon, as the note said his name was, was well dressed, muscles bulging in the expensive, tailored dress shirt he wore underneath the vest straining across his vast chest. He was huge and dwarfed the small table in which he sat, a beautiful woman, next to him, perusing through a notebook. Fallon looked up and spotted her and she frowned at his unusual eyes. The woman looked up, her curly afro tied back with a colorful scarf. It was cute, and despite her nerves, Asa took notes to try the style, though her short curls wouldn't get as big as the woman's. She purposefully kept her hair short. It was easier to maintain when she traveled. The woman's round face was curious, her dark eyes cataloging Asa.

She turned from them and went to the counter, ordering a green tea. While she waited, she took a chance to study them. They looked like they were debating, the woman's hand movements wild. Were they discussing her, and the job? There was only one way to find out. She walked up to their table a few minutes later, tea in hand.

"Fallon?"

He stood and extended his hand. She looked at it for a while and wiped her hand on her pants before clasping his.

"This is my wife, Brianna." His voice was deep, more mesmerizing in person than it had been on the phone.

"Asa," she grasped the other woman's hand.

"Omen," Brianna said and tilted her head.

Fallon choked, his wife grimacing as she patted his back.

"Excuse me?"

"I'm sorry," Brianna looked sheepish. "Your name, it means Omen. I didn't mean to blurt that out. You're very beautiful."

Fallon cleared his throat to interrupt his wife's rambling. "Please, sit."

Asa sat across from Fallon and Brianna. "What's the job?" She bypassed the chit chat stage, preferring to get directly to the point.

Husband and wife shared a look before Fallon turned his attention back to her. "We're here for you."

"Right, what do you want from me?"

"We're here to keep you safe while you wrap up whatever business you have here."

"And then?"

He shrugged.

She snorted, sensing his evasion. "Keep me safe from what? My stepfather is dead, and off the top of my head I can't think of anyone who would want me dead."

Working for them yes, dead, nope, she hadn't made that level of enemy yet.

"We're also looking for a chest," Brianna inputted.

Asa's senses start to tingle, now they were getting to it. "What kind of chest?"

"We don't really have a lot of information about it." The woman admitted.

Fallon pulled a napkin from the small tray between them and started to write. "It would probably have writing similar to this." He slid over the napkin.

Asa's heartbeat picked up. She eyed the two of them and wondered who they were and how they were connected to her mother. The writing on the top of the smaller chest did in fact look similar to what he'd written. She leaned over and looked at the note again and her necklace fell out of her shirt. Fallon hissed and looked at his wife again. Brianna's eyes widened, excitement making her dark eyes sparkle.

"Where did you get that necklace?" Brianna asked.

Asa squelched the instinct to grip the necklace and hide it away. She weighed her words. "My mother left it to me."

"Interesting," Brianna murmured leaning forward to study it more.

Asa picked up the tea she'd ordered and took a sip, moving away from Brianna's prying eyes.

"Show her yours, Fallon."

Fallon gave Asa a long, inquisitive look. He pulled a coin out of his pocket and put it on the table. At first glance, it looked identical to the one on her necklace. She reached for it, needing to touch it to assure herself it was real. The person on the coin was a handsome man, strong chin, arrogant tilt to his lips. A smile that said he knew secrets. She turned it over, and it was another head, identical to the other side. What did it mean? She pulled her chain out and compared it and the coins were the same.

"Who are you?" She asked, the words forced out of her constricted throat. "And what does this have to do with my father?"

The information Chandra had sent her on Fallon Tegan was basic, as far as background went. He wasn't on social media, there were next to no images of him, but that wasn't abnormal in her field of work. The people she worked with and for didn't necessarily want the world knowing about them. There had been no red flags though, so that had made her comfortable with meeting him. Instead of answering, Fallon picked up the coin and put it back in his pocket. He pulled a black business card out of the pocket of his vest. It just said Haven and an address, in gold embossed letters, and on the back, it said plus one.

The room spun for a moment and she gripped her teacup. If she were keeping tally, and she was, that was three separate and distinct ties to her mother's letter. The mention of her father, the coin, and now Haven. She absolutely would not be telling Chandra about the meeting. Asa could well imagine the woman showing up on her front doorstep, vacation forgotten, demanding they head to the Haven. She peered at the address again once she could breathe. The address was in Atlanta, she committed it to memory without taking the card. She made it a practice of never having traceable information on her.

"I can't really talk about it in mixed company." He disclosed, bringing her out of her thoughts.

Asa looked around and noticed they were getting looks, but strangely the place was quiet.

He continued. "If you come to this address, we can explain it."

She snorted. "I'm not hardly leaving the state with a stranger."

"That's fair," Brianna said, putting a restraining hand on her husband's arm. "Just think about it. All the answers and more will be there," Brianna cajoled.

"Is my father alive?" She needed to know if there was a possibility…after so many years…that she could maybe…

Fallon sighed. "I don't want to get your hopes up of seeing your father, that situation is complicated."

Her heart sank, though its rhythm didn't slow. "He in jail?"

Brianna coughed to cover her laugh. Asa narrowed her eyes. Son of bitch, he was. Of course, he was. Why else would Deena keep her from him?

Fallon glared at his wife. "As I said, it's not something I can discuss here."

"Fine, I'll think about going to Haven."

And she would. She was properly intrigued, but she would research as much as she could before she crossed state lines to get into some shit that could be dangerous.

"That's all we ask," Brianna said.

"That, and if you do happen to find a box with that kind of writing on it…don't open it," Fallon warned, his look telling her that he believed her already to be in possession of it.

Chills doused Asa's body and she clutched her shaking hands in her lap.

"And why not?" She managed to get out.

Brianna shrugged and looked to her husband. "We were told it was dangerous to do so."

"Now, you have to know telling me that will make me want to open the box even more…if I had it."

Fallon sighed. "Knowing your father, you may not even be able to open it, but just please…be careful and think about coming to Haven."

She stared at him a while, trying to see past his polite exterior. "As I said, I'll think about it," she said, standing.

"We appreciate the meeting," Fallon said.

Asa left the café, her mind on the necklace, and that little box she'd been unable to open. It was from her father? What was her mother into? Her mother had secrets, and Asa didn't know how to feel about that. It was one thing to have a flush bank account, but strangers and clandestine meetings were different. Though, that feeling she got for treasure started tingling, telling her something was there.

Chapter 5

"I have a few things that require your signature." Adia came into Xavier's office, breaking his concentration.

Xavier grunted and put his thumbprint on her comms pad where she indicated. He looked up and narrowed his eyes at her.

"What's wrong?"

"What do you mean?"

You're…" he stared closely at her face. "Out of sorts."

Her gestures were nervous. She licked her lips. "Prince Khalid pushed back his arrival by a month. There was some issue with his Ileri's family."

She was stiff, just talking about the prince set her off. He didn't probe further, knowing how it upset her. She started to turn but he called out.

"Adia, you know I got you, right? No matter what, you can come to me, understand?"

She sighed and tucked a stray hair behind her ears before nodding.

"You'll come to me before you make any decisions?"

"About what?" She whispered.

He stared her down and she averted her gaze before nodding.

"Promise?"

He knew that once it was confirmed the prince was headed to Haven she would run. He'd need to convince her to stay. And not just for his own selfish reasons. He wanted her safe, and sometimes, a lot of times, Adro wasn't that for the Demi.

She sighed again. "I promise," she said softly.

She turned around and left his office. He didn't bother cursing. It would do him no good. Everything about the Benu's prince's visit had been aggravating, what was one more snafu? Before he could get back to work, Adia popped up on his communicator.

"Fallon is back and wants to talk to you. Let me know when you're ready for him."

He sighed and checked the time. It was nearing the end of Adia's workday. He wondered what his brother would add to his already hectic schedule.

"I cleared the rest of your schedule for him."

He shook his head, it was like she read his mind. "Without consulting me? What if I didn't have time?"

"I've made time."

"No." Of course, he would see Fallon when he came in, but the female was too pushy.

"I'll tell him to come down now." She closed the comms down, her image disappearing.

"No." He called out so she could hear him in the front office.

"This is why I don't consult you." Adia shot back.

He shook his head and contained his smile. It was hard to ruffle that woman. It was why she'd lasted longer than any other assistant.

"You're fired," he yelled out to her office.

"I volunteer for this job." She called back.

"Your pay stub says otherwise."

He knew Adia didn't cash any of the payroll checks they gave her, so she was technically right about volunteering. Even though she'd run away from her betrothal, as far as he knew, she still had access to her family's money.

He listened for her smart ass come back and heard only the movement of her chair as she settled deeper into it. He could see the back of her chair as she swung around to her computer. He couldn't help the smirk that tilted his lips at her lack of reaction. He called down to Liliana's office. She was sitting at her desk, breastfeeding his nephew.

"You didn't have to answer. I could've waited." He grumbled.

She sucked her teeth. "Since when?"

Okay, so he was usually an impatient bastard. "Prince Khalid and his Ileri will be a month late on their post, what have you heard?"

"I'm on it. Adia called earlier. I'm waiting to hear back from some people."

"Why would she tell you before me?" He glared at Lily. "She needs to be fired."

Liliana rolled her eyes. "She is the only person who can put up with your attitude. Plus, I know you like her, cut it out before you hurt her feelings."

"Benu don't have feelings," he said loud enough for his assistant to hear.

Adia's hand shot up over her chair and she shot him a bird, which…he suppressed a smile.

Liliana snickered and adjusted her son. "Have you talked to Fallon yet?"

"I take it you know what he wants to talk to me about?" He growled.

She raised an eyebrow. "I'm not touching that with a ten-foot pole." She shut down the comms between them.

Hung up on again. He was obviously way too lenient with people. Before his brothers had mated, no one would have been brave enough to talk to him the way these females did. He smiled, damn it, they were making him soft. Scenarios of what Fallon could've gotten into spun in his head and the smile dropped from his face.

Fallon and Brianna walked into his office and he glared at the two and their guilty shuffle. "What have you done?"

They both sat and for the next few minutes explained to him where they had been for the past week and what they'd been doing. Xavier had been so far off the mark that he just sat dumbstruck. Of all the things he'd imagined his brother saying to him, working for a hell god wasn't even top twenty.

"So, let me get this straight. Azra sent you to Tennessee to retrieve a woman and a box. You're doing work for a god, other than the one we serve, and did not tell me?"

Anger was boiling under the surface of his emotions but on top? On top was a sticky oily coating of worry and fear. His brother was doing favors for a hell god and had not seen fit to tell him.

He'd been puzzled about the blank spot in Tennessee, it had been bugging him since yesterday. But, now with Fallon and Brianna standing in front of him, it answered some of the lingering questions he had about it in the worst way. If Azra was hiding the woman, it made sense that their Oras wouldn't pick up her location.

Fallon shuffled and shared a look with his mate. Xavier imagined that Brianna was the only reason Fallon was fessing up, and it irritated the shit out of him.

"Explain it to me again, but this time, insert some logic," Xavier said slowly, working to contain his temper. The whorls along his skin came alive despite his effort.

Fallon growled. "It may have been impulsive—"

"May? May have been?"

"X," Fallon sighed. "I'm sorry, it was a foolish thing to do, but I was young."

"And? That doesn't excuse you not telling me, Fallon. You may have been young when you first struck the deal but you for damn sure weren't young a week ago when you left to do his bidding."

"He only asked me to do innocuous shit, X, nothing that would put our family in danger, you know me."

"Yes, and you know the gods. Who's to say that what you did was innocuous. How would you know what sort of long-reaching consequences would come from it?"

"It's already happened, Xavier, there's no use in hollering at him about it now," Brianna interjected calmly.

"I haven't even raised my voice, Brianna," but his power slipped from his control, the space around him glowing as magic filled him. "You probably have researched this enough to know how serious it is."

She winced. "We have it under control."

"We, huh?"

She lifted her chin. "I'll back my husband through whatever consequences."

X slammed a hand down on his desk. He was pissed, but damn if he didn't admire the strength in his sister in law. If Fallon were to get into some kind of shit with his godforsaken quest for magic, at least she would be there to help. He turned his chair toward the landscape hanging over his desk and took deep breaths to calm himself.

"What else did he ask you to do?" He said after he'd taken a deep breath. He turned back to face them.

"I was just supposed to find the girl and make sure she didn't open whatever box she had."

"And how does she play into this power surge?"

"Well, according to the report you sent me, that's the address where I found her."

X cursed. "So the power is connected to Azra, that can't be good."

"I tried to convince her to come here, but Brianna and I didn't have any luck."

"Fuck me." X murmured. He'd already sent Leo to check out the power source, would he find the female? "She can't be roaming around Adro with access to god-like powers, Fallon. Hit Leo up and let him know before he walks into some shit."

Fallon groaned. "I'll handle it, Leo's not the most subtle person."

X stared at his brother, trying to wrangle the fear still clinging to his insides. Azra was not a god to do deals with. A trickster, there was no telling what he'd asked Fallon to do for him and how it affected the world.

Adia walked in and cleared her throat. "Marshal, Leo is downstairs. He says…" she shook her head. "Just…you should meet him in the garage."

X rubbed a hand over his face. "Leo? Already?"

"Fuuucckk, that can't be good," Fallon whispered.

Chapter 6

Xavier and Fallon skidded to a halt in front of their youngest brother. Leo was leaning against a matte black Camaro, his legs crossed at the ankles.

"What have you done?" Fallon asked.

Leo smiled, his eyes flashing silver, the beast in his brother coming alive in excitement. "I've found and secured the power source. You're welcome."

Leo walked to the back of the car and popped the trunk.

Fallon and Xavier both cursed at the woman wrapped in blankets, hopefully just sleep in their brother's car.

"You gotta be fucking kidding me," Xavier murmured.

"Leo, what the hell?" Fallon sighed.

"Your power source." Leo waved his hand like a game show host over the woman.

"Why did you tie her up?" Fallon leaned forward to study the still woman.

"She didn't want to come voluntarily and I don't play games with god powers."

"Did you ask nicely?" Fallon asked.

"Do I look like I ask nicely for things?" Leo parried back.

Fallon shrugged.

Xavier threw his head back and slid a hand down his face. "Why are you so impulsive, Leonalph?"

"Instincts, my brother, finely tuned." Leo smiled and Fallon laughed.

"This is not a joke, you jackasses."

He walked over to the car and turned the woman over. Xavier stepped back with a hiss as he recognized her face from the one haunting his dreams. He whipped to Fallon to see him watching him closely, carefully.

"You know something?"

Fallon shrugged. "That's the woman we spoke with earlier today. I assume Leo nabbed her right after our meeting."

He turned back to the other jackass.

Leo held up his hands. "No one told me anything about a meeting. You said, investigate the power source. I did you one better and nabbed it."

Xavier grunted, not pleased, but now that he thought about it, not surprised by his baby brother's actions. He faced the woman again and frowned. "There is no power coming off of her."

"Right?" Leo said. "But see, here's the thing." He pulled the stone from the inside of his shirt. "This little baby warmed up the moment I stepped onto her porch."

Xavier eyed the stone, Azra, the god of death, had given to his brother to make travel to Azreal easier. He turned and glared at Fallon, pissed all over again. Azra was at the center of this mess for sure, and he could only pray their god Rugaba didn't catch wind of what was happening. They'd be seriously fucked if he did.

"And," Leo leaned over and reached for the front of the woman.

Xavier growled, possessiveness rearing. Leo pulled a necklace, much like his out of the woman's blouse. What the hell?

"I felt the magic as soon as I turned into the gated community, but when I pulled up to her house…nothing."

"Strange," Fallon said. "Now that you mention it, I felt her power when I left my card for her, but not when we finally met."

"Did you physically knock her out," he growled, ignoring for the moment, talk of her power. His beast was becoming possessive at the thought of her hurt.

"Come on, X. You know I don't roll like that."

Xavier breathed out. Of course he didn't. Leo may be lethal, but he would never hurt an innocent.

"The necklace fell out as I was carrying her to the car," Leo explained.

"So, she's been in your trunk for nearly three hours." Fallon thumped his brother's shoulder.

Leo smiled sheepishly. "Well, no. I put her to sleep and into the backseat, but about thirty minutes or so ago she tried to jump out of the car at a red light. I thought the spell would hold longer. I put her under again and slid her into the trunk from the backseat to be sure this time."

Xavier growled. "In the middle of rush hour traffic?"

Leo shrugged. "I mean, there are blankets and stuff and nobody saw me."

Fallon snickered and held Xavier back as he dove for Leo. "Calm down X, he even put a pillow under her head."

Xavier pushed out of Fallon's arms and shot them both a lethal look.

Leo fist-bumped Fallon and they laughed.

"I can't even…" Xavier was speechless, truly speechless. He couldn't even find the words to curse out his brother, he was genuinely baffled by the thinking all the way around.

The woman's lids started twitching, the eyeballs moving around, a sign that she would wake momentarily. Xavier held his breath, wanting to see if her eyes matched the ones haunting him in his dreams. She opened them, and lavender eyes speared him. He didn't think eyes that color existed outside of his dreams and fantasies.

"Elewa," he whispered in shock.

Her eyes widened in first recognition and then panic.

He held up his hands. "We don't mean you any harm."

Her eyes darted to Fallon and she started a frantic struggle to free herself from her ties.

"We're not going to hurt you," he stepped back to give her more space.

She whimpered and wiggled harder. He lifted her from the trunk, pulling the cloth from over her mouth and she screamed, her body fighting.

"Stop, woman, or you'll end up on your ass, but no more free than you are now." He growled, ramping up his pheromones to help calm her.

He walked them down the back stairs to his office. Adia and Brianna both stared incredulously as he brought in the struggling woman. He was fighting both the female and his beast. Her scent wrapped around him, the softness of her curves against him all worked to tear through his control.

"What in the devil!" Brianna followed him into his office. "You kidnapped her?"

Xavier deposited her gently into the chair in front of his desk, both of them breathing hard. He quickly put space between the two of them, going to the far corner of his office. The woman of his dreams was real and in front of him. He needed to get out of the office so he could think. He clenched his hands, his palms itching to feel her skin. Would she be as soft as in his dreams?

"Leo did," Fallon answered, reaching for his wife.

She slapped at her husband's hands. "What the hell is wrong with y'all? You can't kidnap people off the street."

The woman watched the interaction, her eyes calculating. Her amazing eyes. The lavender color bright, the lush lashes surrounding them, thick. She was so beautiful she took his breath away. No, beautiful was too tame of a word. She glowed golden, her tall slender figure making him hard, achy. Her anger crackled around her making her eyes otherworldly. He loved her hair. The curls were short on the side, separated by a side part that then exploded in a profusion of curls on the top. The curls fell across her forehead, teasing high arched eyebrows. The style fit her and complimented her doll face. Her eyes were big, her lips full, her nose regal. She wore some kind of makeup that made her dark mahogany skin shimmer with gold. He wanted to kiss her red lips until there was no color left. Gods, what had gotten into him? He'd dreamed of those lips last night. His body was pumping out pheromones, his beast actively trying to calm her ire. The woman visibly calmed herself as she watched Brianna turn her anger on Leo.

"Have you lost your damn mind?" Hands on her hips, Brianna stood toe to toe with her brother in law.

Leo held up his hands. "Not gonna lie, Bri, it felt faster just to grab her and worry about the consequences later."

Xavier covered his face with his hands and forced air in and out of his lungs. He needed to take control of the situation. Straightening his shoulders, he pushed away from the wall and walked to the chair behind his desk.

"Enough, Brianna." Xavier lowered himself into his chair, his eyes never leaving the exquisite woman in front of him.

Had it finally happened for him? Had he found his mate at last?

###

Asa bounced her gaze from Brianna to the jackass who kidnapped her. She was relieved to know she had at least one person on her side. She was ashamed to say that this wasn't her first or third time being kidnapped, so while she was pissed, she wasn't yet scared. She should have been a lot more alarmed, but her body was relaxed even as she remained alert. She would need to examine why much later. She really should be a lot more scared than she was. She fingered the slender gold bracelet on her wrist and debated pushing the panic button built into it. Chandra was on vacation and it could take her a little while to start rescue protocol. So she hesitated. Plus…she sighed…she wanted to know what the hell was going on.

She turned her attention to the man behind the desk, their eyes meeting and clashing. He'd called her Elewa, just like in her dream. Asa didn't know what to feel. She was pissed, for one, but that was no surprise. The heat traveling through her body…that was the surprise. Mr. X stood before her, his face flummoxed, just as surprised as she was. He was everything she thought he would be. His voice was exactly like in her dreams, the deep timbre heating her skin. He was gorgeous. He studied her intently, heat making his eyes glow gray around the outer edges, the same weird eyes that Fallon had. His hair was shorter than it was in her dreams. The waves cropped tight against his head. Sharp cheekbones, a cleft chin, and skin smooth as silk and dark as chocolate.

She turned her attention to Fallon. "Didn't I say I would think about it? You didn't have to send your goon."

The one they called Leo smirked. Fallon punched him in the arm. "He was not sent to kidnap you."

Asa waved her tied hands in front of her. "Yeah, we're no longer in the 'take Fallon at his word' portion of the negotiations."

"I'm really sorry, Asa, we had nothing to do with this." Brianna rushed to explain, untying her hands.

Mr. X behind the desk was silent, his eyes seemingly taking in every detail of her. His gaze was a caress across her body. She felt every sweep of his eyes. But, until she determined what kind of trouble she was in, she would avoid even looking over there.

"Who are you people?" She should be more alarmed and she supposed once she figured out why they wanted her, she'd get there, but for now, curiosity weighed more.

In her line of work, getting on the wrong side of the wrong people was easy. The amount of money she dealt with brought out the worst in people. These guys seemed like neither smugglers nor thieves. Though, they all had an air of badass. They may not be looters, but they certainly belonged to some type of underground.

"As I told you at the cafe, we were sent to get you, to protect you," Fallon said.

She shook her head. That again? "You gave me that spiel already. The only people kidnapping me, are you assholes." At least today anyway.

Leo coughed to cover his laugh.

"Leo," Mr. X's tone was a warning that vibrated down her spine.

She clenched her thighs together and kept her eyes on Fallon. She'd lose it if she looked at her dream man.

Fallon perched on the edge of the desk. "Your father didn't give me a lot of details."

"Wait, what?" Mr. X sat forward, his face pulled down into a fierce scowl.

Fallon winced and shared a look with his wife.

Brianna stepped forward. "X, maybe we can talk about this after."

Asa flinched. His name was actually X? Her heart raced in her chest and she forced down the panic attack threatening to steal her concentration.

"What's wrong?" Leo asked, looking between the other two men.

"Azra is her father. Was that not a detail I needed to know?" Ice coated X's voice and Asa shivered even though it wasn't aimed at her.

"We were interrupted before I could get to that part."

"The fuck you say," Leo whistled and brushed a hand across his face.

X stared Fallon down, anger transforming his face, his eyes glacial. "Brianna, will you take our guest to the club level."

"Excuse you, I'm not a guest, I am a kidnap victim," she reminded him. "Now, where is 'here' and what the hell do you want with me?"

He turned those freaky eyes to her, hazel completely taking over until it nearly glowed amber. Just like in her dreams. Her mouth dried and for once in her life, she had no snappy rejoinder, her mind had gone completely blank. She didn't avert her eyes though. She held his gaze, her will clashing against his.

X's hands moved in a short pattern in front of her. An image flashed and then solidified, floating to the side of her. The man in the image had the same piercing eyes as her, the face, so similar to her own. She gasped and stood. She moved to get closer to the …hologram? Is that what it was? She would ask someone how he did it later, for now, she needed to get closer. She examined the wavering image.

"Do you recognize him?" Fallon asked her softly, still not answering her question.

She shook her head, a lump in her throat. Though, as she examined the image closer, she realized it looked like the face on the coin of her necklace.

"You knew she was Azra's daughter and you laughed at your brother putting her in the trunk," Xavier said in a growl.

"The shit was funny to me, first of all. Second, how the hell was I to know what *our* crazy as hell brother would do?"

"I'm standing right here," was Leo's dry answer.

"Where is he?" She whispered, breaking into their argument.

"This is where it gets tricky. You'll want to be sitting down, Asa," Fallon told her.

Xavier whispered her name in shock. She turned to him and it took everything in her not to cross the room and go into his arms. It felt like she knew him, how long he'd been in her fantasies. It felt like it would be natural to take comfort from him, the same as she would have in her dreams. She parted her lips to ask if he had the same dreams, but Fallon shifted on the desk and she was reminded of his presence. She saw the worry on Xavier's face along with a hint of fear, before he put a neutral look on his face.

"Sit, Asa," he said.

She did as he asked and sat back in the chair. "Where is my father?"

Xavier sighed. "Let me first answer your questions. I'm Xavier, these two are my brothers, Leo, Fallon, and Brianna you've already met. Currently, you're at Haven."

Her heart started pounding anew, stories that Chandra had told her about the place playing in her head. So, the place was real. What other stories about it were?

Xavier continued. "As to your father…I don't know how to say this in a way you're likely to believe, so I'll come right out and say it. Your father is a god."

She sucked her teeth and crossed her arms over her chest. She knew it was too good to be true. Of course the man she'd fantasized about for a year was crazy. Of course.

"That makes you a Demi-god," Fallon said when she remained silent.

"Lord have mercy," she said and stood. "If you're going to waste my time, you've kidnapped me for nothing. How far from my house are we?"

"I think Asa and I should get some air." Brianna stepped to her side.

"What? Is fresh air supposed to make it all more believable?" Leo mocked.

"I have no problem throwing something at you, Leonalph," Brianna growled.

Leo held his hands up and smirked. "So mean."

Asa stood. "Tell me something that will stop me from walking out of here straight to the police department."

Xavier stood up from his desk, leaning forward on his hands. "I've dreamed of you for nearly a year and I don't want you to go. I won't let you leave."

She sucked in a breath, glancing around as everyone else in the room gasped. Asa stepped back.

"Yeah, air is a good idea." She whispered to Brianna.

Chapter 7

'I've dreamed of you for nearly a year.'

She hadn't quite seen that one coming, Asa thought to herself as she and Brianna walked down another hallway.

"You're going to kill me in these catacombs aren't you?" Asa looked around at the stone walls of the corridors they were passing through. They seemed endless, the turns confusing.

Brianna chuckled softly. "It's the same thing I thought when I first starting coming here."

They continued their path, and Asa stared at the ground, her mind on X's statement.

"That was some proclamation, right?" Brianna startled her from her thoughts.

Asa sighed. "What he said is the only thing in this chaos that makes any kind of sense to me."

She didn't explain further and Brianna let it go. Asa didn't breathe easy until they reached a level where she could see afternoon light from outdoors.

"I have a notebook full of information on Demigods." Brianna offered quietly as they walked through a place that looked like the private club the Internet had purported the place to be. There were tables full of dining patrons scattered across the floor.

"I'm not likely to believe it on page, no more than I believe it coming out of his mouth." She muttered, her thoughts lingering on Mr. X.

Xavier.

A beautiful woman with a baby strapped to the front of her walked up to them, her curious gaze raking Asa.

"Asa, this is my sister in law, Liliana and the awesomely cute kid on her chest is Kell. Lily, this is Asa, we're going for a walk." Brianna introduced them.

Liliana blew out a breath. "Can I come with, I'm feeling stifled. I would love to get out for a little bit."

Brianna hummed in agreement. "Wanna go to the ice cream shop close to here?"

"Yes, please" Liliana answered quickly.

Brianna pulled out her phone and Asa looked around the lavish club. Dark hardwood floors stretched across the large room. There were circular tables scattered across the room, deep leather bucket chairs surrounding them. The ceilings were high, and she craned her neck to count how many floors it went up. There was dark mirrored glass on each floor, probably hiding VIP areas on the higher levels. Chandeliers sparkled above, the gold and glass lending opulence to the space. Asa narrowed her eyes at the patrons dining and speaking quietly at the tables.

There were no vampires or other mythical creatures to speak of…that was, of course, ignoring Xavier's proclamation that she was a demigod. She sucked her teeth and turned to Brianna.

"What kind of place is this?"

"Depends on who you ask," Brianna said distractedly. "It's currently a private club for Demi only, but in a few hours, they'll move all of this and turn it into a club that's open to humans."

Asa rubbed her temples and shook her head. Had demigods been on the list of stories Chandra had collected over the years? She could ask, but that would require her mentioning to her friend that 1: the havens she talked about obsessively were real and 2: she'd been kidnapped. Since she had no plans on doing that, Asa would move past the nonsensical and try to get to the bottom of what these people wanted with her.

"All done," Brianna announced.

"Are we leaving, then?" Asa asked.

"Gotta wait a sec."

"For?" Asa looked around.

Four men materialized seemingly out of the shadows.

"We driving?" A handsome man asked as he came up to them. The other three hung back.

"Nope, just walking around the corner to that ice cream shop," Brianna answered.

The man eyed Asa for a long moment, his gaze speculative. He nodded, and turned back, winding his finger in the air. The men dispersed and Brianna gave her a warm smile.

"Let's go. The sun will do you some good."

Asa frowned. "What does that mean?"

"Well, you're a demigod, so you get literal energy from the sun. It will make you feel better to go outside." Brianna said it as though it were a fact.

Asa swallowed her aggravated sigh and looked at Liliana, who simply nodded.

Liliana's lips moved and the t-shirt she was wearing changed into a maxi dress with tiny straps. Asa frowned and stepped back. She wouldn't panic just yet...but questions were swirling in her mind. Brianna waved at her to follow them. They walked out the front door and Asa was happy to be out of Haven. She looked around for the men that Brianna had talked to.

"They're around," Brianna said noticing her searching. "So, tell me about yourself."

Asa growled. She was most definitely not interested in small talk. "Are those men here to guard me?"

"You, no. Well, I guess technically since you're in danger too. They're our guards, we have to have them anytime we leave Haven." Again, Brianna spoke matter of factly.

It was throwing Asa off.

"Why? Who are you guys?"

"Kokoro souls." Brianna shrugged.

"What does that mean?" she asked exasperated.

Liliana put her hand on Brianna's arm. "I'll give you the condensed version because Brianna here can go on for hours."

"It's interesting," Brianna said defensively.

"At one time, the Demi and Humans were in a war. The humans created an evil entity to help them win. That entity was stronger than they planned for and had nearly destroyed the world. To stop him, the humans and Demi came together to bind him since he couldn't be killed. The three people who did it, their souls were called the Kokoro souls. We are them, reborn."

Asa frowned. It sounded so farcical, but she said nothing and kept walking. Like, what the hell could she say in the face of their delusions? Both women spoke as though they were talking about something as simple as the weather.

"There are factions forming, Demi, who want to free Ofeeree and allow him to destroy everything the humans have built."

Asa gave them a droll look at the gaping hole in their story. "That makes no sense. If he destroys the world, where will they live?"

Brianna and Liliana shared a look. "I think these dumbasses think that after he destroys this plane, they'll be able to bind him again. That's where Kokoro souls come in. The knowledge of how Ofeeree was bound and where, was imprinted into three souls on the off chance that Ofeeree ever escaped his prison."

"And you two have those souls?"

"There are three souls, Asa," Brianna said. Her tone suggested the 'duh' was left unsaid.

"That's," she sucked her teeth. "This whole day has been dumb."

She should've listened to Chandra. Bad enough she'd have to call the woman and tell her that she was sort of being held hostage. Not like she couldn't escape if she wanted to, but she wanted answers, and making them think they had her held here was probably the fastest way to get them. What's one more outlandish thing on top of the day? She kept walking and was loathe to admit that the late afternoon sun was relaxing her.

She had to give Brianna and Liliana both props. Neither of them tried to talk to her, instead, letting a surprisingly easy silence settle over them. They got to the ice cream shop. It wasn't too busy, but there were enough people there that she thought briefly of shouting for help. They ordered and sat at an outside table. Liliana cooed at her baby and Brianna studied Asa.

"You're waiting on me to react." Asa met the other woman's stare head-on.

"I mean, it's a pretty crazy story. You're not reacting. It's kind of freaking me out."

Asa's mouth lifted a little, amused at the woman's bluntness. It was refreshing. "I hunt treasure for a living, crazy stories are my bag."

Though the magic trick of Liliana changing her dress was still throwing her for a loop.

Brianna sat forward, her eyes bright with interest. "Treasure, treasure?"

Asa sucked on her spoon. "Antiques, fabled treasures, yes."

"Oh, that's just cool as hell. Have you found anything?" Liliana asked.

She nodded. It was a knack. One that made her highly sought after in certain circles. Not one to brag, she left it at the simple answer.

"Like what?"

"Brianna," Liliana said in warning. "She'll question you until you're blue in the face if you let her."

Liliana gave her sister in law an indulgent smile. Asa was envious for a slight moment. She wanted that. Outside of Chandra, she didn't talk to other people and she'd never been able to make friends. Not that she hadn't tried. Her mother had always said she had a giant presence and not everyone could handle it. She sighed and scooped up more ice cream.

"What do the guys want with me? Let's leave out the fantastical aspects if you please." Those she could sift through on her own if she decided to take the job.

Brianna shrugged. "As far as I know, your father told my husband to keep you safe. We're supposed to stop you from bringing about the apocalypse."

Liliana snorted. "Bri," she chided.

"What? I'm just repeating what Fallon told me."

"He did not say that."

"Not in those words, no," she admitted.

Asa sucked her teeth again. "Lord have mercy," she muttered.

Brianna smiled. "I personally think you're the last Kokoro soul and your father knows it. Bringing you to Haven is the only way to keep you safe."

"I can't stay here."

"You'll have to take that up with the guys. But, I will ask that you let me teach you about the Demi before you leave. I wouldn't want you just out and about not aware of how much danger you're in."

Asa twirled her spoon. "Chile, please. People have been after me since I first started looking for treasure."

Brianna shook her head. "Not these kinds of people. And they certainly aren't after treasure. I wouldn't be surprised if the 'people' you claim are after your treasure have been after your magic instead."

"Girl, with this magic shit," Asa said exasperated.

"You don't have to believe me," Brianna rolled her eyes. "You can take it up with Xavier."

She could leave any time she wanted and there wasn't a whole lot they could do to stop her, but, she wanted to know about X's dreams, and also, she did want to know about her father, so she'd play along for a bit.

"You guys think my father is a god? Like, a literal one." She eyed the women, studying their faces.

Neither of the women said anything, they simply stared. It was interesting, as far as stories went. She'd tracked down crazier stories, and had seen plenty of things no one would believe. The same sense she'd gotten for treasure started tingling and she made a decision.

"How long?"

"You're the one with the antsy soul, how long do you think you could give me?" Brianna went back to eating her ice cream.

Asa blinked, the only outward sign of her shock at the woman's accuracy. Unless actually on the hunt, she could never stay in one place for more than a month. It had driven her mother's husband crazy, her constant activity.

"Three weeks, a month max," she answered truthfully.

"Deal." Brianna held out her hand to shake when they heard the baby growl.

"Is that your baby making that sound?" Asa asked.

Lily looked up, "yes. We need to go."

They all stood at the same time, just as guards rushed their table. A black SUV squealed to a stop next to them a moment before the table next to them exploded.

"Shit," the guy yelled over the noise of screams. "In the car, now!"

They were shoved into the SUV. Asa's heart was racing. She looked back and found a couple of people standing apart from the chaos, their gaze on the retreating vehicle. Her mind, even through the fear, cataloged their features. Both of the men were overly tall, one on the lankier side, the other built with muscles. Their eyes were what struck Asa. Dead, but there was a glowing ring around their pupils, just like Fallon and Xavier. That complicated things for her. For one, she'd seen those eyes before, and not just on her kidnappers. Brianna's words about 'people' being after her struck her hard and sent nausea reeling in her stomach. If she needed proof, those men were it. She had not seen them before, but she knew she'd definitely seen people *like* them before.

And often.

She whipped back around as they took a turn on two wheels. They pulled into the parking lot they'd left and found all three men outside waiting for them. Each of them in varying states of worry. She only had eyes for one though. Asa let the other women get out first along with their guard before she got out. Xavier was fussing at Liliana about being careful. He towered over her, his uniform all black, intimidating. Asa was impressed with the way the slender woman stood her ground. Liliana was completely different, from earlier. Gone was the light skin woman with short hair. Left was a creature out of a fairytale in her place. Her skin was bronzed and glowing, her hair down her back in a riot of colors. Asa froze in place, mesmerized by Liliana's new appearance.

"We took guards, we were careful," Lily snapped.

"You are carrying around the future king of Legba—"

"You think I don't know my son's birthright?"

"Then move accordingly." He growled. X turned to Brianna.

The woman held up her hand. "Xavier, I know you're mad because you're worried, but I ain't the one. We sensed the danger and acted as quickly as we could."

"She's right, Marshal. They were moving before we got to them," the guard said. He squeezed Brianna's arm and left them in the company of a scowling Xavier.

Fallon pulled his wife's back into his chest and kissed the top of her head. "They're fine for now, X. Let them calm down. Lily, can you find Asa a room?"

Liliana pushed a shaking hand through her hair. "Yeah, I have a place to put her."

Leo cupped his wife's cheeks and dropped soft kisses across her face. There was no trace of the smirking jackass who had kidnapped her. He was gentle as he unstrapped the baby from Lily's front and pulled the infant into his chest, murmuring to him as they turned to head inside. Their love was evident.

Lily turned back to her, her eyes now glowing, same as the two men who'd attacked them. "You coming, Asa?"

She debated it. Was the whole thing a set up to get her to stay? Tensions were high, and she didn't think anyone could fake the panic and relief on all their faces, so she chucked that theory. Still, she should leave. She should get as far as she could away from these people. But, everything Brianna had said to her was brought to life the moment that…bomb went off. Was she in danger, or was it because she was in the company of the two women? She snuck a glance at Xavier. She wanted nothing more than to step into his chest the way Brianna was snuggled into Fallon's but she reminded herself that he didn't know her, and dreams were not real.

Should she stay? Yes, she wanted to know about her father. Yes, she wanted to know more about Xavier, but, no…she didn't like being in close proximity to danger.

"Asa," Liliana prompted.

Xavier stared at her, his copper eyes boring into her. His worry was there for her to read, but there was also longing, and…desperation. He said he'd dreamed of her. She nodded, her heart still hammering, her own trembling contained only by her iron will.

Yes, she would stay.

Chapter 8

Xavier's gaze tracked Asa into the building and only once the front door closed did he breathe easier. His heart was racing and his beast was banging at the control he asserted over his power. He would wait until he got back to his office before he loosed his magic. Fallon watched him carefully.

"Say it." He growled, still pissed at all his brother had hidden from him.

"She's fine, in one piece, we can put that in the win column."

Xavier stormed off, not giving a fuck about a win column. He wanted to go to his mate and reassure her, make sure she was fine, but he had no rights to her. All he had were dreams and dreams were not real.

How the fuck had he found her and nearly lost her all in a day? He didn't know how his brothers dealt with it. Asa had stood there, her face a mask, hiding the fear he could feel coming from her. He wanted to go to her. His beast was demanding it, slamming against his subconscious trying to force his change. He was breathing hard by the time he reached his office, unable to say anything to Adia as he stomped through to his desk.

He closed the door behind him, wincing as it slammed. He paced in front of his desk, his only saving grace that he didn't know what room

Liliana would put her in. It was the only thing stopping him. He could question Liliana, but Leo wouldn't allow it. It took him several long minutes to calm himself enough to sit. No sooner than his butt hit the chair did his assistant come in. One day he'd figure out how Adia knew his moods. She handed him a snifter of Brandy and a file. He noted her trembling hands.

"What's happening?"

"Trouble on Mulu." She answered stiffly.

It was her homeworld, of course she'd be worried. He opened the file, his mind instantly going into work mode. "What kind of trouble?"

She cleared her throat. "It's what's pushing Prince Khalid's visit back. According to gossip, someone is trying to start an insurrection."

"Interesting," he murmured flipping through the file. "Who's newly here from Mulu?"

"I'll find out, what do you want me to do?"

"Send them down to Fallon, I'm gonna fill him in so he can question them."

She nodded and left. A coup? His mind started moving through the different scuffles taking place across the seven realms. He didn't believe in coincidences and there were was too much shaking and moving for the incidents to all be separate. Glad for the distraction, he put his mind into his work. He pushed his comms.

"Adia, call—"

"Already done, Marshal. It will take a little bit, they're taking care of their mates but promised to come straight down."

He closed the hologram and pulled up the security office. There was a buzz of activity going on behind the shift commander.

"We're on it, Marshal. I sent a crew down to the shopping center. We have a contact in the police department, so I should know something here shortly."

Xavier nodded grimly. "Initial impression?"

"Fallon sent a Kira immediately. The spell wasn't set to kill. I think they were hoping to take the females alive."

"Michel said they threw a bomb."

The watch captain sighed. "Doing magic on Adro is iffy, Marshal. Despite the damage to the property, the magic that saturated the area wasn't meant to kill."

Xavier hummed and gripped the arms of his chair. Still, his magic slipped. "I want a report as soon as you're done."

"Yes, Marshal."

Xavier ended the communication and swung his chair around. He stared at the beach landscape above him. It was a spot on Chuita, his home realm, on his family's beach. He gave vague thought of taking Asa and running. Fallon had done it last year with his mate. He'd understood when his brother had done it at the time. He understood it even more now.

"Marshal," Adia called from his intercom.

Fuck! He swallowed the other curses on the tip of his tongue. Unlike Fallon, if he left his office, there was no telling what would happen in his absence.

He'd never once regretted his job…until this moment.

He turned around and got back to work.

###

Asa wandered the hallways of Haven, her eyes taking in the staff moving up and down the halls, along with what appeared to be soldiers. This was no private club. It looked like an army base and she wanted answers. The room they'd given her was nice, better than any five-star hotel she'd ever spent time in. The bed was plush and luxurious, but sleep had still eluded her. Everything on the surface looked like a hotel room, but then there were the odd things that stuck out and let her know she was operating just outside of the norm. The furniture that molded to her body as she sat, the way the whole room looked as if lit by sunlight when she knew for a fact they were underground, but most of all how high tech everything was.

She was still deciding whether or not it was simply very expensive things she would've never had access to, or something otherworldly.

She gripped her phone in her hands, debating whether or not to call Chandra. She likely could get out of this on her own. All she had to do was find the way out and walk away. She didn't need help with that. No, she wanted to call Chandra because she needed someone to talk to about Xavier. She needed someone to tell her she wasn't crazy, that it wasn't poor judgment to see if the man from her dreams was the real deal.

The attack earlier today had shaken her, she'd be a fool to not be wary. In all the trouble she'd got into treasure hunting, nearly being blown up had never happened. Arrested, kidnapped, trapped in a cave or two, those things were part of her normal life. People trying to kill her…that was new. And, she didn't like it. She took a hard breath. So the obvious answer was to leave. Sneak out and initiate the emergency protocol she and Chandra had to get her out of tight places.

And yet…

She looked down at the lounge clothes, she could pretend that was why she hadn't bounced, but she'd hauled ass out of a hotel in a Led Zeppelin t-shirt and panties once. Shame was not something she ascribed to.

"Asa."

She looked up as her name was called. She sucked in a breath as she spotted Mr. X walking towards her. How someone that fine existed outside of her dreams was the question. Now that she was staring, she realized it hadn't been a uniform he'd been wearing. Still, the sight of him in all black had her stomach clenching in desire. The tight black t-shirt he wore was short-sleeved, showing off his muscular arms, it hung down to his waist, tucked into the front of his pants behind his belt. His cargo pants were tucked into some ass-kicking boots and hung baggy around his waist. She wanted them tighter, so she could measure that bulge and see if it matched her Mr. X.

He stopped in front of her and his scent wrapped around her. She leaned over and took a deep inhale. Heat suffused her body, loosening her tense muscles. Lord, he smelled amazing.

"Where are you going?"

His deep voice matched her dreams. She closed her eyes and took a second to savor that. When she opened them, his gaze was serious, tracing her face.

She cleared her throat. "Getting the lay of the land."

He grunted. "Smart. Can I walk with you?"

"Keeping an eye on me?" She narrowed her eyes.

"Putting words in my mouth, *elewa*?" He tilted his head to the side, his mouth lifting in a small smirk.

Hearing that name, seeing that smirk, her breath stalled and a lump formed in her throat. Could it really be him?

She shook her head. "Teasing," she whispered.

He lifted his hand to her face but dropped it before he could touch her. He sighed. "I can go if you'd rather have some time alone."

She swallowed down her nervousness and took a deep breath. She wouldn't get answers fangirling. She needed to remember that.

"No, you can answer some questions while we walk." She straightened her shoulders.

"Fair enough." He moved next to her, turning to face the direction she was going.

She started walking and for a moment, they walked silently together. She wanted to touch him, hold his hand, maybe lean into him. She thought longingly of how easy her dream Mr. X had been to talk to. As they walked, some of the soldiers would pause and salute him, it brought up her earlier misgivings.

"Is this a base?"

"Not in the way you mean. The havens are places where Demis can safely be in the same space as humans. The soldiers here keep the peace." He answered.

She cut him a side-eye. "These big ass men are peacekeepers?"

He chuckled. 'We're dealing with demigods, Asa."

She snorted, still not quite believing that. She thought back to Liliana's transformation. "Everyone looks human." And nothing like the mythological creatures Chandra swore would roam the halls of this place.

"It's required once you leave Haven. The hallways are filled with people going back and forth, so they tend to stay in that form until back in Demi space."

She took a moment to process that. She went over the small snatches of information she and Chandra had collected over the years and tried to fit them into what he was saying. The whole concept of the havens had been like tales of El Dorado to her. Yes, such a place may have existed, but she knew years of oral tales could change the true meaning of a legend. With the talk of demigods, Asa could see where some of the more outlandish tales of haven had been born. One sighting of a demigod in something other than the 'human form' Xavier talked about had probably fueled stories of otherworldly creatures.

Her mind drifted back to Liliana. The woman had looked straight out of fairy tale.

"You're not going to ask me about what I said?" His voice brought her out of her musings. A sharp edge of longing stole over her.

"I was getting there," she mumbled. She slid a look at his profile. His face was serious, his eyes scanning around them, as though he never took a break from work.

"You can't imagine my surprise when I saw you in the back of my brother's car."

"Trunk," she corrected. She planned to cuss his brother smooth out when she saw him next.

He grimaced. "I'm sorry about that. Your neighbors were complaining about a power source and you were the likely culprit. Leo got a little overzealous."

She stopped and spun to face him. "What do you mean my neighbors were complaining? Why would they come to you?"

"Your mother somehow bought a house smack dab in the middle of a Demi neighborhood," he commented casually.

She shook her head. "That's not...I bought that house for my mother. I picked out that neighborhood."

His eyebrows raised. "That makes more sense. I'm would imagine it felt safe to you."

It had. She'd felt safe and comfortable from the moment she had gotten out of her rental car. Deena had been skeptical, but she'd gone along with it for Asa. Had she subconsciously felt the Demi there?

"What about the power source? What does that mean?"

"I'm still working on that one." He rubbed a hand down his face. "One of the many things I'm trying to figure out about you."

"I can answer for myself," she said defensively.

"I do not doubt that, Asa." He grabbed her shoulders and moved her aside as an employee passed with a cart full of food floating in front of them.

She swiveled her head to watch him, fascinated once again by the technology she found in this place. They started walking again. The whole thing was getting very bizarre. They lapsed into silence.

"Were you having the dreams as well?" His voice was curious, careful.

"For a year now," she admitted.

He put a hand on her arm to stop her movement. "What do you think it means that we've both been dreaming about each other and you show up here?" His heated gaze caressed her face and she lowered her eyes.

"I don't…" she lifted her eyes and met his. "It's the only reason I'm staying. I want to find out."

A hungry growl was his answer, but he made no move to close the distance between them. She wanted him to. She wanted to see if the heat between them was real. His cologne reached out to her and she leaned closer, her lids dipping low. He sighed and released her arm, stepping back.

"I'm having the hardest time with my control around you," he said softly.

She stepped closer, chasing his elusive smell. "I can't tell."

"The very fact that you look drunk off my scent says otherwise," He muttered, cupping her cheek. "Let me walk you back to your room."

She sighed, not understanding his words, and frankly not caring. Especially since it seemed he wouldn't do anything about the lust bubbling up between them. She gave him a small smile that was barely a lift of her lips, hopefully hiding her disappointment.

"I'm sorry about your mother," he said as they stopped in front of her room door.

Her eyes clouded over, and sadness covered her face, "thank you."

He cupped her cheek and dipped down, brushing a light kiss across her lips. "Don't leave yet, okay? Give me time with you."

She sighed, her mind in turmoil. She wanted time with him as well. Her sense of self-preservation warred with that need. His dark eyes traced her face, the edges of his pupils glowing the longer they stared at each other. She nodded finally and his shoulders relaxed. The smile he gave her melted her heart, as well as areas a lot more south than her chest.

"I'll see you later, then?" He whispered against her lips.

Asa tiptoed and kissed him deeply, sighing at her first real taste of him. She wanted to drag him into her room for more, but she stepped back, reticence taking over.

"I'll see you later," she promised.

Chapter 9

Asa couldn't pinpoint what had awakened her. Hell, she was surprised she'd managed to fall asleep if she were being honest with herself. She been kidnapped and nearly blown up on the same day. As far as adventures go, this was panning out to be one of the wilder ones. It didn't quite beat the time she'd been kicked out of Turkey and accused of stealing national treasures. Nothing compared to the fear of a dozen or so rifles pointed directly at her.

The only reason she hadn't lavished in a prison there was partly because of Chandra, but also, she'd had no intention of actually stealing any of the antiques she'd found. She'd happened upon the ancient ruins entirely on accident chasing down a client's stolen Matisse. It happened all the time, her stumbling onto ancient ruins and the treasures within. Normally she alerted local universities and went about her day. In this instance, curiosity had won. The military police happened upon her as she was being nosy.

She stretched and rolled over on her side, burrowing deeper into the most comfortable mattress she'd ever experienced in her life. It was like sleeping on a cloud, the way it hugged her body. Her heart lodged in her throat as something moved in the shadows beside the bed.

It was a man.

He was sitting in the shadow, his silhouette visible, his legs crossed, arms on his knee. Her heart was racing. With the thumb of her right hand, she rubbed across her ring finger. Her token was absent, marking the interaction as a dream. She calmed down and turned to the stranger invading her dream.

She propped her head on her hand. "Can I help you?"

The shadows around him lifted and once again her heartbeat took flight. The man was beautiful, otherworldly, his lean figure fit perfect in slacks and crisp white shirt, a vest buttoned on top. He smiled and her body relaxed without any input from her mind. It was when she reached his eyes that she scrambled to a sitting position. Lavender, and in the same almond shape of her own, same as in the picture Xavier had shown her earlier.

"Who are you?" Though she already knew the answer, she wanted to hear it from him.

"Give it a minute," he said, his deep gravelly voice filling the space in her bedroom.

"You're my father?" It made sense that she would dream of him.

"Got it in one," he said, his chair gliding closer to her bed. He stared at her for long moments. "You look so much like Deena, yet like me, it's uncanny."

"This is a dream." She reminded herself.

"Alas, the only way I'm able to visit with you."

She bunched her brows. "You can't come to Haven?"

"I can't come to Earth at all, but that is not what I visited you to discuss."

"What then?" She whispered through her dry throat.

"I wanted to see you, see you acknowledge me since I'm free to make my presence known to you."

"What was stopping you from before?"

"Deena and I had an agreement." His jaw clenched and he looked away. "I could never tell her no, even right up to the end."

"You visited her?" Rage filled her. "You saw how she lived, why didn't you do anything?"

His eyes lit, his anger matching hers. "Deena made choices for both of us. I was bound by my words to her."

"Why are you trying to get into my life now?"

"You're in danger, I have always protected you, will always protect you."

She took a deep breath and calmed her anger and reminded herself that it was all a figment of her imagination. She sighed and rolled to her back. She wanted to be dreaming about X, not a man she'd never get to meet.

"You're going to ignore me?" Surprise colored his voice.

"What, dream daddy, can you possibly tell me with the limited information that I have on you?" What was the use?

He snorted. "You're disgustingly practical and entirely too much like me for my comfort."

She chuckled at the thought of that. Was she like her father? "I wonder why you sent Fallon to get me."

"With your mother's death, some of the hold on your magic was gone, I had to get you away before more vultures started circling Deena's neighborhood."

Asa frowned at that, trying to imagine any of the nice people on her mother's street as vultures.

"Why didn't you save her?" Her throat clogged, grief barreling down on her.

"Deena didn't want to be saved, Asa. I tried until she cut me off. She blocked me from even her dreams. It's a rare power your mother held…you hold."

"You sent her money?" She thought about all the money in the accounts her mother had. Where had that money come from? Here in her dreams, she could pretend it came from some sense of honor her father held.

"She felt betrayed once she found out who I was, it was no wonder she wouldn't allow me to see you. I don't know if she even spent the money, but it was the least I could do."

"She found out you're a god?" Asa mocked, shaking her head. Straight up nonsense.

"Not just any god, daughter of mine, but a hell god. Worse, a trickster god. Deena worshiped my brother, Rugaba, she was brought up to believe me an evil entity." He grabbed her hand, pressing it against his as though comparing their differing size. "Still, she wouldn't denounce me, no matter the pressure from her people. But, she did cut me off from the two of you, her compromise for an untenable situation. She came to me when you turned thirteen, your power was waking and swelling too big for her to control."

Asa frowned because she didn't know what he meant. Her mother had served no god as far as she knew. They'd never gone to church, didn't so much as say grace. Where had that thought come from? A god of hell?

Her father let out a frustrated sigh. "You still don't understand your power, nor the power your mother held over the world of dreams. How many visits with me before you start believing, I wonder?"

He moved her over and lay down beside her. A comforting warmth wrapped around her. A tear escaped and she closed her eyes to trap the others behind it.

Asa clutched the necklace at her throat. "Did you leave this for me?"

"I did. It keeps your magic concealed from others."

"Why didn't I need it before?"

"You did, technically. I hadn't realized Deena was using her magic to conceal you. One more way she hid who I was from you," he said forlornly.

Oh lord, now she was buying into the concept of magic. She thought about Liliana and the way her hair glowed, she still hadn't come up with a scientific excuse for that.

"So I'm a demigod?"

"A very powerful one, daughter of mine."

Asa rolled over and stared at him, her eyes tracing his face. "I wish you were real."

He gave her a sad smile and kissed her forehead. "You'll find out how real I am soon enough, *okan mi*."

Asa forced herself awake and sat up in bed, her heart breaking into a million pieces, lonelier than she'd ever felt in her life. Her thumb automatically went to her ring finger. Finding the simple silver band there reassured her. She wiped a hand over her face and rolled over to leave the bed. She needed information. Her dream had left her lonely yes, but curious more than anything. She needed to find Brianna.

Xavier walked into his office after a fitful nights' sleep. He'd wanted desperately to go to Asa. Even in the small snatches of sleep he'd claimed, she'd eluded him. His magic was flaring wildly around him this morning, out of control. He'd had to force his beast down, wrestling with his power to get into his human form. The attack from yesterday was still unsettling him. He'd come close to losing Asa and he'd reckoned it would be a while before he could shake that feeling.

He looked at the pile of files he'd left on his desk last night after giving up trying to work. It was bad enough that he'd finally met his mate, but to find out she was Azra's daughter. He'd had a lot on his mind last night. And now he had to make up for all that work. He sighed and rounded his desk.

He'd made notes about the trouble on Mulu. His brothers had stayed with their mates the rest of the day and he hadn't had the chance to talk to them. He pulled up his comms, to demand their presence when Leo walked in.

Xavier looked up as Leo walked into his office in his Cagyn form, his black hair flowing to the middle of his back. He was tall and bulky in this form, the copper power lines all Cagyns had glowing up and down his skin. His brother wasn't as dark as he and Fallon were, instead his mixed heritage making his onyx skin closer a dark chestnut.

"Is Lily alright?"

Leo nodded and took a seat. His brother's hands shook as he grabbed one of the many files Xavier had pulled out for them to go over.

"These reports are on thefts on the Gu realm. Adia said you wanted to talk to us about the Benu realm."

Xavier grunted. "I think they're related."

"The Gu are known for their weapons, but who'd be brave enough to take on the giants to steal them? What would be worth that?" Leo flipped through the pages.

There had been thefts on Mawu, highly dangerous weapons, ones that hadn't been used in centuries. On the surface, it wasn't anything to garner their attention, but together with everything else…there were too many coincidences. As Leo said, there weren't a lot of Demi crazy enough to take on the Iron Giants. The Gu made weapons for the Demi, weapons made of iron, and various Earth metals. Their weapons were coveted, and the strongest made across all seven realms. For that reason alone, Mawu was one realm that was protected by more than one monarchy. It was political suicide, not to mention actual suicide to mess with the nine-foot-tall creatures.

Leo flipped through the pages, his gaze intense. "I have a few spies on Mawu, I'll put some feelers out." He frowned. "Some of this shit is ancient, who would steal weapons this old?"

Xavier dropped another file in front of his brother. "Now couple that with this treaty dispute on Minona. The Mina claim that there have been Demi using their meeting place without their permission. The Benu who are doing so are claiming that there was an agreement in place that allowed anyone use of it."

"The meeting place where the Mina store prophecies?" Fallon asked from the door.

Xavier nodded, catching his brother's eyes. Fallon was also in his Cagyn form, his nearly seven-foot-tall form folding into the chair next to Leo. Instead of the normal suit and tie his brother wore, Fallon was in mission gear, all black from head to toe, his powerlines lit, and the points of his fangs visible. He could only assume from his brothers' appearance that their beasts were still jumpy after yesterday's incident with their mates. He couldn't judge, he'd fought his own beast this morning to get back into his human form.

"Bri?"

"She's shaken up, but fine. She says they're restless. Nothing has happened in so long, I think they thought it would be okay." Fallon said quietly. He pushed a hand through his hair, his black-tipped claws sharp and long. "Look, X, I'm sorry about yesterday. I know you're dealing with a lot of shit, I didn't mean to add my shit on top of all that."

"Fallon, you could've…" Xavier sighed and waved away the thought. "Just be careful."

Fallon nodded and just like that, the air between them was cleared. "So what's this about a coup on Mulu?"

He caught Fallon up on what he and Leo had been discussing. Leo looked down at his communicator as it beeped, letting out a low whistled.

"There are a lot of rumors flying around," Leo said.

"About Mulu?" Xavier leaned back in his chair.

"Just a second," Leo murmured, typing furiously.

"What are we going to do about Mulu?" Fallon asked, turning his attention back to Xavier.

"Outside of making sure the Amanda there are neutral, what do you want us to do?"

"What if a coup happens?"

Xavier sighed. "You know how the Benu are. We don't have any authority in that realm outside of that portal station. Order your men to keep the portal safe and functioning, that's all we can do."

Fallon let out a frustrated breath. "And if they take out the monarchy?"

"It's not our job," Xavier told Fallon.

"Can we live with that?"

"We'll have to." It wasn't a decision Xavier made lightly. It wasn't their place to save the monarchs. "I won't risk our men, not in this. Bigger troubles are coming. All we can do is switch out the Benu for soldiers who have no alliance to make sure they stay out of it. All I care about is that protocol at the portal entry is followed."

Fallon stared at him a while before nodding.

"If you get different information, we'll assess again." He promised his brother, wincing at the concession. It wasn't for them to intervene.

"That's all I can ask then," Fallon said finally.

"I want instructions to get Adia's parents to a safe location if needed though," He added softly, glancing towards his front office.

"Already in place," Fallon assured him.

"You won't believe this, X" Leo cut in. "I have a few people monitoring some of the illegal portals we've found over the years and they have become a hotbed of activity."

Alarm skittered down his spine. "This after an attack on the Kokoro souls?" Another coincidence? Not likely.

"Interesting," Fallon murmured.

"That's one word for it," Leo shook his head. "I want to chase this down."

"We need to close as many of those illegal portals as we can," Xavier ordered Fallon.

Fallon nodded, his fingers moving across his communicator.

Leo stopped typing and looked up. "So…are we going to talk about your dreams of Asa?"

"Let's get into it," Fallon said, leaning forward.

"None of your fucking business," he grumbled. "Why are you changing the subject anyway? There are other things to worry about."

"I personally have time to talk about both," Fallon crossed his legs.

"I don't want to talk about it."

"But, like, what kind of dreams? That's all I wanna know." Leo prodded.

Xavier groaned, knowing neither of his brothers would drop it. He was surprised it had taken them so long to ask. They had both relaxed falling back into their human forms, their magic contained, though still flowing tightly around them. He was glad they'd calmed. The last thing he needed was either of his brothers prowling Haven in their beast's form on a hair-trigger.

"Do you think she's your mate?" Fallon asked.

Xavier's stomach dipped, his nerves skittering. "Yes."

Leo and Fallon shared a smile and they both stood.

"Then we'll drop it for now," Fallon gave him a smug look and stood to leave.

Leo followed suit.

Xavier frowned at them both. "You're leaving here to tell your mates aren't you?"

They both gave him wide eyes. Xavier shook his head. That's exactly what they were going to do. Bunch of gossips.

"I'll keep you posted on the other thing," Leo said, leaving.

He sighed. Shit, if they told their wives, then the chances were Asa would know soon. He hadn't talked to her since yesterday and even then the conversation had been short. He needed to change that.

Chapter 10

Asa leaned back in the chair, slouching lower as Brianna handed her yet another book.

"I don't know what you want me to do with all these books."

"Don't you research before you go 'treasure hunting'?" Brianna lowered her fingers from her air quotes and gave Asa a chastising look.

Asa snickered and turned another page. "Nope, I go on instincts alone," she lied.

Brianna snorted. "Whatever, bitch."

Asa laughed. "No, but really, my assistant Chandra does the research, I'm on the ground. I use my gut for a lot of my work."

Brianna hummed and went back to reading. Asa sighed, clearly the woman wouldn't be swayed from her research. Liliana had warned her. That's what she got for going to Brianna for information. But, she was anxious to know about her father.

"So what are we looking for exactly?" She ruffled the pages between her fingers.

"Well, I want to know how you were…made."

Asa snickered. "Should I explain the birds and bees to you, then?"

Brianna glared and went back to her book. "Everything I've read about Azra says he can't come to the mortal plane, so I'm curious as to how you came to be. Plus, you don't have any, like, outward power. I want to know why."

"What does it matter to you?"

Brianna shrugged. "I'm curious like that."

Asa looked around the library and propped her legs up on the chair across from her. "Tell me about the Demi."

Brianna sighed, "You don't believe us about you being Demi?"

"Do I think I'm a demigod? I'm gonna go with no."

"You're Demi?" A sharp voice asked. It was an older woman, her eyes glowing with curiosity.

"Penny, hi, I didn't see you when we came in."

"Who is this?" The woman asked.

Penny's eyes were dark, but ringed with gray as with the other 'Demi' Asa had seen walking around Haven. The woman's kinky hair was sandy brown and pulled back into a bun, but the soft edges were haloed around her face as though fighting to work out of the tight confines of Penny's chignon. Freckles dotted across the woman's wide nose and high cheekbones, her skin light brown, but in a way that looked kissed by gold. She was beautiful, with a studious air about her. Penny studied Asa as thoroughly as she studied her.

"I'm glad to see you, actually." Brianna sat taller. "This is Asa. She's the daughter of Azra."

Penny frowned. "That's not…" She scanned Asa's face and Asa, unbothered, continued to stare back at the woman. "You look like every depiction of him I've seen. That would make you the first pure Demi born in more than a millennium. Who is your mother? Is she human?"

"Was," Asa told her.

Penny's face transformed with empathy, as though she'd just realized what kind of questions she'd been asking. Which gave her points in Asa's book.

"I'm sorry for your loss. How old are you?"

"Thirty-ish." More -ish than thirty, but this lady didn't need to know.

"Thirty…" Penny sat in the chair across from Brianna. "That's…I don't sense any power in you."

"A mystery," Brianna murmured, her eyes going between the two women.

"Has a Kira seen you?"

Asa shrugged, "I don't know what that means."

"X doesn't want a lot of people knowing about her yet," Brianna spoke up.

Penny nodded and ran a hand across her hair.

"Explain to me what the Demi are." Asa pulled her feet back underneath her and sat up, putting her elbows on the table.

"I already tried to do that," Brianna pointed out.

"I want to hear it from her," Asa inclined her chin towards Penny. The other woman's disbelief was intriguing to her.

"Well, our legends tell that the gods created human, the Divine, molded them out of clay and breathed life into them. It was said that some gods fell in love with the others' creations."

"So they started having sex and the Demi are the product?"

Penny nodded. "What would you like to know beyond that?"

"Why are you surprised I exist?" It was the more pertinent question, especially since Penny was staring at Asa like a specimen.

"For one, there hasn't been a pure Demigod born in centuries. Long centuries. The gods were punished during the war between the Divine and the Demi. They were set apart from humans. Never to intervene."

"The same war you were telling me about yesterday?" She asked Brianna.

The woman nodded.

Penny took a deep breath. "They were fighting because the Divine were covetous of the power their offspring had."

Asa shook her head. "Always about power. My mother said she grew up in an Esin, what's that?"

Brianna gave her a sharp look. "You grew up in an Esin?"

Asa shook her head, she didn't even know what that meant. "I only saw mention of it in a letter my mother wrote."

Penny hummed. "So a pure Demi. Interesting."

"Esin's are like…" Brianna bit her lip. "It's a Divine community. They all live and worship together."

"Like a cult?" Asa frowned.

"Thank you! People act like I'm crazy as hell when I say it," she muttered.

Asa shook her head. "Anyways, finish what you were saying."

"What started as petty squabbles became worse when the Divine made a sacrifice to the gods to beg for more power." Penny picked the story back up.

"What kind of sacrifice?"

"The human kind," Brianna answered.

Asa shuddered. Jesus.

"The humans' lifespan was shortened and then the fighting started in earnest." Penny sighed.

"If the Demi were so powerful, why didn't they just crush the humans?"

"Ofeeree," Penny said.

Asa looked to Brianna, "from yesterday?"

Brianna nodded. "Ultimate evil." She put down the book she was holding and sat forward, pushing through some of the texts and journals scattered on the library table. She lifted a heavy volume, flipping through the pages until she came upon a landscape covering two pages. She opened the book wide and set it in front of Asa.

Asa's heart started thumping and she leaned forward, blown away by the scene depicted in the artist's rendering. It was war. Bloody, messy war, one side with creatures in all different type of forms, and on the other, humans, their faces twisted in hate, their hands tightly gripping weapons. Behind the humans loomed a darkness not quite formed, but menacing all the same. In the clouds were what she could only assume were gods with their backs turned to the carnage.

Asa was fascinated by how beautiful it was but, mostly what had her rendered mute was the fact that she'd seen the artwork before. Her hands shook as she grazed her fingers across the page.

"I've seen this depiction before." She whispered.

Brianna whipped to her. "What? Where?"

Asa racked through her brain to remember where and what circumstances. She'd barely been able to make out the art at the time, due to its condition, but she would never forget the gut punch she'd gotten from it. "It was on ragged tapestry in a cave somewhere in South America…maybe." she shook her head. "Maybe kidnap number two?"

"Lord, how many times have you been kidnapped?" Brianna gripped her arms.

Asa shrugged. "It comes with the job. Everyone wants treasure, and I'm damned good at finding it."

Brianna and Penny shared an incredulous look.

Asa shrugged, her eyes riveted to the page. She pointed to the dark cloud, bringing the subject back around from her kidnappings. "Does darkness represent Ofeeree?"

Penny nodded. "The Divine created him and loosed him on the world. It killed anything and everything in its path."

"But the Demi eventually won?" She sat back and gave Penny her attention.

"If one can call it that." Penny drummed her fingernails on the table. "The gods' final act for us was to create realms where we could escape the humans. But Offeeree wanted all."

"Why didn't the gods help?" The artist was clear that the gods hadn't helped.

"The gods had lost control of their creation and the primal source punished them for it, forbidding them from getting involved and raising the stakes and loss of life. Ofeeree was something I imagine no one saw coming. To create a being with no soul, nothing to tether it to the Earth, it was evil, unspeakable. With the gods out of the picture, there was nothing stopping the Divine."

An interesting story, but as far as Asa was concerned, it was just that…a story. Not to say she didn't love a good story. The artist rendering did bring it to life for her, though. It gave credence to their legend. Not so much that it was real, but more so that it was a legend that went beyond Brianna and her friends making it up. Clearly more than one group of people believed it.

"And how did we get to here?"

"Eventually, the Divine and Demi came together to stop Ofeeree. They bound his physical body, and hid him from his followers."

Asa hummed, it matched the recap Liliana had given her yesterday. "And the world as it is currently? I've never heard of the Demi, so I assume you guys squirreled away to your dimensions? What are the havens for?" Would Penny's answer match the one Xavier gave her? Asa leaned forward.

"The Demi are still connected to the Earth's essence. At least once a month, they must pass through to Adro in order to replenish their life force."

Asa looked at Brianna for clarification.

"They come to soak up energy from the sun."

"Ah. So your dimensions don't have that?"

"To an extent," Penny commented. "The Havens serve as a place for Demi to pass through and be counted. It keeps some of the more dangerous of us from overrunning this realm."

"How many kinds of demigods are there?"

Penny bit her lip. "Excluding you. There are eight. The Kira, Eshu, Benu, Cagyn, Dzivas, Gu, Mina, and the Abiku demons."

She licked her lips and debated her next question. But what the hell…"What kind of Demi is Xavier?"

"Marshal Tegan?" Penny's eyes widened. "His family are Cagyns. They're basically shapeshifters in that they can change into anything they want. Most Demi have two forms, their Demi form and then the human one. That and their pheromones make them among the strongest of us. It's why you see so many in the Amanda."

Asa pursed her lips. "Interesting. And Liliana?" She thought back to the riot of colors in Liliana's hair and the way her skin glowed.

"She's Eshu. 'Messengers of the Gods' they're known as. They control most of the commerce for Demi. Lady Tegan's family in particular is very wealthy. With Commander Tegan being the son of the King of the Eshu, their son is the Crown Prince and will eventually become king."

Asa whipped her gaze to Brianna. *Very* interesting. It brought more context to the argument Liliana and Xavier were having yesterday. She thought about the long list of Demi and shuddered at the thought of demons. She didn't want to know just yet about them. She changed the subject back to what she really wanted to know.

"What do you know about my father?"

"Your father, Azra, is a hell god."

Asa's heart started beating faster. Her father had said that last night in her dream. She thought about his words. "A trickster god?" She whispered.

"Some would agree with that." Penny conceded.

Asa put a hand to her head. She pulled the necklace from under her shirt. "In my dream last night, he said that he left me this to hide my power."

"You dreamed about your father?" Brianna grabbed her shoulder. "Why didn't you tell me?"

"That I had a dream about my daddy? Why would I tell you something like that? It was just a dream."

"I guess," Brianna grumbled. "What else did he say?"

"What does that mean?" she ignored Brianna and watched Penny for a reaction.

"I don't know." The librarian reached out and touched the necklace. "I don't, I can't sense anything from you or this necklace. Though I'm not as powerful as some, my powers lay more in line with Brianna's. Information and research are where I'm strongest. I could probably find out for you."

"But, ok…ok, wait. Let's think this through. Asa, what else did he say in the dream you had?"

"Why is that important?" Asa finally gave her attention to Brianna.

She cleared her throat and gave Penny a nervous look. "I have read that Azra can visit people through dreams, so I'm curious about what you experienced."

"He said he could only visit me in dreams, and that we could never meet in person."

Penny nodded in agreement. "He's very powerful, but he's anchored to Azreal."

"Why?"

Penny shrugged, "one of the big mysteries."

"What's gossip say?" Brianna leaned closer.

"That he tethers Ofeeree to the spiritual realm."

Brianna sat back and frowned, "Of all the gods, why him?"

Penny shrugged again and Asa slumped in disappointment. She'd never get to meet her father.

"But then, how did he procreate with her mother?" Brianna asked.

Penny raised her eyebrows. "That is a very interesting question. One of many about you, Asa." Penny mused. "I have a few places I can check to find some of our answers. I'll let you know what I find," Penny said standing.

Brianna waved as she left and Asa turned to her.

"She didn't mention the Kokoro souls you were talking about, why not?"

"Honestly, Penny is the Head Archivist, and the sharpest researcher I've ever had the pleasure of meeting. I wouldn't put it past her to know. But, Rugaba is making us keep it to ourselves."

Asa flinched at the name. "He's real."

"Who? Rugaba?" Brianna asked.

"Yeah, in my dream, my father mentioned Rugaba. I don't…that name is not familiar to me, so it's not something I could have thought of."

Brianna pursed her lips. "You know, when Fallon has 'visits' from Azra, it's when he's sleeping. I didn't want to say anything in front of Penny, because Fallon doesn't tell a lot of people."

Asa's eyes widened. "You mean to tell me that that dream was real, that I was actually visited by my father."

Brianna shrugged, "was there other stuff said that you wouldn't have known."

She nodded, remembering how odd some of the things he'd said were.

"Well, there you go."

Oh God, she was visited by her dad. Excitement threatened to seep in through her cynicism. "Do you think I can ask him why he's tethered to Azreal?"

Brianna frowned, "I mean, I don't know that he'd tell you. Just from my dealings with Rugaba, the gods kind of tell you what they want you to know and nothing else. If your father— man, that is so weird to say that your father is a god—" Brianna shook her head and scribbled something in her notebook. "Anyway, if your father doesn't want to tell you, he won't. But, I mean, I guess he won't scorch his daughter for asking."

"Scorching is an option?"

Brianna shrugged.

"So, how do we find Ofeeree?" Asa changed the subject. She could go down the rabbit hole that was figuring out her dreams, or she do what she always did and find treasure.

Brianna's eyes widened. "Umm, we don't. Are you in a rush to end the world?"

"No, I just…I mean, it's what I do. Find things that are hard to find."

"This is one mystery you should leave alone. Finding him will lead to some demigods torturing and killing us to free him, so…see if you can refrain," the woman said dryly.

Asa smirked because she found Brianna hilarious. She would leave the mystery of Ofeere alone for now, if only to focus on the mystery of her father and how he met her mother. Could she get him to visit her in a dream again?

Chapter 11

Xavier's head lifted at the knock at his door around midday. Brianna and Lily stood at his door, their faces unsure. Xavier cursed that they were wary of him. He'd only ever wanted to keep them safe. He knew that sometimes it didn't come out that way.

"What's wrong?" He kept his voice quiet.

"We're not here to apologize, Xavier. We've been cooped up inside these walls since Bri was kidnapped. It shouldn't be a big deal for us to walk down the street for ice cream."

"Did you come to fight with me, little sister?"

He sat back in his chair and slid his shoes off and thought longingly of coffee. Adia was due back from lunch soon, he could probably wait that long. He was running analysis on all the information coming in from Leo's spies, trying to connect enough of the dots to form some kind of picture. He rested his elbows on the arm of his chair and lay his head back against the headrest. He studied the two women, seeing the signs of strain in their eyes. Residual fear from the attack was there too.

"We didn't come to fight." Brianna was more subdued than normal.

He didn't like it one bit. But what could he do? Their very existence threatened the whole world, how did one go about keeping them safe without crushing the very spirit that drew his brothers to them. He waved them into the chairs in front of his desk.

"Fallon told me about the dispute with the Mina. I came to help." Brianna pulled out her comms tablet.

Xavier raised an eyebrow. "In what way?"

"Well, I can find anything." It wasn't bragging, just fact. Brianna was a helluva researcher. "I found some info about the meeting area and who has rights to it."

He was stunned. "How did you find that out?" He reached out his hand and she passed him her tablet.

"You just have to know where to look. The problem was with how long ago the area was established. It's technically only supposed to be a resource for librarians and historians. But, about a million years ago—not literally—the current Benu monarch had a succession dispute. Minona was the only truly neutral place where they could mediate. Long story short, it was the first time prophecy was actively used to determine a king. It opened the flood gates to others requesting the use of prophecy."

He thumbed through the journal entries she'd found. "What does it say about revoking the privilege?"

"I imagine it's as easy as getting squatters off your land" She shrugged.

He winced.

"I don't agree with gatekeeping, but if you want, I can get with Penny to find out how the Mina can revoke free use of it."

"Do you think there's another prophecy about the Benu monarchy?" Liliana asked suddenly. "Could that be why there's an issue of the place being used?"

"I'll be damned," Xavier said softly. He smiled at his sisters-in-law. "Do you have any idea how much work you just saved me?" He passed Brianna back her tablet after sending the information she'd found over to his own and stared at her in wonder. She was so damned clever.

She brushed a hair off her face and scowled. "What?"

"Nothing. Thank you, I really appreciate this."

She shoved her tablet back into the leather bag she carried everywhere. "Of course. It's. what. I. does." She said, playfully dragging out the word. "Researching my demise has been, quite frankly, depressing."

He shook his head. "You're so dramatic, female."

She growled. "Quit calling me female, I'm not an animal. I'm a human. A woman."

He rolled his eyes. "Fine, sorry."

Her face lit, "you just apologized." She put a hand over her chest. "To moi."

He smiled, loving that Brianna was finally becoming comfortable enough with him to joke around. "Anyway. I have a couple of other things if you're bored. I just got through talking to your mates about it. There are a string of strange things happening on the realms. Problems that shouldn't be problems all cropping up and clogging my desk."

"You think on purpose," Liliana asked perking up.

"I think someone is trying to keep me distracted with petty shit, yes." He'd come to that conclusion as he'd flipped through the reports steadily clogging his inbox.

"Interesting," Brianna leaned forward. "I'll be more than happy to help. Can I ask a favor in exchange?"

He narrowed his eyes. "Like what?"

"Like, we're all feeling a little cooped up, can we do a club night?"

"Cooped up? It's been mere hours since the last time someone tried to kill you guys. You cannot be restless that fast." He swept them both with incredulous looks.

"I'm perfectly content to read in the library but there are others to consider." Brianna put on an innocent face and tilted her head towards Liliana.

"You're so ridiculous, Brianna," Lily laughed.

He sighed. "Fine."

"Without the magic. I want to dance without wanting to hump the floor." Brianna added.

He snorted. "Fine." He passed her over the files he was having issues with. "Is Asa settling okay?" He kept his voice casual.

Liliana got a sly look, seeing through the farce. "You could ask her yourself."

"Oooh, so she is your mate," Brianna cackled.

He stared at his sisters, not sure if he wanted to answer.

Brianna snorted. "That means yes." She announced to Liliana.

The two of them leaned forward.

"I'm not talking about this with you two. Thank you for your help, now get out of my office." They gathered the files he'd handed them and Brianna stuck out her tongue at him on their way out.

He growled because now, all he could think about was Asa. His head was throbbing from his lack of sleep and proper feeding and she was the reason why. He needed to feed. He was already a hypocrite for waiting as long as he had. But the dreams that kept him up at night, kept him from feeding. He thought about his dream with Asa a few days ago where he'd fed from her. It had given him a momentary boost, but had still been not enough.

He needed to feed in real life.

Not that his beast or magic was cooperating. Every time he even so much as looked at a woman, his body rebelled. Now that Asa was under the same roof as him, he understood why. His mate had been calling to him from their many miles apart and now no other woman would do. He wondered how much of what they shared in dreams were real.

He sighed and looked at the pile of files on his desk. How the hell was he supposed to get any work done? That question was answered a short second later.

And the answer was: he wasn't.

His mother waltzed into his office without a knock or warning. Xavier groaned. He hated when Adia left her desk empty. Sharine was dressed to the nines as usual. She was so beautiful and conniving. Her face told him she was up to something. Gods, he loved the messy woman so much.

"*Iya.*" He greeted.

"My firstborn," she said in a syrupy tone.

"Don't come in here starting shit, *iya.*"

She pouted, but then laughed. "I promise I'm not."

He sighed and closed the screens he was working on to give his mother his undivided attention. Sharine was highly effective at getting the things she wanted, even before she deployed her Cagyn wiles. She sat in the chair across from him.

"How are you doing, sweetheart?"

He sighed, "I am actually exhausted."

She crossed her legs. "I've talked with a Mina."

"About?"

"You."

"Me?"

He was caught off guard, firstly because she shouldn't have been able to talk to a Mina, at least not about prophecies about others. But, curiosity had him filing that away for later. He wanted to know what she found out.

"Why?"

She cleared her throat. "Well, Xavier, out of all my children—"

"Mom." He sighed.

"There's something going on with you. I know it, Fallon knows, hell, even Leo says something is happening with you, and you know

Leonalph notices nothing outside of his new family. What can I do to help?"

"What did the Mina tell you?"

Her gaze got sly. "This girl, Asa, is there anything going on with her?" Sharine changed the subject.

"Asa is my mate."

His mother's eyes widened. She must have thought he would lie about it.

"Then why aren't you doing anything?"

"It's complicated."

She frowned. "You're avoiding her, and according to the Mina, it won't go well for you. You need to start your mating, there are bigger troubles coming, Xavier."

He perked up. "How much did this Mina tell you?"

"I am not without my contacts, son. Your father didn't run the Haven alone, despite his arrogant assertions to the contrary."

He shook his head, he wouldn't fall into his mother's machinations. He laid his head on the desk, prepared for the launch of his mother's vitriol about his father. He peeked up when that didn't come.

"What?" She said.

"You're not…"

"I'm done with this war between me and Ranolph, it's not healthy, and especially in light of what's to come, it's not helpful." Her expression was worried a moment before she wiped it clear.

"What can I do to help you, omo mio?"

He stood and marched around the desk to his mother. He kneeled at her feet and laid his head in her lap. Her pheromones wrapped around him, the scent comforting and bringing with it a host of memories from his childhood.

She rubbed her hand across his hair. "I've done so much damage to this family, and I'm sorry for that, Xavier. I'm working on it and promise to do better. Just tell me what you need to make your life easier and I'll do it."

He sighed. "I don't know, iya. Asa's like a fantasy I can't have. Everything about her screams too good for me."

Sharine scoffed. "Too good for my baby? Tuh."

He laughed, relaxing under his mother's comfort. She rubbed the top of his head.

"I don't have time to start the mating process, Iya. If all of this falls out the way I think it will, I can't afford to be distracted by the mating frenzy."

"I understand what you mean, all I ask is that you keep your mate close. She's important in all of this, though the Mina won't tell me how."

That wouldn't be a problem since he had no plans to let Asa out of his sight. Here at Haven, she'd be safe and he planned to keep her that way.

"Come take a break, omo. We're all meeting upstairs for dinner." His mother said after a moment of silence.

"I have too much work, Iya," he murmured, lifting from her lap.

"You can spare your family an hour," she fussed.

He looked over to his desk and back at his mother. "Fine, will baba be there?"

Sharine shrugged. "He and Leo are still at odds, so I don't know if he'll show up."

Xavier sighed and rubbed his forehead. He could feel a migraine coming on. Something had to give between Leo and their father, he just didn't know what to do to fix it. Usually, Fallon handled the messy part of their family, and he was starting to realize how much his brother did to keep it from affecting everyone.

He stood. "I'll be there."

Sharine stood also and kissed his cheek. "Good, I'll see you later then."

She left the office and Xavier walked out to Adia's domain to find her back from lunch and at her desk. She smiled up at him. "It's good, you need a break."

"Eavesdropping, huh. So that's how you know when I need something?" He sat on the edge of her desk.

Adia snickered and continued typing. "I'll clear your schedule for the rest of the evening. I'm leaving here, shortly since you don't have any other meetings, but there were a couple of conference calls that can wait. Don't come back after dinner, you've been rubbing your forehead all day, which means a migraine is sure to follow."

He growled and clenched his hands to keep from doing exactly that. "You know what I want to know."

She gave him a sly smile. "As far as I can ascertain, she's fine. She was at the library earlier with Brianna but has been wandering around Haven. She doesn't ask questions like Brianna, she just…" Adia made wavy motions with her hands, "glides around observing."

He grunted.

"Soooo…mates, huh?"

Xavier stood and walked away.

"You can run, but I always find out!" She called out behind him.

He shut the door in her face and fought a smile. It was time he talked to Asa himself.

Chapter 12

Asa garnered stares as she walked around. A part of her hoped it was because she looked her best. She had to borrow a dress from Brianna. Pants were out of the question. Besides the fact that she was a good six inches taller than the other woman, Brianna had an ass that Asa could only get with a good surgeon. The woman was a curvy bombshell.

Brianna had surprised her and used 'magic' to make her a dress. Asa was still trying to digest that part. The deep maroon garment was beautiful, the silk fabric like air against her skin. The wrap dress had a deep vee that showed off her cleavage well, and her long legs peeked from the middle slit with her every step. She reached Xavier's office and paused outside of the door. She wished she'd passed a mirror so she could give her makeup a final check.

She took a deep breath and went over the story she would use to get past his assistant. Satisfied that she had it together, she tugged down on the skirt of the dress to give herself a little more cleavage and opened the door. The front office was empty, his assistant was gone, and her computer shut down for the day. Asa smiled, one less obstacle. She could hear typing sounds still coming from the back which meant Xavier was still in. She walked further into the office and stood at the doorway to the inner office. She cleared her throat. The typing stopped immediately and his head lifted, an irritated scowl bunching his brows. That was until he got a good look at her. Surprise flitted across his face followed swiftly by a heated lust.

"Am I interrupting?" She asked.

He swallowed and licked his lips. God that man was too fine. His black vee neck sweater fit him like a second skin, showing off his muscular frame. The sleeves of the sweater were rolled up to his elbows, and the corded muscles of his arms flexed as he clasped his hands together on his desk.

He shook his head and stood. "I'll always make time for you."

Her heart took flight at his words and she begged herself to calm down. It was just words. He'd been ignoring her all day. Their walk was the last time she'd been able to see him. If the talks they had during their dreams were real, then she knew his job kept him busy. It wasn't like she'd spent her time pining for him. Brianna had kept her busy in the library with her endless factoids on the Demi. Still, Asa hadn't been able to stop checking around every corner for him.

He held out his hand and indicated she take the seat in front of him. It only took three or so steps to reach the desk, but she felt the caress of his gaze the whole way. He kept standing until she sat. She liked the chivalrous move. She adjusted the skirt of the dress to show off her legs. His eyes followed her hand movements like a hungry predator tracking its prey. They sat in awkward silence for a moment, him staring at her until he shook his head and gave her a sheepish smile.

"I'm sorry, you're just so beautiful."

Her cheeks heated. "Thank you."

"Are you settling okay?"

Small talk, then. "Yeah, the room is comfortable. Considering I'm being held hostage, everyone is being so nice."

He winced. She studied his face, noting the strain lines of stress around his mouth.

"Work stressing you?" It slipped out, her falling into the habits that they had in her dreams.

He sighed. "As usual."

"Have you eaten?" She wanted to go behind the desk and touch him and run her hands across his head, the way he liked. Or at least the version of him in her dreams.

He shook his head. "I told my mom I would join the family for dinner, but you know how everything has been lately." He cursed, "I mean…"

She nodded, understanding what he meant. "Leo and your father still fighting?"

He gave her a sharp look. "Someone told you that?"

"You," she whispered, holding her breath.

"So the dreams were real?" His eyes softened and longing suffused his face.

A lump formed in her throat "Tell me I'm not the only one feeling this." Fuck, why did she say that? She should've played it a little cooler.

He rose from behind the desk and moved to her, "It took everything in me not to go to you. I've been aching to have you in my arms."

"Then why you've been avoiding me?"

He sighed. "I'm a lot to take, *elewa*. I wanted to give you time."

Asa stood and closed the distance between them, not yet touching though. "And if I'm ready?"

He lifted his hand and slid a finger down her cheek. "Are you?"

Was she?

"How is this possible?" she asked to stall.

He shrugged. "Is it bad that I don't care?"

Her eyes traced his face. She raised a shaking hand to his cheek. "You cut your hair."

He shook his head. "I wear it like this when I work. Human form, remember?"

She nodded, their conversation from their walk coming back to her. He'd had longer hair in her dreams, so had that meant he was comfortable coming to her in his Demi form? She would ask him later, for now, she smoothed down the wrinkle between his eyebrows.

"You're getting a headache."

He let out a breath and cuddled into her hand. "You can't possibly know that."

She scoffed. "Every time you complained of a migraine, the next night I wouldn't see you in my dreams, so I memorized the signs. I thought you were getting them checked out."

"Fuck," he hissed and closed his eyes. "This shit is real, it's really happening." He opened them and the copper color had completely encompassed his eyes. "I need… can I kiss you?" His voice was barely audible.

She nodded because she really needed to know if that part was real as well. She raised on her toes and tentatively touched their lips together. Xavier growled and gripped her waist, bringing her flush with his body. His tongue traced her lips, coaxing her mouth open. Heat flooded her body the moment their tongues touched. She scratched the back of his neck and his body shuddered. His kiss turned more possessive, his tongue plundering her mouth. She pulled up to breathe and he nuzzled into the side of her neck.

He pulled back. "Why did we never exchange names?"

She laughed, a tear escaping as she realized that her Mr. X really existed. She patted her wet cheek. "I actually don't know. We talked about everything else."

"You knew my nephew's name before you knew mine."

"I called you Mr. X." She admitted.

His smile was sweet, bemused. "Will you have dinner with me?"

"Do you think your family will behave just because I'm there?"

"Fuck, you do know me. I'm going to have to get used to that," he leaned over and kissed her again.

They pulled away from each other at a knock at the door. It was a beautiful woman. For a moment, jealousy reared its ugly head.

"Oh, Asa, I'm so glad to finally meet you." The woman sauntered up to them with her hand out. "I'm Sharine, Xavier's mother."

Asa shot him a surprised look. The woman looked so young! But then she remembered, they were Demi-Gods, perhaps they aged differently. He just shrugged. She clasped the other woman's hand. "Nice to meet you, Xavier's told me a lot about you."

Sharine's eyebrows shot up. "When exactly?"

"*Iya*," he said in a warning voice.

Sharine hooked her arm beneath Asa's and pulled her towards the door. "You can tell us all about it over dinner."

Asa heard Xavier curse behind her. She couldn't help the laugh that escaped, this should be interesting.

###

Xavier followed behind his mother and Asa, his eyes lingering on the sway of his mate's ass as she walked. He refused to let his mind linger on the conversation they'd just had. The dreams he'd been having for a year were real. How was that possible? He knew one person he could ask, but the moment he did, Brianna would tell her husband and once Fallon knew, it would be over. His brother would worry him to death. Sharine gave him a sly look over her shoulder and he sighed. Never mind, it didn't matter. His mother knew and was currently up to something, so Fallon nagging him to complete his bonding was probably a better outcome.

They were going up to the roof, which meant they'd have dinner among the other Demi who used the rooftop to sunbathe. The pool was on one side, surrounded by grass turf where patrons could lay out on blankets with cabanas and café tables scattered throughout the rest of the roof. It gave the Demi a place to eat while they were spending time in the sun, soaking up its energy. He was relieved to find the place not quite empty, but not as full as it would be if the sun was high in the sky. There were some families still scattered around, some getting ready to have dinner it seemed.

He took pride in the space that he'd built. In the decades since he'd implemented it, it was working to keep the peace. It kept families who didn't want to venture around humans or get into human form, a place to go. Unlike the other Havens, he'd had suites built below where they were allowed to stay, a hotel that stayed busy. The rooftop area featured a restaurant and Liliana had started having events, which increased traffic to their Haven.

He spotted his sister in law and Liliana waved him over. The evening lights were starting to come on with the descending sunlight.

Asa breathed out as she looked around. "Wow, this is beautiful."

"Xavier implemented it. It's one of the reasons this Haven is so popular." Sharine bragged.

"Are there a lot of Havens?" Asa asked.

"All over the world. We use them as a way to pass from our home realms to the Earth one. Not all Demi are nice, so the Amanda keeps track of who comes through the portals."

"Who is Amanda?" Asa asked, turning back to him.

"The Amanda. We're like the police of the Demi," he answered.

She cocked her head as though digesting that. She turned back as they arrived at a decked-out dinner table. Xavier leaned over and kissed the top of Brianna's head in greeting. Kissing Liliana's proffered cheek.

"This looks amazing, Lily," he greeted her.

"Thank you! I wanted to welcome Asa in an amazing way," she said slyly.

"Cut it out," he warned.

She gave him a mischievous smirk and moved to greet his mother and Asa. He found a seat next to Leo and sat. His mother guided Asa into the empty seat next to him. He gripped her hand under the table.

"Are you okay with this?" He asked her quietly.

She nodded. "This whole place is amazing."

He turned and found everyone staring at them. "Cut it the fuck out," he barked.

"Doesn't get any sweeter than that," Brianna muttered.

Asa snickered next to him.

He shook his head. "Don't encourage her. Fallon already has her spoiled rotten."

"Whatever," Brianna rolled her eyes.

"We are all going to have a pleasant dinner," Sharine ordered. All eyes turned to her at the head of the table. "And to that end, I've invited Ranolph."

Leo cursed next to him and moved to stand. Xavier put a restraining hand on his shoulder. Liliana was whispering furiously to his brother. Leo's growl had heads turning towards them.

"Leonalph, please," Sharine's strained plea paused Leo's exit.

Xavier rubbed the front of his forehead, his migraine building steam. Asa's hand was cool on the back of his neck as she started kneading the muscles there. His whole body tightened, need heating his blood. A tense silence gripped the table as Ranolph walked up to their table, taking place at the other end. His father's eyes took in them all with more emotions than he'd ever seen in his life. Ranolph's eyes landed on Asa and the calculation in them was a familiar sight. Xavier swallowed his sigh. He couldn't even imagine what his father was planning for Asa.

"Now, we're going to have a normal family dinner, even if I have to tie every last one of you to your chairs," Sharine barked.

"Normal is a reach, Sharine," Brianna said calmly, perusing her menu as though there weren't two hundred and fifty pounds of pissed off male directly across from her.

He tightened his grip on his little brother and prayed they made it through dinner without showing the staff their entire ass.

"*Ife,*" Fallon muttered.

"What, just saying. Y'all ain't never seen the other side of normal, no use in pretending. We'll have a Tegan dinner and pray that doesn't include broken dishes." Brianna said matter of fact.

Asa's shoulders shook and she moved her hand from the back of his neck, picking up a napkin and covering her mouth.

"Bri," Lily said on the other side of Leo, her lips twitching as she tried to conceal her own smile.

"I don't know what the three of you find so funny," Sharine said, raking the three with a chastising look. "But Brianna's right, we can only be ourselves. So let's please try and be civil.

Xavier looked around at his assembled family. Yes, they were dysfunctional, but, they were still together. Some days that's all he could ask for.

Chapter 13

Asa huffed out an irritated breath and turned over in bed. She was bored. That was never a good thing. She got into trouble when she was bored. She'd been kidnapped for…two days and she was going out of her mind with boredom. Last night, she thought she'd made progress with Xavier, but after that disaster of a family dinner, he'd dropped her off at her room and told her he'd see her later. Some kind of alarm had gone off while they were at dinner that had all three men scrambling from the table.

Not that she'd been expecting sex, but…some sex would've been nice.

His mother had explained that the alarm signaled that a Demi had been caught doing something to a human. There had been no explanation as to how they monitored that kind of thing, and she chalked it up to Xavier's job and left it alone. She picked up her phone and ignored the rising pile of emails, focusing solely on the time.

It was barely nine a.m., way earlier than she normally woke up if she wasn't on a job. She could call Brianna and have her teach her how to do 'magic'. The other woman had promised to teach her about the Demi before she left and that was something she could do. Except, she didn't want to do that. Sitting around in a library was not her idea of fun, but, she had to admit, her mind had been activated. She now sought treasure, unlike anything she'd ever hunted. Yes, she knew she couldn't free an evil entity that would destroy the world, but the fact that no one on the planet knew where the being was bound…that lit up every one of Asa's pleasure centers. She wanted to find him…it…she didn't know what to call it, but it was lost and now she wanted to find it.

Problem was, she thought better while her knitting needles were clacking and Leo hadn't had the decency to let her pack a bag before he'd kidnapped her. Maybe Brianna could abracadabra her some, but, she wanted her own. She wanted them and that meant going back home for her stuff. Also, if she was being honest with herself, she wanted to see Xavier. She enjoyed spending time with him last night, despite the bickering going on around the table. She wanted to talk to him about what they'd started in his office.

She opened her door and looked up and down the hallway, debating how she would get to his office. She was in the family wing, Liliana had told her, so there were only five doors, she could knock on them all. Maybe whoever answered would help her get back up to his office. She bit her lip and looked up as one of the doors opened.

A woman she recognized as Xavier's assistant came out of the room. Asa narrowed her eyes; that room must be Xavier's, otherwise, why would the woman be in this area. She made quick steps to the woman before she could leave. Asa put on her most non-threatening smile and sidled up to the woman.

"Hi, I'm Asa." She thrust out her hand.

"Adia," the woman gave her a curious look as she shook her hand.

Asa smiled brighter. "Is that Xavier's room?"

"Yeah, he's not feeling well today, so I brought him some stuff from the office."

Asa frowned. "If he's not feeling good, he probably shouldn't be working."

"Believe me, I've told him." Adia blew out an irritated breath.

"Does he need anything, like help?" Asa ramped up to her most charming smile, the one she used when she was trying to get information from someone.

Adia blinked. Asa moved closer to the woman.

"Well, I don't…"

Asa clicked her tongue in sympathy, interrupting her. "I can just pop in and see if I can do anything. I'm sure you have a lot of work you could be doing and don't have time to babysit." She placed a hand on the other woman's shoulder.

Adia nodded, her face a little dazed. "Yeah, I always have work."

"Right?" Asa patted the woman's hand in commiseration. "I'll take care of him, one less thing for you to worry about today." Asa eyed the keypad and pretended to type in the numbers. "Shoot, I can't remember…" she trailed off.

Adia turned around, "I'm sorry, let me." She pressed in the code for Xavier's room and opened the door.

Asa gave her a winsome smile and Adia blinked again slowly. "Thanks so much, and put it out of your mind, I'll take care of your boss."

"Oh, of course," Adia gave her a dazed smile and left.

Asa was shocked by how well that worked. She usually had to do a little more coercion than that to get what she wanted. She paused in the doorway. She'd been able to talk people into all manner of things her whole life. Was it because she wasn't human? What other clues had she'd ignored over the years? She'd known she was different, but who didn't think they were different?

She pushed it out of her head and turned her attention back to Xavier. Asa closed the door behind her and blinked at the complete darkness. She pulled out her cellphone and used the flashlight on it. She found a light switch and pressed the middle button. It would keep the light dim, at least it did in her room. She walked through the living room and came to the bedroom. She gave a light knock and when she didn't get an answer she opened the door. The room was just as dark as the living room. She heard a growl and it froze her footsteps.

"Xavier." She called softly. She heard the rustle of blankets.

"What are you doing in here?"

"Your assistant said you were sick, I wanted to see if I could help."

He growled again. And she froze at the animal sound. "You need to leave."

She flipped the middle light switch again and gasped as she saw a giant…she didn't know what it was in the middle of Xavier's bed. It was certainly shaped like a man, but, he was darker, more muscular, and had marbled copper lines flowing up and down his body. He growled again, and the lines on his skin lit. She was fascinated.

"Xavier?" She brought the light up to his face.

He flinched but didn't look away. He looked at her, the amber eyes definitely his. He closed his eyes and let out a rough breath, before laying his head back down on his pillow. The gold light emitting from him dimmed to nothing.

"What's wrong? How can I help?" She rushed to the side of the bed.

"Exhausted, just need to rest today."

"Is this like, your normal form?"

Asa now understood what he'd meant about them changing forms. Penny had said Cagyns could change into any form. Her curiosity was peaked. Damn it, now she would have to call Brianna and get trapped in the library. She needed to know what the hell she was dealing with.

He nodded then winced. She recognized the sign of a migraine. He made that face many times in her dreams, right before he left. It would be days before she would see him again. Her heart banged against her chest as she realized just how hurt he'd been when he hadn't shown up in her dreams. Did he go through this every time?

"Do you have pain pills you can take?"

"*Elewa*, please shut up and turn off the light."

She narrowed her eyes and decided whether or not she wanted to be offended. He groaned and turned to his side.

"You need help, do you guys have doctors in this place?"

"I need," he gasped. "I need you to turn the fucking light off and stop talking."

She sucked her teeth but got up and did as he asked. She didn't leave though. Instead, she used her phone flashlight and found his bathroom. She wet a cloth and walked back to the side of the bed. She put the cold cloth to his forehead and he hissed but let out a sigh after a moment. She doused her flashlight and sat next to him. His breathing was a little ragged, but calmed the longer she sat there. She kicked off her shoes and put her legs up on the bed.

Xavier growled low and pulled her closer to him. He lay his head across her stomach and she ran her fingers through his hair. It was way longer in this form and felt amazingly silky as she played in it. Just like her dreams, she massaged his scalp with her fingertips the way he liked. It was probably a dumb idea, but nonetheless, she sat there quietly. Not once had fear entered her mind. He was literally the man of her dreams. There were dark days when she'd had only her dreams and him for company. She wanted to help him in any way she could. She pulled out her phone and pulled up her kindle app and read, her fingers dragging through his long hair. His breathing evened out and he fell asleep.

Xavier tensed. There was someone in his bed. He inhaled and filtered through the scents that were supposed to be there, to find the one that was not. A spicy cinnamon smell overtook him and his beast growled. *Mate.* His head was in her lap, and while that in and of itself was strange, the strangest part to him was his lack of a migraine. Was he dreaming? There was nothing that could stop the debilitating headaches when they were upon him. He'd tried medicine, and even the Kira were only able to take the edge off. He knew part of it was the fact that he wasn't properly feeding. The skimming was no longer working, but in the year since he'd been having dreams about Asa, no other woman was doing it for him.

"You're awake."

So not a dream.

He sighed and debated giving up his comfortable spot. "How did you talk my assistant into letting you in here?"

"I'm quite charming you know."

He snorted.

"Feeling better?"

He took stock of his body. "I am." She didn't make any moves. He settled into her lap again and closed his eyes. Not sleeping, simply soaking in the feel of his mate.

"How long was I out?" he asked after a moment.

"Hmm,"

He looked up and her attention was on her phone. "What are you doing?"

She growled, "Reading, shhh."

He didn't quite know what to say to that, so he did what she asked and got quiet. He wrapped his arms around her waist, sighing as he settled his head back into her lap. After a moment, her hand went through his hair. There was magic in her touch, literal magic that soaked into him with her every stroke. Did she realize what she was doing to him? He started to ask, but then he realized he was still in his Cagyn form. His beast was silent, content. She'd seen him in his Cagyn form and had said nothing. In the dreams he'd had of her, he'd sat like this in her lap sometimes and told her about his hard days, but never in his Cagyn form. He wondered what she thought of it, of him. He closed his eyes and let the magic from her hands soak into his body. He went back to sleep.

He didn't know how long he'd been sleeping this time, but his beast had awakened him with a warning. He stiffened in her lap, a long growl releasing a moment before his front door beeped.

"X," Fallon called out.

Xavier relaxed but didn't move from her lap. The light in his room came on next, which irritated him. It meant his brother had no plans to leave until he talked to Xavier.

"We can't find…" Fallon trailed off. "Girl, do you realize I have all of Haven looking for you?"

She waved the phone in her hand. "Why didn't you just call?"

Fallon rolled his eyes and cursed. "Nobody has your phone number."

She shrugged and tapped the top of Xavier's head. "I'm hungry, you gotta get up."

He sighed and squeezed her tighter, loving the feeling of her in his arms. "Get out Fallon, but call up for food on your way out." He ordered.

Fallon sucked his teeth and walked out of the room, seemingly to do as he'd asked.

"I still need to get up, you know." She smiled at his put upon sigh.

"Fine." He watched her as she left the room, his gold eyes following her every step.

Once the bathroom door closed he breathed out and wiped a hand down his face. He should find his brother and punch him in the throat for interrupting his time with Asa. He looked up as she came out of the bathroom. He tugged on her shirt as she got close to him and pulled her down into his lap.

"We need to talk," he murmured against her shoulder.

He inhaled her scent and closed his eyes as feelings overwhelmed him. It was unbelievable to him that she was real, and in his arms. He kissed her neck and she sighed, turning to straddle him.

"I wanted to talk you anyway," she dropped a kiss on his forehead. "I like your hair like this."

"My favorite part of my dreams was the way you would touch me," He murmured against the hollow of her throat. He took a deep inhale. "One thing the dreams didn't get, though."

"What's that?"

He nibbled against her skin and she shuddered. It took everything in him not to pull her down and roll over onto the bed. "Your scent. You smell amazing. That never translated."

She sighed and clutched him tighter. "So many sensations are so much better in person." She kissed his forehead. "So, do you get the migraines often?"

He paused, fidgeting. "They started this year. I've been under a lot of stress lately."

She nodded and they lapsed into silence.

"Yo, X!" Leo called from the other room.

He sighed and clutched Asa tighter as she moved to stand. "Just ignore my brothers."

"That doesn't seem like it would work," she whispered. She lifted his chin and kissed his lips lightly before standing.

Leo came into his room with Kell on his hip. His nephew gurgled and reached for him, nearly jumping from his father's arms. Xavier smiled as Leo dumped him into his lap. "Oh, sorry. Fallon said we all had to talk."

"Who is 'we all'?" Xavier growled, irritated.

Leo shrugged. "He's bringing lunch"

"Good, I'm starving," Asa said as she walked out of his room.

He bit his lip, his eyes following the sway of her ass. Leo snickered and shook his head, leaving the room. He sighed and stood.

"Nobody asked for a guy session," Xavier protested heading after his brothers and Asa.

Kell snatched at his hair, his drooling, smiling face washing away Xavier's irritation. Not like it would phase his brothers if he was mad anyway. He carried his nephew into the kitchen as Fallon was laying food all over the table, and his stomach rumbled. He didn't have breakfast, so the scents of the lunch was welcoming. Usually, he wouldn't be able to eat when he had migraines. He was thankful for Asa all over again. He waved his hands and a high chair appeared at the table. He settled Kell in and sat next to Asa at the small table in his kitchen. He looked down in surprise as Asa set a full plate in front of him. She leaned over and kissed his cheek and started fixing food for herself.

"Why were you looking for me?" She asked Fallon.

Fallon sighed and rubbed a hand across his face. "I had a visit from your father. You were supposed to bring the beacon with you."

Her hand hovered over the salad she was scooping. She shook her head and resumed fixing her plate. "What beacon?"

"I'm guessing the box we talked about at the cafe," Fallon said.

"Well, I didn't exactly get a chance to pack," she shot Leo an irritated gaze.

He had the nerve to look sheepish. "What? I was told to get the power source. We all," he waved his hand over the whole table, *"all of us* thought it was the girl."

Fallon growled. "She needs to go back and get that beacon."

Leo shrugged and starting feeding his son.

"How important is it?" Xavier asked.

"Azra is insistent," Fallon murmured.

Xavier shook his head. "You'll get no sympathy from me. You're the one who entered a deal with a hell god."

"That reminds me. Y'all keep calling my father 'a hell god' is he like the devil?" Asa asked chomping on a cucumber.

Leo shook his head. "He's more like the gatekeeper to the Underworld, our version of hell."

Asa's frown cleared from her face. "And you say 'a hell' because, of course, there are pantheons a plenty. That makes sense." She went back to eating.

Xavier smiled at her practicality. For someone in his position, it was a trait he admired. His job was tough and there were difficult decisions that had to be made on a daily basis. He loved that his mate wouldn't shrink at his duties.

"So, this beacon," Leo prodded.

A flash of light startled them all. Rugaba stepped through a portal, and he and his brothers hit the floor on their knees. Asa sat in her chair, turning her bewildered gaze on them all. Xavier reached for her arm, intending to bring her down with him. Except, Rugaba moved closer to her.

The god studied her, his face serious. "You are Asa."

Chapter 14

Asa turned another nervous glance at Xavier. His head was down, as were his brothers. What was going on? Who was this man? She was intimidated, to say the least. The three men had gone down to one knee, panic was written all over their faces. Not to mention the power that came off this man in waves. And Jesus, how had he just popped into the room? She rubbed her right ring finger and swallowed when her thumb met the metal of the ring she kept there. So, not a dream.

She nodded, finally answering the man's question. The man came to her and his hand lifted, but then he dropped it.

"You are my brother's child." He whispered.

Her eyes started watering. "You're Rugaba."

He nodded. "I've only just learned of your existence."

She cleared her throat. She didn't know what to say to that so she said nothing. Hell, she was just finding out about her father's existence, so they were both in the same boat. His gaze traced her face and his eyes softened. He turned to Xavier.

"Where is the beacon?"

Fallon spoke up, "my lord, we didn't…it's not here."

The room shook and Kell whined. Asa grabbed the baby, and Leo shot her a grateful look, still kneeling.

Rugaba turned his gaze back to Asa. "You were supposed to be in possession of the beacon."

"I don't know what a beacon is."

"Your mother left things for you." Not a question, it was barked out as a demand.

"She did," she agreed.

"Why did you come here and leave those things behind."

"I didn't exactly…"

All three men shot her a warning look.

She closed her mouth, not wanting to snitch on them.

"Up, all three of you." The men stood. "That beacon needs to be secured."

"Of course, my lord, I'll see to it myself," Xavier said.

His brothers shot him a surprised look.

Rugaba took one last look at her. He touched the coin pendant at her neck. "If you ever have need of me," the metal glowed and he turned it over. On the back of the coin, in place of the face that was there before, appeared a sun with thorns surrounding it. "Call to me."

She nodded. "Can I see my father?"

He gave her a pained look. "Not on this realm, no."

"But you can visit?" She was confused as to why her uncle was able to travel but not her father. But then she realized what Penny had meant about him being tethered.

"Any time you have need of me, Asa." He promised.

"And if I just want to talk?" She whispered.

He gave her a small smile. "For anything."

He disappeared and everyone in the room took a deep breath. Leo grabbed his son and pulled him close. Asa was shocked. Had she just encountered a god? There was a marked difference between Rugaba and everyone else. He exuded power. And…he was her uncle.

Xavier came to her and put his hands on her shoulders. "Are you okay?"

"Yes," she moved her eyes reluctantly from the spot Rugaba disappeared. "Rugaba is a god."

"The god of fate," Fallon said, sitting hard in the chair. "We need to go back to your mother's."

Asa nodded. "Okay. I'm ready."

Fallon cleared his throat. "It can't be tonight."

"And why not? Am I the only one awed by the god that just flashed in here?"

The three brothers shared a look.

"Asa, the magic you carry around would be a call for anyone, I don't know how long it would take someone to find you once you left Haven. We need to make the proper preparations." Xavier answered.

"For what kind of people?" She frowned.

He just looked at her and she sighed. Brianna had warned her that there were people who would happily use her for her magic. The frank woman hadn't lied to her, or even tried to sugarcoat any of the information she'd given Asa so far, so Xavier's warning felt like confirmation. The men from their attack flashed through her mind and she shuddered. More and more she was reconciling her old life to match their explanations and stories. Was that a mistake? The trip back to her mother's house would give her much needed distance.

He just looked at her and she sighed. Brianna had warned her that there were people who would happily use her for her magic. The frank woman hadn't lied to her, or even tried to sugarcoat any of the information she'd given Asa so far, so Xavier's warning felt like confirmation. The men from their attack flashed through her mind and she shuddered.

She held up the coin still warm from Rugaba's touch. "I have the necklace on. I can go back to mom's house and get my stuff and her things. I'll wait until we get back here to look through them."

"Tomorrow would still be best," Leo spoke up.

Something was going on between the three of them and she didn't have the headspace to deal with it so she dropped it. Whether it was today or tomorrow, she would leave and that was what was important to her at the moment. More and more she was reconciling her old life to match their explanations and stories. The trip back to her mother's house would give her much needed distance. She needed some perspective before she let these strangers rewrite her life's story.

Asa sighed and stepped out of Xavier's arms, her mind spinning with the fact that she had an uncle who was an actual god. "I need to go…" she needed some space to think about that.

She gripped the necklace at her throat. Could she call her father to her in another dream?

Xavier watched her leave and turned to his brothers. They were both staring at him. "What's the deal? Shouldn't take but a day to grab her stuff and come back."

"You're going to take the time off?" Leo asked, his eyes narrowing.

Fallon grunted in agreement.

"I could use it, and I gave my word to Rugaba."

They still stared.

"Fuck you guys, I rest," He grumbled.

"Yeah right," Leo muttered.

X sat back at the table and continued eating, ignoring his brothers. A road trip with his mate. It would give him a chance to see if she was like the woman in his dreams.

"You need to feed." Fallon sat across from him.

"You don't give me orders," X said automatically.

"Bro, your aura is weak as shit," Leo fussed. "You'd never let us leave Haven like that."

"You're her only protection when she leaves the ward over this place," Fallon added.

"I wouldn't want to be the one who gets Azra's daughter hurt," Leo chipped in.

Xavier grit his teeth. "I haven't been able to feed," he confessed.

Fallon cursed, "Since when?"

X sat back in his chair and crossed his arms. "I've had nightly dreams about Asa for the last year, I haven't been able to look at another woman since."

"Damn, you haven't had sex in a year? I guess we now know what happens when you ignore the ancestors call to mate." Leo shook his head and spoon-fed Kell.

He avoided their gaze and answering that question. He definitely would not be telling them about his last dream of Asa. "I haven't ignored shit, I didn't know she existed."

Fallon scoffed. "The dreams started before or after the migraines?"

"Before," he reluctantly admitted.

"Mmhmm," Fallon said in answer.

They were right. He should've known something was up.

"There wasn't exactly time. Between saving your mates and averting a fucking war, I haven't had a moment to myself."

"Moot point now," Leo said. "You'll have to ask her to the club floor tonight if you're leaving in the morning."

Fallon nodded.

"I can't ask her to do that." He protested.

He didn't want their first sexual encounter to be her feeding him. The dream he had about her days ago didn't count.

Leo snorted and wiped his son's mouth. "Uncle X is pretending not to understand English." He said in that baby voice he used with his son.

"That's not—"

"X quit being a jackass." Fallon stood and started collecting empty dishes.

They cleaned up and left, leaving him staring into the empty room. He'd expected the migraine to have him down all day. Now that he was fine, he could go and get some work done. He needed to arrange his schedule with Adia for the time he'd be gone. And yet, he couldn't move. He looked down at his communicator, sighed, and dialed.

Brianna picked up, her head bent down over whatever she was reading. "Yeah."

"You still want your club night?"

Her head popped up and her eyes lit with excitement. "Yes!"

"I have to take Asa back to Tennessee tomorrow. I'll arrange it so that you have the dance floor to yourselves for the first few hours." It would take some wheedling but he would manage it.

"Thank you, Xavier. I'll tell the girls," She breathed out happy, clapping her hands before leaning forward and ending the transmission.

He dropped his communicator on the tabletop and put his hands behind his head. He would feed from his mate tonight. His beast stirred, and his magic flared at the thought. Yes, he could keep others from storming the dance floor but would he be able to stop himself?

He sat forward and picked up his communicator again. Taking Asa out of the safety of Haven reminded of him of something he'd meant to have happened days ago. He pulled up a familiar contact and waited. Tahir's image floated above his communicator, the Kira somewhere deep in the forests of his homeland.

"What's up?"

"I need a favor."

Tahir pursed his lips. "You know I don't work for you anymore, right?"

Xavier sucked his teeth at the reminder. "I said favor, but now that you've brought that up, why didn't you tell me Fallon had made a deal with Azra?"

Tahir was Fallon's best friend and had been traveling with his younger brother for most of the decades Fallon had traveled the world.

"I told you I could no longer in good conscious pass you information about Fallon," Tahir rubbed the back of his neck. "I couldn't spy on your brother for you then, and I won't do it for you now."

Xavier growled. "It's not spying, I sent you to him to keep him safe. You think making deals with hell gods is safe?"

Tahir looked chagrined. "That happened before I got to him."

Worry reared up all over again at the thought to the mishaps Tahir and Fallon had gotten into as they traveled. The magic his brother searched out was dangerous, reckless, and sending Tahir after Fallon had been the only way Xavier had been able to sleep while Fallon was gone. The 'spying' as Tahir called hadn't lasted long. He and Fallon had bonded quickly and the Kira had refused to divulge any information to Xavier outside of general updates.

"Nevertheless, that's not why I called you."

"What do you need, Marshal?"

"My mate…" He paused as the sound of that settled him. "Asa's power is bound, I'd like you to take a look. When can you come to Haven?"

"Give me a few days, gotta tie up some loose ends," Tahir murmured.

"Thanks."

Xavier closed the call, not bothering to ask what Tahir had to handle. The powerful Kira no longer worked for him and was none of his business as he just reminded Xavier. He stood, and put the call from his mind. Now that he'd agreed to let the girls have a club night, he needed to get up to the club level and make sure it was safe for them to do so.

Chapter 15

Asa crossed her legs as much as the leather miniskirt would allow and leaned closer to the mirror. Liliana and Brianna were chatting behind her, the conversation flowing over her as she concentrated on getting her cat-eye straight. She didn't particularly care for clubs anymore at her age, but the others were excited. It was different being around a bunch of women. Not that she was around a lot of people, per se. Her job was a solitary one. Find treasure, give it to the person that commissioned its finding, collect the check, repeat.

She was happy to dance off the restless energy plaguing her, though. She wanted to be on a hunt…*the* hunt, but as Brianna had cautioned her. Once she found it, then what? There was so much they didn't know. She rolled her shoulders. In lieu of hunting for Ofeeree, she could use her skills to hunt other prey. Though, now that she thought about it, while she was with Xavier seemed to be the only time she wasn't restless. She'd sat in his room for hours without moving.

That was new for her.

Would the sex be as good as it was in her dreams? There was one sure-fire way to find out. But, did she want to start…she snorted. Hell yeah, she did. If he was even half the person he was in her dream, she was going to find out. She started to do the other eye when the room got quiet. She looked up and both women were staring at her.

"What?" She swiped the other eye and dropped the eyeliner in the makeup bag Liliana had brought to her.

"You do that so easily," Brianna said.

"I love makeup." Asa shrugged and changed the subject. "The top floor didn't look very club-y when we were up there."

Liliana sat on the bed and stretch out. "You're going to be shocked by the difference."

She hadn't been to a club since college, so she wasn't sure how much had changed. She went back to her makeup, the deep vee of the silk tank top she wore dipping as she leaned back into the mirror.

"What did you do all day?" Brianna asked.

Asa cursed as she poked herself in the eye with the mascara wand. "I spent the morning at Xavier's.

Liliana sat up on the bed, her eyes excited. "Do tell."

"There's nothing to tell. He had a migraine, I sat with him for a little while. Then your husbands came in."

"Cock blockers," Brianna said with a shake of her head.

Asa smirked. "Are you always so blunt?"

"She has no filter," Liliana said dryly.

"Fallon said y'all were visited by Rugaba." Brianna leaned over her shoulder.

"Why are you so close to me, girl?" Asa said, staring at her in the mirror.

"Well?" Brianna prompted, not moving.

"If you already know what happened, what are you asking me for?" Asa muttered.

"How did you feel meeting your uncle?" Brianna asked, finally moving back.

Asa shrugged. "I'm still processing it."

"That's fair," Brianna said. "Now, hurry up, Xavier only gave us a couple of hours to ourselves on the dance floor."

"We're supposed to dance by ourselves?" Asa turned in the chair, sending them a confused look.

"The magic in Haven gets intense on club nights. Xavier's going to hold it back for a little bit." Liliana answered.

Intrigued, she hurried through the rest of her makeup. A club full of magic, what would that feel like?

Nearly forty-five minutes later, she knew what it looked like. The understated décor of a private country club was gone and in its place was opulence that was very much overstated. The dark wood floors, so elegant during the day seemed to shine in the mauve lighting. The lighting was a slow throb, toggling between red and a darker pink that brought her body to life. The music was loud, the beat rattling her chest.

Brianna shuddered next to her. "Lord, this is without magic?"

Asa couldn't answer, because she knew what Brianna meant. Her skin flushed, and warm, languid heat invaded her body. She wanted to dance, more to say, she wanted to dirty dance. That slow press of bodies together that left a person hot and sweaty.

She looked around the swanky place, searching for the one person who she wanted to more than dance with. She looked up, her eyes scanning first the balcony of the second floor, and then up to mirrored windows of the third. Her eyes went immediately to one window, and though she couldn't say for certain how she knew, she knew her dream man was behind the glass. She lifted her lips in a smile, and put a little more sway into her hips as she followed Liliana and Brianna to the dance floor. Her mission: to entice Xavier down from his tower.

###

Xavier stood at the window one of the VIP suites watching his sisters-in-law and Asa dance. He clenched and unclenched his hands, his mouth damn near watering as Asa gyrated on the floor. Between the three of them, magic floated around them, drawing everyone in the club closer to them. He threatened to put his foot in the ass of the first person that approached them. He promised Bri a couple of hours and he would damn sure deliver.

All the same, they'd attracted a crowd. He stared at his mate, fascinated by the way she moved. The short skirt she wore was slowly inching higher on her thighs with her every dip and need clawed his chest until he could barely breathe. He wanted that skirt around her waist, and his dick deep enough inside her body to leave his mark. He growled in hunger.

"How long have they been down there?" Fallon came into the room, startling him out of his thoughts.

His brother had gone to the Mulu realm to make sure the guards that they had over there were keeping themselves neutral. They were all keeping an eye out on the disturbance happening on the Benu realm, Fallon making sure their soldiers wouldn't have any issues.

"An hour, easy," he answered his brother.

"Dancing the whole time?"

"Yep." He pointed out the guards he had flanking the women. "They're okay."

Fallon stared a moment, mesmerized. "Their magic is…"

Xavier sighed and wiped his face. "Yeah. I'll have to pull them in a moment. I can't imagine how much longer the Demi circling them will be content to just watch."

Fallon grunted.

"Are we gonna talk about it?" His brother said after a few minutes of silence.

"No, mom," Xavier mocked.

Fallon sighed. "I've only ever wanted to make your life easier, arakunrin."

Xavier turned and faced his younger brother. He grabbed the back of his neck and brought Fallon closer. "At the expense of your own?

I would never ask that of you. No matter how many times baba has asked you to accommodate us. I don't want that for you."

He backed away and went back to the window. "That harridan down there," he pointed to their mates, "she is everything I could've wanted for you. She takes care of you the way you do others, but doesn't put up with your shit."

Fallon laughed and wiped his face. "I'm worried for you, X." He held up his hand to stall his argument. "It's my prerogative and habit. I worry that you are working yourself too hard and now that I know you haven't been feeding properly... Please, I'm asking you to come to us if it gets too much."

Xavier nodded. "That's fair."

"This trip, it's a lot," Fallon added.

"We'll be fine."

"With the added pressure of her being—"

Xavier interrupted his brother as he queued up his lecture. "Fallon." He growled.

Fallon stared at him a moment longer and then sighed. "You should feed before you pull them off the dance floor."

"Arakunrin," Xavier said softly, stepping closer to his brother. "I will handle it."

He knew Fallon would worry regardless of what he said. His brother had done so his whole life, no matter how many times him and Leo had told Fallon to take care of himself.

Fallon touched their foreheads together without saying anything. He turned and left Xavier alone. X turned to the window one last time to watch Asa. The way she moved, he remembered from his dreams. He'd memorized everything about her in his dreams. He wondered if any of it held up to the real thing. Was she a figment of his imagination, the things he'd dreamed? The other day, Asa responded to him with things she'd only know if she shared the dreams. Did that make them real? Only one way to find out. He walked down to the dance floor.

Asa spun around and caught his eyes. Her smile was triumphant and smug. She'd been dancing that way on purpose, he realized. His beast raised its head. She crooked her finger and sped his steps, his palms itching with the need to touch her. She wrapped her arms around his shoulders once he'd reached.

"I wondered if you would come down."

He didn't say anything. He couldn't really. His tongue felt swollen, desire for her made him mute. "Dance with me," he managed in a hoarse whisper.

She smiled wider and moved closer to him. They danced, the swaying of their bodies, natural, in tune, as though they'd done it for years. He leaned over her neck, a spot he'd kissed her on many nights in his fevered dreams. She shuddered and her hands gripped his shoulders. He traced a light kiss across her skin, inhaling her scent. She sighed and her hips moved against him. He closed his eyes and enjoyed her nearness. Yes, he wanted to be inside her, but this…this closeness with her filled him in places he'd long thought dead, never to be revived. He was well past the age where most were mated. He'd thought it'd never happen for him.

He spun her around and pulled her into his chest. He nipped the bottom of her ear. "Do you know how many nights I dreamed of holding you like this?"

His pheromones surrounded them and he was lightheaded. She whipped around and tiptoed, pulling him into a kiss that damn near blew his head off. He loosened his hold on his magic and felt the moment it overwhelmed his mate. Her body went pliant in his arms, and her eyes lit, the lids dropping midway.

"Feed me?" He asked, knowing his eyes were copper. Not something he would've been able to stop.

She swallowed, her eyes widened, and she nodded. His beast bucked against his chest. She remembered. They'd discussed the dreams being real, every time he got proof of it… He closed his eyes and pushed his beast back a little, not wanting to devour Asa on the dance floor in front of everyone. They danced a little more, his pheromones dancing around them. Even though it was his magic, he seemed to fall under her spell, with their every movement. Was it possible to love someone from just dreams? Would it be real, would it survive the real world?

Looking into her eyes, feeling her against him, he wanted with everything to bet on them.

His fingers traced her thigh, sliding under her skirt. Her mouth parted, her lids drooping, hiding her beautiful eyes. He sucked the skin of her neck into his mouth, determined to leave a mark one and all could see. He touched the core of her, shuddering at how wet he found her. He brushed across her clit and her gasp brushed air across his neck. His hands shook, his body tense as anticipation took over.

"Oh God, X," she gasped and he sped the rhythm of his fingers, the heat of her sex hardening him like a steel pike. "Almost there," she panted.

"Open for me, ife," He ordered.

She opened her mouth and he leaned over her, pinching her clit. She exhaled and the power released from her dragged him under. His body was inundated with it until his beast tore from him. Fallon and Leo surrounded them, raising their hands, a shield going up over them to hide them from the other patrons. He didn't care. He closed the distance between him and Asa's mouth, devouring her, their combined magic coursing through their bodies. Lights danced within the shield of his brothers, their magic escaping them and flashing around them. He saw her soul, saw their connection already in place although they'd technically just met. The feeding he'd done in their dreams was no comparison to the raw power they exchanged.

He lifted her legs, needing to be inside her.

"Xavier!" His brother's voice crashed over him, bringing him back from the edge he was hovering over.

"X, damn man, pull back." Leo barked.

Asa pulled back first, her hand covering her mouth, wonder filling her eyes. He tightened his grip on her waist, before helping steady her as she moved her legs back to the floor.

"Goddess above, Asa." He whispered. He leaned over her neck and licked a path across her collar bone.

"You saw it too?" She whispered.

He nodded. She traced the whorls over his skin, her touch soft, her lips parted with lust.

"Yo, X." Fallon called out, "I'm not keeping this shit up all night."

Asa's eyes widened and she stepped back. "Oh, Lord."

"It's okay," he whispered. "No one saw."

She stepped back into his arms and put her forehead on his shoulder. "We nearly had sex in the middle of a crowd."

He chuckled. "No need for the recap."

She snorted and laughed. She looked up, her face serious. "My room or yours."

His mouth dried. He finally stuttered out… "mine?"

She nodded and grabbed his arm.

"We good, Fallon." He said hoarsely.

His brother lowered the shield over them and shook his head. Brianna smirked and gave him a thumbs up before the two of them moved to keep dancing. Leo waggled his eyebrows before grabbing his wife around the waist and leaving the two of them in the middle of the floor.

"Let's go." Asa pulled him towards the back entrance of the club that led to the caverns below.

###

They barely made it through the door before he was on her. Asa moaned as Xavier lifted her by the back of her thighs, propping her against the door. They kissed, their tongues dueling, their desperation evident in their heavy breathing as they broke apart. His form had completely changed. There were lines going up and down his skin, pulsing with their matched heartbeats. She traced his arms as he walked them to his room, the silence between them thick with lust. He set her down in front of the bed.

"Strip," he ordered.

Asa obeyed, instantly, heat flushing her body. His eyes were glowing, the hunger in them spurring her faster. He was slow to undress and her eyes took in every inch of muscled skin he revealed. She inhaled sharply when his pants hit the ground. His body was bigger…everywhere. She couldn't wait to feel him. He sauntered to the bed and she pushed back towards the headboard. Xavier pulled on her legs until she was directly underneath him. He kissed along her stomach and back up to her mouth.

"I can't wait to be inside you," he whispered against her lips before devouring her mouth.

He gripped the back of her neck with one hand, lifting her hips with the other. She reached between them and guided him to her center. She gave a small thought to a condom, but it was drowned in the lust and magic flowing between them. She sucked on his tongue, moaning as he moved slowly inside. They both threw their heads back and released a heavy sigh when he was seated fully. He looked down at her and smiled, the heat in his gaze clenched her belly. He growled as her sex squeezed around his shaft.

He started moving then. He stroked in and out and she closed her eyes, holding tight to the sensations. He was here, and they were together in the real world. She'd dreamed of him for so long, and having him in her arms…she was overwhelmed with emotion. Their bodies were wet with sweat as they moved against each other, the air around them hot and wavering. Xavier kissed down her neck, his teeth scraping against her skin. Asa gripped his shoulders, wrapping her legs around him tightly. She met his thrusts with her own, wanting him deeper.

Between the need built up on the dance floor and him whispering in her ear, it took her no time at all to explode. He rode out her climax but then turned her over onto her stomach. Before she could get her breath, he was back inside her, clutching her hips, stroking deep. Her eyes crossed and she arched her back for more. Xavier rode her until she was a quivering mass of nerve-endings, every thrust hitting her deep.

He reached around the front of her and gripped the column of her throat. His cologne filled the air, and her body responded, tightening and vibrating until she went careening into another orgasm. She screamed, her arms collapsing beneath her as they turned to jelly. Xavier was right behind her, one last deep stroke before he came, calling her name.

He collapsed on top of her and she let out an exhausted giggle, euphoria overtaking her body.

"That was better than I could've possibly imagined," he murmured in her ear.

She snorted. "I didn't realize how much I needed that."

He laughed, removing his weight from atop her, gently pulling from her. She sighed when a cool cloth swiped across her tender sex. She frowned, turning her head towards him.

"Where did you get that?"

"Magic," he whispered.

The cloth was gone into thin air in the next second and he pulled her towards him. She snuggled into his chest, sleep making her eyes heavy. He brushed a kiss across her forehead.

"What time are we leaving in the morning?" she murmured.

"Early, early, *elewa.*"

The circles he was making on her back with his hands should have been lulling her to sleep. Instead, her body warmed, and her clit started throbbing with her heartbeat. She licked across his sweat soaked skin, moaning at his salty taste. She threw her leg over his waist and he peeked down at her smiling.

"That's how you feel?" He asked as she climbed on top of him.

"One more round." She nuzzled into his neck, taking a deep inhale.

"Anything you want, love," he whispered, before pulling her head up and kissing her breath away.

Chapter 16

Asa sighed and looked around. She was once again thrust back to her childhood home. She looked around at the threadbare furnishings and shook her head. The small two-bedroom apartment was immaculate. Though they'd been poor, her mother was meticulous about keeping their space clean. She growled as she thought about the money her father said he sent. She'd seen the proof of it in the bank statements that had been neatly stacked in the desk her mother had at her new house.

So many things Deena hid from her.

She now saw her childhood memories through a different lens. Her initial anger at Deena squirreling away money was assuaged when Asa remembered that she hadn't had to pay a red cent for college. Yes, she'd taken a job while she studied, but Deena had insisted Asa keep the money for herself and use it as spending money. So much about her life was put into a different light with Deena's death.

Asa walked back to her bedroom, sliding her hands against the wall of the short hallway. She stopped at the door and gasped in surprise. Brianna was wandering around her childhood bedroom, looking around.

"What are you doing here?"

Brianna looked introspective. "I think you called me here."

Asa frowned. "What does that mean?"

"I mean, I was just doing dirty things to my husband in my dream a second ago, so…" Brianna picked up the small ceramic horse her mother had gifted her on her eighth birthday.

Asa swallowed the lump in her throat and walked up to her, pinching Brianna's arm. If this was anything like her dreams with Xavier, then—

"Ow, damn!" Brianna rubbed her arm. "What was that for, and why the hell did it actually hurt?"

Brianna looked around more carefully, her mind spinning. Asa herself was equally stunned.

"This is real then?" Asa whispered.

"Just like Fallon's dreams of Azra. Interesting. I'll be spending my day tomorrow in the library," Brianna said more to herself. She turned back to Asa. "Why did you summon me?"

Asa sat on her bed stunned. "I didn't, at least I didn't mean to. This makes me very confused about me and Xavier. I've had dreams about him for months, do you think I summoned him on purpose?" Had she manipulated his feelings for her?

"You'd never met him before you got to Haven right, so how?"

Asa breathed out a relieved breath. "Right, you're right."

Shock had her knees weak. Her mind spun back over the months of conversations she and Xavier had had. She should be done being shocked about the dreams being real, but every bit of proof had her stumbling. Everyone talked to her about the power and magic Demis had, was the dream thing one of hers?

"How is that possible?" She whispered, more to herself.

"I have a few ideas, but I need to check." Brianna sat next to Asa. "What's up, I assume you needed someone to talk to."

She'd only just met Brianna, why would she not call Chandra, a woman she'd known longer and had certainly shared more with than Brianna.

Asa looked around. "I spent a lot of nights in this room wishing I could be somewhere else. Weird that every time I have a problem I come back here in my dreams."

"Not so weird now that you know you're purposely doing it. It's home base, no matter how much you hate it."

Asa sighed and laid her head on her thin pillow, stretching out on the worn quilt of her childhood.

Brianna followed suit. "Spill, girl."

"I slept with him."

"Girl, duh. If you didn't sleep with him after all that hunching on the dance floor, you'd be crazy. How was it? Is he all tense and growly like he is every day?"

Asa burst out laughing, Brianna's dry tone relieved the pressure on her chest. "Jesus, Brianna."

"Nevermind, don't answer that."

"What am I going to do?"

"Huh…he hasn't told you about mates yet. You should ask him when y'all wake up."

"Mates?"

"Yep, soulmates. How many hours to Tennessee, seems like time enough to talk about it."

"That's…" Asa sighed. "Is it possible to love him already?"

She didn't mean to say that last part, but it was out and she tensed waiting on Brianna to answer.

"Yes. You probably both let your guards down because you thought you were dreaming. That's enough to build a bond, know what I mean?"

"I do," she whispered, knowing she'd told Xavier things she'd never say aloud in public. She turned and faced the woman she was starting to regard as a friend. "Should I worry about people trying to blow us up on our trip?"

"Probably," Brianna said bluntly.

"Have you ever tried sugarcoating?"

Brianna snickered. "I'm going to bed now, have a good trip tomorrow, and be careful. I'm going to find out if I can help you do magic when you come back."

Brianna left with that, and Asa laid there more confused than ever.

Xavier kept his eyes on the road, his eyes straying back and forth between his rearview and side mirrors. He was alert, vigilant, making sure they weren't being followed. He was actually surprised his brothers hadn't sent back up. So far, he and Asa were one of a few cars on the early morning road. Now and then, his eyes drifted to Asa. She was quiet, her head leaning on a pillow against the door. They'd been in the car for an hour and a half and she'd maybe said a total of ten words to him. Was she regretting last night?

She sighed. "I can feel your gaze."

Her voice was sleepy, which made sense. He smiled, his body warming. Despite her claim of having him just once more, she'd rode him until they both collapsed. They'd managed to get two hours of sleep before his alarm had awakened them.

"I'm just wondering if you're okay."

She turned and looked at him. "I am."

"Knowing that won't stop me from looking at you. I find you gorgeous, so you'll need to get used to me staring." He saw her smile out the corner of his eye.

"Explain mates to me."

He glanced at her, her lavender eyes serious, and watching him closely. He cleared his throat. "Explain in what way?"

"Since we know our dreams were real, then you know how I am, X," she warned him.

She didn't like games, word games in particular. Asa liked plain speak, he'd learned that early in his dreams. She'd rather he not answer than to lie to her. He sighed.

"You'll need to ask a specific question if you're looking for a specific answer, elewa." He turned his gaze back to the road to avoid her probing stare.

"What are mates?"

"You've heard of the concept of soulmates, right? For us, fate gets a little bit of help from our ancestors, the Eminzu."

"And I'm your mate?"

"I believe so. Pray it's so."

Her hand reached out and rubbed the back of his neck. "What does that mean for us?"

"It means, that these feelings swirling around us are natural and that you've become the most important person in my world."

She gasped and he spared a look at her. She smiled and shook her head, her hand kneading the muscles in his neck.

"I like that," she said softly.

He released the breath he was holding. "How close are we?"

She moved her hand and picked up her phone. "Another hour, it says."

He grunted. At least they'd gotten the difficult conversation out of the way for now. He glanced at her as her phone rang.

"What's up Chandra?"

"Hey, you're not kidnapped!" Came her friend's enthusiastic greeting.

Asa put the phone on speaker. "Haha, heifa. What's up?"

"Where are you?"

"Atlanta," Asa cut him a look.

"For how long?"

"I don't know. A while, I think."

"Of your own free will?" Chandra snickered. "This isn't like Rome is it?"

Xavier turned his face to hide his laugh. Asa glared at him.

"Not at all. I'm taking a vacation."

"Good, you need it. I just wanted to check in with you. You haven't called me in a couple of days which is unusual. I'll put off the jobs that have come in until you tell me different. I'll let you know when they become persistent."

"Sounds good. Thanks, Chandra." She turned her body to him once she ended the call "Why were you snickering?"

"Isn't Rome where you were kidnapped until you agreed to help them find a stolen sculpture?" He laughed remembering the story.

Her eyes widened. "I really was minding my own business that time, too." She sucked her teeth. "Those dreams cut out a lot of the 'get to know you' phase. I don't know how I feel about that."

He smiled at her. "You regret telling me all your secrets?" He waggled his eyebrows.

"Not at all, now I don't have to pretend to be normal."

He laughed and reached out for her hand. She wound their fingers together and pulled his hand up, nibbling on his knuckles.

"Normal wouldn't survive a day in my world," he assured her. "Did you find it? You never said."

She snorted. "It wasn't theirs. But, yes I found it and returned it to its rightful owner. I let the Carabinieri sort out the rest."

He snickered and turned back to the road. He kept driving and the rest of their time passed with an easier silence between them, Asa drifting in and out of sleep. He kept the smug smile to himself. The morning sun was high by the time they pulled into her mother's house. He got out of the car and stretched, eyeing the single-story craftsman. The neighborhood was nice, quiet. Clean sidewalks and manicured lawns stretched the length of the street. Power flowed throughout the neighborhood and he understood why Asa had subconsciously felt safe when she'd bought it. There was a goodwill spell over the whole street and probably over the whole neighborhood. He didn't bother probing to find out.

Their presence didn't go unnoticed. The curtains in the window across the street flickered and a few neighbors, all at the same time, decided to check their mail and take out the trash.

"Your neighbors are nosey," he noted.

Asa snorted and came around the car. She stood in front of him, gripping his waist. "I wouldn't know." She laid her head on his chest.

He wrapped his arms around her and kissed the top of her head. "It's hard to be here now?"

She nodded and sighed, stepping back. "Should we just grab her stuff and go back today?"

He watched her eyes, hurting for the turmoil swirling the lavender depths. "Just like that?"

"I don't..." She shook her head and looked around. "You're right. I can feel their eyes."

He followed her up the porch, his eyes combing the street. So far, though they stared, none of the neighbors had left their property to investigate. A rush of power swept across his body as he crossed the threshold into the cool interior of the house. Her mother's house was warded. He wondered if Asa knew. He frowned at the scattered boxes.

"Still packing?"

"My mom never unpacked," She said over her shoulder. She walked over the fireplace mantel and picked up a box. A small datebook fell to the floor. She picked it up and frowned.

"What is it?"

"Phone numbers from my mother's friends. Someplace called an Esin," she murmured.

"Your mother belonged to an Esin? Why were the two of you living in the way you described if that was true? Most Esins stick together." He frowned and stepped closer to her, peeking over her shoulder at the book.

"Really? You think my mom was tossed from hers?" Asa looked up at him.

"Only your mom and maybe someone from that Esin would know that," He said, nuzzling the top of her head.

He inhaled her scent and closed his eyes. He burrowed his head into the space between her shoulder and neck, dropping small kisses. What were the chances he could talk her into quickie before they left?

"I'm going to call them." She spun around, her eyes excited.

He swallowed his sigh, so no quickie. He nodded.

Asa pulled out her phone and called the first name on the list, putting the phone on speaker. He prayed she'd get the answers she wanted.

Chapter 17

Xavier propped his head on his hand and stared down at Asa. She was beautiful, even in sleep, energy pulsed around her. He trailed a finger down her cheek. They had spent yesterday packing her mother's things. Today they were supposed to visit an Esin to see a friend of her mother's. The whole process was hard for her, echoes of her pain flowed down the tentative bond that was strengthening with every minute they spent together. He finally pulled her away from the tasks, taking her out to eat to get her out of the house.

It had worked, and when they got back, he'd spent the rest of the night in Asa's bed making her forget everything but him. He leaned in and nuzzled against her neck. His power flared, his magic trying to start their mating process. He'd meant what he told his mother. He didn't want to start the mating frenzy until they'd figured out what they wanted to do about the constant attacks on the women. He needed his head together, and couldn't afford the distraction of the frenzy. Even without it, he was having a hard time keeping his hands off her. He traced the soft curves of her breasts under the sheet.

She sighed and her arms reached for him, even though her eyes were still closed with sleep. He pulled her closer, turning so that she lay on top of him.

"What time is it?"

"Does it matter?" He murmured, gripping her ass and positioning her over his straining erection.

She snorted. "Yes. We're supposed to meet Breesha this afternoon."

He hummed and pulled her down.

"Wait, gotta pee," she scrambled off him and headed naked to the bathroom.

He adjusted his plans and waited until he heard the toilet flush before getting up to follow her. He grabbed his toiletries and headed for the guest bathroom they were using. She was standing over the sink brushing her teeth when he walked into the bathroom. He smiled at her and started the shower. She watched him, her eyes narrowing. He grabbed his stuff and stepped in. He kept his eyes on her as he brushed his teeth, fascinated by her morning routine. How many steps did it take her to wash her face?

When she was done, she turned to face him. He rinsed out his mouth and set his toothbrush aside. Her lavender eyes traced his body, glowing in heat. He poured the soap into his hand and stroked his shaft, meeting her gaze. She crossed her arms over her chest, her mouth parted, her eyes lowered to half-mast. He stroked across his dick, slow, twisting movements and licked his lips.

She mirrored the motion, her tongue dragging across her full bottom lip before gripping it with her teeth. He hissed and gripped his erection tighter. It felt amazing, and her watching was throwing his lust into overdrive. She stepped closer to the bathtub, her heartbeat thumping at her neck. Her chest rose and fell, her needy pants filling the bathroom. She lowered her arms and his eyes latched onto her beaded nipples, his mouth watering.

"Come here, elewa," he ordered.

She stepped close enough for him to touch, but he kept his hands to himself. Torturing them both.

"Touch your breasts for me."

Her eyes widened, and she sucked in a hungry breath. She did as he ordered though, cupping her handful of breasts, her fingers caressing the tips. His erection jumped in his hand and a growl rattled his chest. He released his pheromones, need ripping through his chest.

"You always smell so good," she murmured, her hand softly trailing her stomach. "Your sisters-in-law warned me about your pheromones."

He growled, not because he was bothered by that, he just didn't want to talk about them. He wanted to watch her hands disappear inside the gripping channel of her sex. He made a promise to himself that he'd taste Asa before the day was done.

"Spread your legs wider, I need to see you touch yourself," was his gruff order.

The pheromones were pumping from his body, the scent taking over the bathroom aided by the steam from the hot water. Whether or not it was working on his mate, it had him dazed, and ravenous as fuck. Asa smiled and dropped to her knees. He stopped stroking and tightened his grip on his erection. He had to or he wouldn't last. She laid down, her back on the fluffy rug, her legs wide, displaying her sex to him.

Fuck he had to taste her.

He rinsed quickly, damn near moaning as her fingers parted the lips of her sex. He jumped from the shower, splashing water across the floor. Her skin slipped in his wet hands as he pulled both legs around his shoulders. Asa's laugh turned into a gasp as his mouth latched onto her sex. He speared his tongue between the folds, licking at the core of her. He ravished her, nipping and licking until she was squirming beneath him. His tongue flicked against the bundle of nerves at the top of her sex and she bucked, whispering his name. He closed his eyes, savoring the taste of her. Her thighs tightened around his head, her hips rising as she moaned. He flicked his tongue over her clit, tugging it with his teeth. She gasped, her body tightening in orgasm. He wanted to let her come down from it, let her ride it out while he wallowed in her taste, but damn he needed to be inside her.

Raising to his knees, he guided his erection to her pulsing center, gritting his teeth as he worked through her pulsing walls. Her sex pulled him in, gripped him and he damn near was sent over the edge. His magic slipped out of his control, surrounding her. His beast demanded they mark her. He shook his head, fighting his instincts. By the time he was fully seated he was sweating with the effort it took to keep the mating magic in check.

But then Asa swiveled her hips and he was lost.

He loosened the reins over his control as fucked his mate, deep dragging strokes that had them both cursing. He held her hips down as he drove deep. Electricity skimmed across his skin as he shed his human form. Asa's fingers trailed his hands, the light from his whorls casting shadows on the walls around them.

"Yes, X, more," she panted.

He lowered her legs and lowered his body so he could kiss her. He lifted her back and she circled her legs around his waist, taking his every stroke.

"There, there," she chanted, her nails scoring his back as her sex clenched around him.

He was right there with her, his orgasm barreling over him. He called her name and drove in one last time before exploding. Gods, this woman was everything. He clutched her tightly to his chest, their breathing erratic, loud as they both fought for air. It took a solid five minutes before either of them were able to catch their breath.

Asa leaned against his shoulder. "The water's probably cold by now."

He snorted, finally feeling the hard floor against his knees now that the haze of sex was cleared. "I swear you steal every ounce of control I try to have."

"Control is overrated," she said around a yawn. "Come on, we have to shower and make that appointment."

He groaned. He didn't want to go anywhere. If they were like this before the mating frenzy kicked in, he'd be a goner once it started. He made a promise to himself that they would be taking their bonding period far away from everyone and every responsibility when this was all over.

###

Asa ran her hands over the leather of the steering wheel and stared at the guard gate. She took a deep breath and shut off the app as it announced that they'd reached their destination. She'd hopped in the car and drove to the address her mother's old friend Bresha had given without giving herself enough time to think about what she was doing. Xavier hadn't questioned her, just simply got into the passenger side and rode quietly next to her.

What were they getting into?

She wanted some answers, but perhaps her impulsive actions weren't the way to get them.

"What was I thinking?" She whispered.

She should've stayed in bed with X all day. That would've been a better use of her time.

"That you wanted answers." Xavier grabbed her hand and sandwiched it between his warm palms.

She groaned. He was right. She wanted answers. She likely wouldn't come back to Tennessee once she was finished packing up her mother's house. There was nothing holding her here. So it was better to meet with Bresha now, than pretending she'd get around to it later. Besides, she would bet anything that Brianna would ask her a million questions about her mother's Esin when she got back. She knew nothing about her mother's past and this was the only person who could tell her.

"Are the guards normal?" She nodded towards the guard shack.

"As far as I know," he said, releasing her hand. "They're a secretive bunch."

Asa took a deep breath and drove up. The guard was an older black man, his face serious as he looked down into the car. He stared a moment and then nodded over towards a parking area.

"Pull off to the side, please," his deep voice was serious, unfriendly.

Asa looked at Xavier. He cocked his head, but nodded at Asa to do so. She pulled over to the parking lot area of the guarded gate. Another guard, this one a younger fit version of the first walked towards him, his dark bald head gleaming in the sun. Asa and Xavier stepped from the car. Xavier leaned against the passenger side, propping his arms on the top of the car.

Asa looked back at him. "I can handle this."

She headed for the guard. She could maybe try and use the charm she normally employed when she was treasure hunting. She met the guard halfway.

"What are y'all doing here?" He asked gruffly.

Asa smiled and relaxed her body, putting on her best ditzy expression. "I'm here to see a friend of my mother's. Her name is Bresha."

He didn't return her smile, instead, looking down at the clipboard in his hand. "Asa?"

She nodded, upping the wattage on her smile.

He grunted. "Your name's on the list, but she didn't say anything about Demi." He glanced back at Xavier. "She'll need to meet you somewhere else. We don't allow Demi into our Esin."

She tried a different tactic, changing the tone of her voice. "Really? Well, I'm sure I can convince him to wait out here. It's important that I speak with Bresha."

The guard blinked at her and cocked his head to the side. She thought for a moment that it would work, but then he shook his head and frowned. "Lady, you're exactly why we don't allow the Demi in. Leave, and don't come back."

She frowned, straightening her body. "What does that mean?"

"Don't think I don't understand what you just tried to do. It's especially why we wear protective spells." He pulled a necklace from underneath his uniform, the sun, surrounded by thorns, the exact symbol of her uncle. "You're not welcome here. No disrespect to Marshal Tegan. If he needs to get in, he can make an appointment with our Oliri."

He walked away and she stood there stunned. They were protected by the god Rugaba? What did that mean? She walked back to X and he raised a brow.

"What happened?"

"They don't allow Demi in."

Xavier grunted but said nothing.

"Why aren't you surprised?"

"The peace we have with the Divine is tentative on good days." He shrugged.

"He knew who you were," she squinted her eyes, "but that's not surprising to you either? Who are you?"

"You know who I am Asa, I've told you more about myself than I've told any one person in centuries."

Her stomach fluttered at the reminder and the nonchalant drop of centuries. Dare she ask how old he really was? "But, like, who are you in this world?" She waved at the gates of the Esin.

"I'm head of the Amanda. We police the Demi, but especially so when they come to Earth. It's in the Divine's best interest to stay on my good side."

"Bresha is a Divine like Brianna has been telling me about?"

Her mind was spinning because that meant her mother was as well. Which…she sighed, was exactly what Brianna had been telling her.

She looked back at the guard, then at Xavier. "He said we could get in if we made an appointment with their leader."

He eyed the gate for a moment in silence and then inclined his head towards the car. "Let's get in."

She opened the door and climbed back into the driver's side. "What did he mean?"

He slid into the passenger seat. "How important is this meeting?"

"Well, maybe Bresha can tell us something about my mother that helps me understand her a little better."

He grunted. "Can you meet with her outside of the Esin?"

"She seemed reluctant," she grudgingly admitted, thinking about the phone call she'd had with the woman earlier.

"The thing is, Asa, if I go into that Esin, I'm not going as a person, but as the head of the Amanda."

"And all the protocol that entails," she finished his sentence.

He nodded.

She looked back at the guard who was watching them. "He said they have protective spells to guard against me."

He cursed, "you specifically?"

She shook her head, "I don't know what he meant though. I mean, I tried to convince him to let me in, but it's not anything different than—"

He cursed again. "You tried to spell him, Asa?"

"I don't know any spells or magic."

Xavier grabbed her chin and turned her to face him. "Love, you're Demi, you may still be in denial, but you're purely Demi, one of the first born of a god in thousands of years. Despite your denial, that carries weight. You need to be careful with the way you talk to people and you need to start being aware of the way you move around others."

She thought about what Penny had told her. Hearing it from Xavier and observing the way the guard got pissed, she now understood that no matter what she protested, her powers were there, whether she believed in them or not. She needed to talk to Brianna when she got back to Haven.

She sighed, "I'll try."

"Not try, do." He told her softly.

"I'll call Bresha and see if she'll meet us someplace else." She said, pulling out her cellphone. "I can't get through the gate." She said as soon as the other woman picked up.

"Why not?" Bresha's voice was suspicious.

"They…I'm Demi."

A weight from her chest lifted and she felt lightheaded as she admitted for the first time aloud what she was. She cleared her throat as tears gathered at the corners of her eyes. She looked away from Xavier.

"I'm Demi," she said in a clearer voice, "so I can't get in."

"How? Deena didn't say…the hell god." Bresha whispered. "You're the child she had with the hell god? I thought maybe…I won't meet with you."

Her heart dropped. "I just want to know about my mother and her…power." Panic had the words rushing from her mouth.

It was so weird to think of her mother having power after everything she endured, but there was no more time for her to close her eyes to the facts revealing themselves to her.

"Your mother was powerful, and arrogant in that power. She dabbled when she shouldn't have, and now you're the result. What more do you need to know?"

"Why were we cast out on our own? You people left her to die. I just want to know where I came from."

"Your mother was one of us, but you never were. All Deena had to do was denounce the hell god and she would've been welcomed back." Bresha said harshly.

Asa sucked in a breath and clenched her phone tight.

Bresha continued. "Herman loved Deena, but he couldn't take the humiliation. He stuck by Deena even after she insisted on having you."

Her breath stalled in her chest. "He killed her. That was not love," She whispered.

"He was obsessed, yes. He'd always been obsessed with your mother." The woman admitted.

Asa didn't want to talk about Herman. "Tell me about my mother's powers."

"I shouldn't even be talking to you, never mind giving up Divine secrets. Ask your father," Bresha snapped.

"My mother was kicked out, offered no help, and now you won't even respect her memory enough to help her only daughter," Asa growled. "I thought she was your friend."

"She was my best friend, but she knew the consequences and still chose him over us," Bresha answered.

"Oh, fuck you, lady. I hope every one of you suffers every day the way my mother did."

Asa hung up the phone and threw it into the back seat. Xavier didn't say anything, just gripped the back of her neck, the warm weight of his hand settled there. She leaned forward on the steering wheel. Asa downed the window intending to let loose her temper on the guard at the gate.

Xavier tightened his grip. "Aht aht, love, anything you do represents me as well. Let it go," he whispered.

She turned to him, her face burning in her anger. "I want to burn their shit to the ground."

"Your father may not be able to travel to this realm, but you're connected to him. What do you imagine he'd do to these people if he found out this Esin purposely hung your mother out to dry?"

She cursed and put the car into gear and peeled out.

She drove his car fast, the window still down. Xavier lowered his as well and the wind whipped through the car aggressively, matching her mood. She drove fast, and he let her, knowing what she needed. The muscle car growled as she put her foot further on the gas. They drove in silence for an hour until they came to some mountains. Asa pulled over onto a lookout shoulder and got out. He took his time getting out. He walked to the back of the car and sat on the trunk, pulling her in between his legs and into his arms.

She cried, her shoulders shaking, her anger and grief a swirling miasma inside of her. They sat in silence, occasional cars passing them by. She soon quieted and her arms tightened as she snuggled into him. She sighed and turned her cheek into his chest, staring out at the mountains.

"I'm so happy you're real." She whispered.

He kissed the side of her hair. But said nothing.

"I thought I made you up."

He chuckled. "Trust me, I understand that. Dreaming about you was the only thing that got me through this last year, despite the fact that I wasn't able to feed. You were a bright spot in an otherwise shitty time."

She lifted her head and kissed his lips. He deepened the kiss, his hand holding her head in place as he plundered her mouth.

He pulled back, "better?"

"Is it strange that I love you?" She whispered, her eyes luminous, the lavender orbs tracing his face.

"No stranger than me being in love with a figment of my imagination."

She smiled. "You were in love with me that long?"

He nodded and kissed her lightly. "You can imagine how good it feels to know you're real, and the mate chosen for me."

She sighed and hugged him. "Thank you for being here."

"Always, Asa." He whispered, tightening his grip.

"Nothing is holding me here anymore," she looked back out into the mountains.

"Your home is with me, elewa."

She laid her cheek against his chest. "I like the thought of that."

"Let's go get your mother's things and get the beacon safely to Haven."

"Can I still treasure hunt, do you think?"

"Would I be able to stop you?" He asked.

She snorted. "Right. With this Kokoro business, I don't know that I should be gallivanting across the world."

He kept silent, working not to pressure her. "We'll figure it out when we get home."

She nodded.

Chapter 18

Asa looked around at the boxes Xavier had helped her pack, relieved to be done with the hard part. He'd told her to take only what was necessary for the moment. She'd leave the boxes in the house and make arrangements to have movers pick them up and move them into storage. Chandra could easily sell the house and then…that would be that. She sighed. Xavier had claimed that her home was with him, but she still needed to see on that. But if she were being honest with herself, falling in love with him had already happened. There was no backtracking about it.

She had her large rolling suitcase with her clothes, a duffel bag for her toiletries, and a single cardboard box that held the things her mother deemed important enough to put into her safe deposit box. She was as ready as she could be.

She was still pissed about the trip to the Esin, but there was nothing to be done. Xavier had explained more on their drive back how secretive the Divine were. Why then did Bresha invite her in the first place? Though, Asa could admit that she'd had to coerce the woman to meet with her. One more instance of the magic she'd been wielding unknowingly over the years.

She could work on contacting her father once she got back to Haven. There had to be a way to get him into her dreams. She fingered the coin on the end of the necklace and smoothed over the raised ridges that outlined her father's face. She would ask him about her mother. It was still early enough in the day that they could get back before nightfall.

"So, when we get back will I still have my own room?"

Xavier grunted, moving the last set of boxes against the wall. She smiled, taking his disgruntled look as a 'no'. They both paused at a knock at the door. Frowning, Xavier moved to the window facing the street and peeked outside.

"Should I answer it?"

He shook his head and went to the door. "Yes?"

"I was…I wanted to check on the girl and see if she needed anything." Came a muffled reply.

Xavier frowned deeper, stepping back from the door. "Asa, grab your things." He ordered quietly.

She didn't think, doing exactly as he asked. She grabbed her duffel, swinging it across her chest and picked up the rolling suitcase, situating the cardboard box on the top, snapping it into place. Xavier's body was tense, his hands up in front of him in a defensive position.

"What's happening?" She whispered.

No sooner than she asked, the air seemed to pressurize around them before a thump sounded on the door. A scream was next and then silence.

"Stay back," Xavier ordered as Asa rushed forward to see what happened.

Xavier looked both ways before going out of the door. There was a man slumped on her porch. She gasped as Xavier slid him inside and shut the door again.

"Who is that? What happened?"

"Your mother's house is warded and this fool just tried to use magic to get inside," he answered tersely, checking the man's pockets. He cursed when he didn't find anything. "Is there a back door?"

"Of course, out through the kitchen. The car is in the front though," she rolled her suitcase towards the window.

Her heart started thundering when she saw a crowd of people gathering on the street in front of her mother's house.

"Umm, X, we may have a problem with that," she whispered.

"No shit," he muttered. "Let's go, out the back. If we're lucky, the yard isn't warded and we can get out that way."

She didn't understand what any of that meant, but it didn't stop her from rolling her suitcase after him, the duffel slapping against her back as she rushed to keep up. She was no stranger to sneaking out of places. The house shook again and she swallowed her yelp. They'd barely reached the back door when it happened again, this time, the boom louder than all of them before.

"Hurry, Asa." Xavier gritted out as he kicked out the back door.

She winced. That would definitely affect the resale value. Her mother's back yard was fenced in and she breathed easy to see that no one was hanging out there. Xavier on the other hand cursed again.

"The whole place is warded." He dropped the man he'd slung over his shoulder and walked over to the fence. "What's behind here?"

"Umm, woods I think."

Asa racked her brain to remember the layout of the neighborhood. Her mom had picked the house in particular because she had no neighbors behind her. Xavier held out his hands, she understood what he wanted her to do. She set her suitcase aside and put a foot in his clasped hands and he lifted her towards the top of the high fence.

"Yep, nothing but woods," she said softly.

"Over you go, then," he said.

She scrambled across the fence cursing when the duffle bag slapped the back of her head as she landed. She winced as he tossed first the cardboard box, then her rolling suitcase over. Next came the man that had tried to get into the house. Xavier hopped over the fence next and her eyes widened at the feat. The air around her warmed and started to once again pressurize.

"Umm, X,"

"I know, *elewa*, hold on tight," he said a moment before his arms starting moving quickly, his hands making a pattern.

Xavier pushed out and Asa wobbled on her feet as his magic clashed against something. Probably the same something that was shaking against her mother's house. She turned towards the structure and winced as lightning and heated shafts of air pushed against the place. If she could see it from over the fence, how powerful was the magic they were up against? She now understood what Xavier meant by wards. Her mother's house was taking a beating which each new assault.

Xavier turned and nudged her forward and she followed his unspoken instruction, going deeper into the woods. She pushed through the oak trees, carefully picking her way through the dense brush on the ground. The air around them vibrated and instinctually she ducked. The tree closest to her splintered apart and she cursed but kept going.

A sense of disorientation hit her as they went deeper into the forest. One tree looked the same as the next and she'd lost track of which direction they were going. From her peripheral, running alongside them, and gaining closer were creatures she'd never imagined. The sun glinting off their scales caught her eyes and her steps slowed. The iridescence was mesmerizing, the color of their skin changing right before her eyes. Red eyes, sharp teeth, and air of evil broke the spell quickly though and she sped her footsteps.

A swoosh sounded and a gust of air pushed Asa down to her knees as a large man…bird…what the hell ever reached out for her. A hot sting of magic caressed her back and right before the thing could grab her, it went flying back into a tree with a hard thud.

"Keep going, Asa. I'll get us out of here as soon as I get a clear path." Xavier grabbed her arm, jerking her up to a standing position.

She wanted to stop and assess, but magic pressed down around them as the people chasing them geared up for another attack. Xavier cursed and slung the man he was carrying back over his shoulder. Her skin heated and panic skittered down her spine, this magic was closer than the last. The coin on her chest started heating and a battle cry sounded off to their left. The woods really came alive then. Asa's mind didn't even have time to process the different kinds of creatures, who she now assumed to be Demi that poured through the trees.

Power saturated the place to the point where she could hardly breathe the air. A bright white light opened right next to her, and Xavier grabbed her arm and dragged her and all her stuff through that light. Asa blinked, her heartbeat thundering in her ears. Her eyes were having a hard time focusing, the bright light of whatever Xavier did still making her disoriented.

Fallon was standing behind a large desk when she could focus. They were back at Haven? Xavier dumped the male on the ground and he started groaning. Asa released the tight grip she had on her rolling suitcase and wiped a hand down her pants. Whatever he had done was handy. There were a couple of times she wished she had something like that. Would've made escaping way easier.

"He needs to go in a cell for questioning," Xavier ordered Fallon, his voice breathless from their mad dash.

Fallon nodded and got on a fancy phone. Less than a minute later, two big giant men came through the door and hauled the man up.

Xavier cupped her cheek, "are you okay?"

She nodded, dazed, not sure how she felt if she was being honest. "I could totally use that teleportation thing."

He kissed her forehead, "yeah, the ward over your mother's place reached farther than I thought. We need to talk about how calm you were during this."

She snickered, "was I supposed to be hysterical?"

His lips quirked. "Something like that."

"I will have an adrenaline crash here soon if that makes you think I'm normal."

He shook his head, a bemused smile on his face. His fingers lingered against her cheek and kissed her forehead again.

Xavier closed his eyes and took a deep breath, reminding himself that he'd gotten her home safely.

"I assume I'll need to send someone to go pick up the car," Fallon said dryly.

Xavier sighed at his brother's interruption. "Yep, get right on that, I'm taking my mate to my room. Come get me once the male has been questioned."

"What happened?" His brother asked.

Xavier lifted the duffel bag from around Asa's chest, pulling it up on his arm. "Just a forest full of mercenaries. Easy day." He gave her the cardboard box and grabbed her suitcase shooting Fallon a shit-eating grin. To which his brother returned and saluted him.

"Come, elewa."

Asa followed behind him, not asking any questions. He would take time later to figure out why his mate didn't have to be coached about getting away. Right now he was grateful she wasn't hysterical. She set the cardboard box on his dining room table as they entered his apartment and followed him to his bedroom. He put her stuff on his bed and walked back out to the living room, ordering dinner to be sent down. His hands were shaking by the time he was done, that adrenaline crash she was talking about hammering through his body. He pushed them into his pockets.

Asa was putting her stuff away in his closet when he got back. Dark, possessive pride expanded his chest. She was his, moving around in his space, a space that would become theirs. It made him very happy. She walked out of his closet and gasped as she caught him watching her at the door.

"I ordered dinner," he said with forced calmness.

She nodded and ran her hands over her hair. "Thank you, something sweet I hope?"

"I remember, elewa."

She smiled at him and walked over to him, wrapping her arms around his waist.

Easy.

From the very first moment, he'd stepped into her dreams it had been easy between them. He was happy to know that part transferred over into their waking life. Her body was trembling, but there was no fear wafting from her. She was strong, steady and it relieved him like nothing else he could imagine.

The doorbell rang and she tensed.

"It's probably the food," he murmured against the skin of her neck.

She nodded. "I'm starving."

She settled at his dining table while he picked up the trays from his front door where the staff had left it. Carrying them to the table, her eyes lit.

"What's this?"

She grabbed at the green pear on top.

"Fruit from the Demi realm." He answered.

She bit into it, closing her eyes. "Oh my God, this is amazing."

He smiled, even as he hardened at her rapturous expression. She moved the cardboard box aside so he could put the rest of their food down. He sat across from her and they dug into their dinner. There was a small knock on his door before Liliana barged in, her eyes wide and curious. He assumed rumors of their adventures had already gotten back to her.

"There you are," she rushed towards them. "There were some rumors…" she broke off.

He snorted. That woman had more spies than even he.

Liliana moved to the table, curiosity on her face as she looked at the box. Her eyes glazed over as she stepped closer and pushed it open.

"Excuse you, nosy," Asa snapped.

A glow started emitting from the cardboard box. Liliana reached out and it pulsed. Xavier held her hand right as she was about to touch it.

"Lily?" His voice seemed to pull her from a trance.

She shook herself. "I…I'm sorry, are you guys okay? I came as soon as I heard what happened."

Her eyes were still watching the box. Xavier opened the flaps of the cardboard, wondering what from inside would be glowing. He pulled the wooden box Asa said she believed to be the beacon from it. It emitted a small pulse before going dark. Liliana's eyes were wide, her gaze never straying from the box.

"What it is about the box, Lily?"

"I've been dreaming of it," she whispered, reaching for it again.

Xavier gripped her arm again to stop her, shock straightening his spine. "In what way?"

"Of my mother's box?" Asa asked, putting down her fork.

Liliana shuddered, seeming to fight whatever compulsion held her. "I keep having nightmares about Ofeereee. In the nightmares, he shows me a box like that and a spell I can do. I can program it to find him." She shuddered again and her eyes were luminous with unshed tears.

Fear skittered down his spine. "Have you told your mate?"

No way Leo would've known something like that and not have told him. Well...he could hope. Fallon had been keeping a doozy of a secret from him, who knows what his brothers had been hiding.

Liliana shook her head, "I didn't want to worry him. I've never seen anything like that, I didn't think it existed." She cleared her throat. "Or if it did, since I didn't know where it was, I wouldn't have to worry about it." She hugged herself.

Asa put a hand on her back but looked at Xavier. "Why would my mother have something like this?"

Xavier shook his head. Hell if he knew, and the only person, or rather god he could ask may or may not answer that question. He studied his mate. "Have you tried contacting your father?"

Asa's eyes went wide. "I was going to."

He nodded, "I think you should try and do that tonight. Lily, you need to tell Leo about this."

Liliana sighed and closed her eyes, but nodded in agreement.

Xavier stood and kissed her on the forehead. "We'll meet in my office in the morning. Will you be okay?"

"None of this is okay," Lily stated.

That was true, but there was nothing he could do to spare them what was ahead.

Chapter 19

"Are you worried about her nightmares?" Asa reached out and touched his hand.

He was gazing on the other side of the room, his face bunched in thought. He shook himself at her touch and blinked, focusing back on her.

He cleared his throat. "I want you to see someone for me."

Instead of answering, she waited him out. Xavier pulled back his hand and wiped it down his face. He stood and walked over to the fancy panel he had on the wall by the door. His voice was low as he talked into it. Whatever the conversation was, it didn't last long. He came back to the kitchen table and sat, sighing.

"We have a race of healers, they're called the Kira. I want to have one check you over."

"For what purpose?"

"I want to get a handle on what type of powers you have. If Liliana is already having nightmares about Ofeeree, that means things are moving faster than I anticipated. That attack at your mother's house was almost full scale. His followers have never been that bold before."

"What are you worried about, can you explain it to me?"

He picked up the beer in front of him and took a swig, studying her face. A small smile tipped up one side of his mouth. "It feels good to be able to do this with you in real life."

She gripped his hand. "I like that we can still talk to each other."

He nodded and sighed. "Ofeeree was bound in a prison with no escape, his power bound with him. If he's able to infiltrate Liliana's dreams, it means he's awakening."

"The people who are trying to free him would love that," her mind went back to her first conversation with Liliana and Brianna. "Do you think they can feel it?"

"That's but one of my fears. If they can, it means they'll come harder for the Kokoro souls."

If the fight they'd just escaped was 'almost' full scale, she shuddered to think what else they'd throw at her and the girls. All the bits and pieces of the stories she'd heard from the ladies were coming together.

"Because they need us for his prison break."

"Yep."

A shudder of fear went down her spine and she sat back in her chair, clutching at the necklace on her chest. A knock at the door sounded and Xavier went to answer it. Her eyes widened when a tall, lanky man followed him into the kitchen. The man was handsome, his face a study in perfection. High cheekbones, large, heavily lashed dark eyes and full lips, he gorgeous. Could a man be called gorgeous? His hair was in locs, long enough to reach the middle of his back. He wore pants that swept past his ankles, covering his feet. He was shirtless, his body muscular, lean. Her gaze traced the tattooed circles on his shoulder and chest, curious as to what they meant.

His eyes were kind as they raked her. He smiled and she sighed, her body instantly relaxing.

"Cut it out, Tahir," Xavier growled.

"My apologies, she is restless, anxious, my immediate reaction is to comfort." Tahir's voice was deep, soothing. There was a hint of mischief in his eyes.

"Asa, this is Tahir, Tahir, my mate, Asa." Xavier introduced them.

Asa reached out her hand and Tahir clasped it, his palm smooth, and cool to the touch.

"Where would you like her?" Xavier asked.

Asa's brows winged up with curiosity. What were they going to do?

"If we can relax in the living room that will be best," Tahir answered.

She followed the two of them into Xavier's living room, digging her toes into the plush carpet, nervous and unsure of what was about to happen. Tahir smiled at her and she relaxed.

"Just sit here, cross-legged in front of me," he ordered.

She did as she was told, crossing her legs and resting her hands on her knees. Xavier sat next to her on his knees. His presence was reassuring and she was happy for it, because though her body was relaxed, she was still feeling apprehensive.

"How shielded is your room, Marshal?" Tahir asked.

"You know me," was Xavier's answer as he started to move his hands and murmur under his breath.

Tahir snorted and turned his attention to Asa. She shivered as something danced across her skin, raising goosebumps. Was it more magic?

"Don't worry," Tahir said soothingly. "Just the ward going up."

He started breathing deep, closing his eyes. Asa looked at Xavier, not sure what she was supposed to do. Xavier rubbed her back and nodded, which she took to meant this was normal. Tahir's eyes opened, and they were a deep brown, with a lighter brown ring around the edge of the pupil, glowing.

"Okay, remove the necklace." He ordered.

She gripped the pendant, reluctant to do so. He didn't say anything to pressure her, just waited silently. Stock still, serene. It was eerie how still he was able to sit. She took a deep breath and removed it. He frowned once she put it on the table behind her.

"I need to touch your forehead, is that okay?"

She nodded. Tahir slid his body closer to her and lifted his hand. It was warm over her head and an electric shock went through her. He hissed and moved his hand. She looked at him and he was frowning. He touched her forehead again and this time, the current was a little stronger, raising the hair on her arms.

Xavier grunted next to her. "What's wrong?"

Tahir shook his head. "Pass me the necklace, Asa."

She handed it reluctantly to Tahir. He picked it up and hummed. He handed it back to her. And she put it back on. It was warm as it settled against her chest. As a matter of point, her whole body was warmer. Heat flushed across her skin and she closed her eyes as the smell of wood smoke drifted to her.

Tahir hummed again and she opened her eyes. He nodded as though coming to some kind of decision and turned to Xavier.

"Her magic is definitely bound. This is much different than what happened with Brianna though. This was purposeful and expertly executed."

"By the necklace?"

Tahir shook his head. "No, coin on the necklace is a token. From her scent and the power, it was her father who did it."

"What's a token?" She looked between the two men.

Tahir ignored her question, his focus still on Xavier. "You said she's able to pull you into a dreamscape?"

Xavier nodded, and Asa's cheeks heated, though she knew the man would have no idea what they did in their dreams.

"Rugaba has also put his mark there, so if she wanted, she could call either of them to her. It's very powerful." Tahir continued. "Azra has bound Asa's magic, I'm guessing he also added some kind of dampening magic to the necklace. It's why her power can only be felt once she's removed it."

"Can anyone use the token?" Xavier frowned.

Tahir nodded, a grimace marring his face.

"How can the necklace be used?" She asked.

"By someone other than yourself?" Tahir asked stretching his neck. "It can be used to request an audience with either god, not something easily attainable. There is usually a high price attached. Your necklace cuts the oracles out of the equation. Not necessarily a good thing."

"Why not?" She was new to this gods thing and, she realized, slightly out of her depth.

"Going through a god's oracle prevents you from making life-ending mistakes. All gods have their quirks. Who better to know how not to piss them off than the ones who speak for them."

Her shoulders slumped. "So I don't have access to my powers?"

He shook his head. "I can't say that. Some of your charisma and instincts are natural parts of your magic and are very evident in your aura. There is also the fact that you're able to pull the Marshal into your dreams. That in itself is powerful magic, one I've rarely heard of, never mind seen in action. I'm curious to know what your father deemed too powerful for you to have access to and what he bound within you."

"How do I—"

Tahir pointed to her necklace before she could get out the question. "Your father is the only person who can unbind your power."

She gripped the coin and stared at the face chiseled into the metal.

"You've talked to him." Tahir's expression was curious, his head tilted.

She nodded. "He's come to me before."

"There is your answer, then. If you don't mind, I would like to sweep you, though."

"Sweep me?"

"Your grief and confusion are drowning your aura," he said quietly.

She nodded, understanding what he meant. "How will the sweeping help? How do you do it?

"The grief is yours to carry, but I can lighten the load of it on your soul. I'll use my magic to dissipate some of the strain on your aura."

She nodded and he touched her forehead.

"Close your eyes for me, Asa," he said quietly.

She did as he asked and closed her eyes. She flinched when she felt the wind from his hands as they passed over her, but kept her eyes closed. Soon, a peace stole over her and tears fell from her eyes. Her body shuddered and she took a lungful of air in. Her body felt light and untethered.

"All done," Tahir announced and she flinched, the sound unexpected.

She wiped her face and lowered her head in relief. "Thank you," she whispered.

Tahir stood. "It's no problem. The ward, Marshal."

Xavier cleared his throat, his arms moving until her ears popped. Tahir left them with a smile and a wave. Asa stayed on the floor, unsure of what to do. She turned to Xavier. He was sitting patiently, his face empathetic.

"What next?"

He slid backward until his back met the sofa and stretched his legs out. "Nothing for now. We rest, because if what I fear is happening, is actually happening, then I don't know the next time we'll be able to."

She stretched her arms up and rolled her neck. She hadn't realized how much stress she'd been carrying around.

"Come here." Xavier held his arms out.

The deep baritone of his voice moved through her and she shuddered. She turned her head to face him. His eyes said he wanted to soothe her, but her body had other ideas. She scrambled into his lap, laying her head on his shoulder. She nuzzled into his neck and need for him overwhelmed her body. Her limbs, already pliant from Tahir's magic buzzed with energy and heat. She straddled his lap and cupped his cheeks. She stared into his eyes, memorizing the hazel depths, relishing the love she saw reflected back.

"Need you," she whispered, leaning in for a kiss.

Xavier grabbed the back of her head, holding her in place for his plundering tongue. She pulled back and rolled off him, fumbling to remove her pants. He did the same, shoving them down his legs. She resumed her position across his legs, rubbing her wet center against his erection. He sucked on the side of her neck, his hands gripping her hips. She reached between them, grabbing his shaft. She closed her eyes and slowly slid down on his dick.

He groaned and nipped her chin with his teeth and then her lips. She opened her mouth sucking his tongue in as she raised her hips. She sank down again, pleasure washing over her.

"Love you," he murmured against her lips.

"Love you too."

She gasped when his hips rose, pushing into her harder. He pumped into her again and again, holding her hips in place for his strokes. She arched her back and rotated her hips, taking him deeper, grinding her clit against his groin. Her inner walls flexed and throbbed, clenching against his shaft. She raised higher, slamming back on top of him, smiling at his growl. Xavier bucked against her, and she gripped his legs with her knees holding on for the ride. She released his shoulders and pulled her shirt off, flinging it across the room. Her bra was the next thing to go. His eyes lit, the copper ring around the iris glowing, his greedy gaze going straight to her breasts. She grabbed his head and guided him there, hissing as he bit her nipple before licking it and soothing the bite.

Urgency gripped them both, their bodies moving in synch, both desperately reaching for that peak. She came first, her yell sending him over behind her. They were panting, clutching each other tightly as they worked to get their breath. The worry she'd felt earlier was momentarily pushed aside, for which she was grateful. She would hold tight to that feeling for as long as possible.

Chapter 20

Asa moved around the small bedroom anxious. As she'd told Brianna, her childhood bedroom was one place she returned to in her dreams, over and over. She thought about her father, unsure how to 'call' him to her. Was it just a matter of thinking about him? How did one summon a god?

"For someone as powerful as you, it's fairly easy."

Asa whipped around and gasped. Her father was standing at the door, his gaze not on her, but sweeping her old bedroom. She stepped closer, her heart racing. It had worked! What she'd done to accomplish it, she didn't know, but she was going to take the win.

"Dad," she whispered, awkwardly. Did she call him that?

His face softened into a surprise as he turned his attention to her.

She cleared her throat and stepped forward. "I needed to talk to you."

He nodded but turned back to her bedroom. "You grew up in this room?"

"It's the one I spent the most time in." She looked around at the sparse decorations that Herman allowed. "There were others, but this one was…steady."

For a moment, a pained expression crossed his face before he cleared it. "One day, when things aren't so urgent, I would love to hear about how you grew up."

Tears clogged her throat and she turned away.

"Asa." His voice was soft as he laid a hand on her shoulder.

She swallowed and blinked the tears from her eyes. "I went to visit my mother's Esin." She cocked her head, curious as to how he would feel about that.

"She used to take care of Rugaba's temple there." He sighed and a chair appeared behind him right as he sat down. "The first time she summoned me to her dream was…" He shook his head. "She'd found some kind of text about me while she was cleaning the temple library. It made her curious."

Asa smiled, because like her mother, she often stumbled onto things in her curiosity.

"Did you love her?"

"As much as one such as I have the capacity to love," was his answer.

She dropped down on the bed, sitting in front of him. "She was booted from the Esin. No one would tell me why."

He nodded. "She was pregnant, and under pressure to denounce me. Their leader's son wanted her, and would have her by whatever means he could."

"If it was the leader's son, why did they kick her out?" she still didn't understand.

Her father sighed. "According to your mother, he couldn't take the talking behind his back."

"Coward."

"One of many things he was," Azra agreed. "She and Herman reached some type of compromise, and your mother banned me from her dreams."

Her heart ached, knowing that was the only way he could travel to Earth.

"I sent oracle after oracle to talk to her until she finally came to me, begging me to stop." He leaned forward and pulled one of her hands between his.

She snatched her hand back, realizing the direction he was going. "You're going to blame not being there for me on my mother? What was stopping you from coming to *my* dreams?" Her voice was a hoarse whisper.

He watched her, his eyes tracing her face as though memorizing it. He sighed as he seemed to come to some kind of decision. "I want to show you something, I don't know how you'll react, but I find…I don't want your disdain."

She nodded, nervous, for what he could show her. Her heart skipped as the room swirled around her until she and her father were standing in a park she recognized. It was one near the last apartment they'd lived in together. Her stomach dropped and her breath caught in her chest as she saw a glimpse of her mother. Deena was younger, her face panicked as she looked around carrying what Asa could only assume was her as a baby.

There was a flash and her father stepped from a bright light. Deena rushed to him. He looked the same as he did now, save the anger on his face.

"You're done ignoring me?"

Deena took a shaky breath and moved the blanket from the baby's face. *"I wanted to give you the chance to meet your daughter."*

Asa gasped at the pain she saw cross her father's face. His hands shook as he reached out to the baby, dropping his hand at his side before lifting it to the baby's face.

"You were such a beautiful baby," he said softly, next to her.

Her heart broke for him.

Past Deena lifted baby Asa and set her into her father's arms. Past Azra's smile was tentative as he stared down at the baby. His eyes filled, and a look of awe-filled them. Asa felt awkward, as though she shouldn't be witnessing his vulnerability.

"She has my eyes." Past Azra whispered.

Deena nodded, tears falling down her face. *"This is the last you can see of her. I'm afraid of what he'll do if he knows that I still visit you."*

"I can have him killed," Past Azra said it so casually, his eyes never leaving baby Asa.

Deena's face went ashen and she stepped back. *"Let me deal with him,"* she said cautiously.

"And my daughter? Will you allow me to see her?"

Deena looked away. *"I'll do what I can."*

The scene shifted, the days and nights blurring as time passed. Still, she and her father stood in the same spot until time stopped. Her mother was older this time, her face bruised, her eyes wild with panic. She rushed up to Past Azra, who had been pacing the park.

"She's going into puberty," was Deena's panicked statement. *"Her powers are manifesting."*

Asa tried to remember how old she would've been. What had been happening in their life at the time?

Past Azra stepped closer to Deena, cupping her cheek. His hand glowed as he healed Deena. *"He's done this to you."*

"It's Asa, she reminds him of what I did." Deena hurried and explained.

Asa sighed in frustration because her mother had made many excuses for Herman throughout her life.

"You were mine before he was even a thought." Past Azra insisted. *"Is that why you've not brought Asa to see me?"*

Deena gave a wry chuckle, *"he hates knowing that. You have to do something to help me control Asa. For her protection,"* she hastily added.

He growled, cutting her off. *"Bring the child to me, and I will bind her powers."*

Deena nodded and disappeared. Another whirl of the world and her mother appeared again, this time with a preteen Asa in the background, sitting on a picnic blanket.

Asa's eyes widened as memories of that time flooded her. She'd gotten her first period and had been wildly out of control, fussing at her mother and step-father. It was the year he'd started hitting Deena. She never understood why. It wasn't as though Herman had ever acted as a father toward her, but until that year, he'd never shown his hate for Asa.

Past Azra appeared near a tree, longing on his face. His hands moved, the atmosphere around him swayed and he tugged at the air. Twelve-year-old Asa rubbed her chest and then disappeared. Asa rubbed her chest in the present as the memories played out. She remembered waking in a cold sweat that morning, feeling as though something was missing. She'd walked around in a fog for weeks after that, with Deena saying it was hormones.

Past Azra walked over to Deena with a chest in his hand. One she recognized as the one she'd found present day in Herman's closet.

"There is a necklace within, one that will allow her to call to me until she has full use of her power. There is also a beacon, it connects directly to me. When she is ready, give this to her and she will be able to travel to me so I can release her magic."

"A visit to hell?" Deena's eyes widened.

"She is my daughter, Deena!" he snapped. *"You've kept her from me in all this time, will you do so even when she's old enough to choose for herself?"*

Deena held up a hand to placate him. *"Of course not. I'll give it to her when she's of age."*

Past Azra's eyes narrowed and he hissed, pulling up her arm, seeing the bruises. *"Again?"*

"He doesn't mean it."

"Let me help you."

"You have to stay away from both of us. He'll kill Asa, he's sworn it."

Anger flushed his face. *"I will take our child from that place."*

Deena gripped his wrist *"you can't, he'll never let me leave alive. You're a hell god, Azra, I don't want that for Asa. She could still join an Esin, so long as you're not…"* she paused and sighed. *"Promise me that you'll not visit anymore. If Asa breaths a word about you, it will set him off and she'll be banned from any Esin."*

"She's Demi, Deena, they'll never have her." His jaw worked, anguish on his face.

"Promise me," tears streamed down Deena's face, her petite body trembling.

He stared at her for a minute before saying, *"I can protect you at a Haven. There is one not too far from you."*

"No. He'll kill us both."

"I'm a god Deena, though I am imprisoned in my own realm, I can still protect you. Let me protect you!"

She shook her head and stepped back from him. *"Promise. Leave Asa and me both alone."*

"She's my daughter, Deena."

"Please, it's the only way."

He growled and turned his back. He turned back around, *"when she leaves your home, you can no longer keep me from her."*

"Asa is headstrong, if you tell her, she'll confront him. She's so much like you. You can't tell her, he'll kill us!" Her shrill cry rang out in the empty park.

His shoulders slumped. *"I can't promise you this, Deena, she's mine."*

Deena went to her knees sobbing. Asa saw the struggle on her father's face. Watched the dilemma play out, her chest tight with grief.

"If you leave him?"

Deena's face lifted, her eyes hopeful. *"I will tell her, I swear."*

He nodded, *"then I will not contact either of you again until you reach for me."* He disappeared and left her mother in the park.

Asa closed her eyes as anger, grief and so many other nasty, undefinable emotions swirled within her. When she opened them again, she was back in her bedroom. Azra was standing in front of her, pain on his face, longing for her to understand the promise Deena had extracted from him.

She wiped her cheeks. "She never told me."

"I'm aware." He clenched his jaw. "She never came to me and told me she left."

"The box that Herman lured her with had the beacon inside," she whispered, now understanding why Deena had walked into his trap.

Asa had long ago looked up why a battered woman would stay and Deena was a textbook case. She needed to understand why her mother had made the decisions she did. Even now in her anger, her mind went through the psychology laid out in the books, empathizing with Deena's plight.

Asa wanted to be angry, though. Angry that her mother had kept her father from her. But, Deena had been right, had Asa known her father was out there, nothing would've stopped her from seeing him.

A chill went down her spine as she realized something… "You killed Herman?"

 His jaw clenched. "Yes. With her death, I was released from my promise to her." There was no hint of remorse on his face.

She wanted to know how Azra had managed it, but there was a question more important to her than that. "Why didn't you do it earlier?"

His eyes lit in anger. "I'm a god Asa, my word cannot be broken. I promised Deena I would stay out of it. I found out she was in danger when it was too late to do anything."

His eyes were luminous and she saw the pain on his face and her anger melted away at him. He was hurting as much as she was.

"Is there a way…" she trailed off, afraid to ask.

"I can't see your mother, she's beyond me."

Asa nodded and turned her back. He touched her shoulder, at first tentative, then with a firmer grip. He turned her and pulled her to him. She burrowed into his chest, her grief too big for her to hold back. He said nothing, simply held her as she cried. She stepped back and wiped her face.

"I need to go, I need to think about this." She gripped the pendant at her neck. "Can I see you any time I want?" She whispered.

"You've only to call to me, *okan mi.*"

She nodded and forced herself to wake up.

Chapter 21

Asa gasped as she sat up in bed. She wiped a hand across her face and took a deep shuddering breath. Xavier was sleeping beside her, his arm thrown across his eyes. She needed to get out of this room. Restlessness rose and she nearly screamed with the pressure of it on her chest. She had to get out. She pulled on a pair of jeans and a tank top with some slides. She could go on the roof for a walk. She didn't want to risk leaving the Haven.

She tiptoed out of the suite, careful to close the door softly. Brianna was leaving her suite when she spotted Asa.

"Hey." Brianna wrapped her robe around her tighter. "Can't sleep either?"

Asa shook her head. "I was going to go up to the roof."

Brianna touched her arm. "What's wrong?"

Asa sighed. She couldn't get the words out just yet. Brianna narrowed her eyes but nodded in understanding. She followed Brianna's lead through the tunnels, her mind on the memories her father had replayed. Could he be lying about the images? She rubbed her chest, her memories matched at least one of the visions he'd showed her so she would say no.

Her mother had purposefully kept her from her father.

It went through her head like a mantra. Why would Deena stay with Herman when a much more powerful god had offered to protect her? All in the hopes of one day going back to her Esin? She'd been right when she'd called the Esin a cult and Brianna had confirmed it. Asa didn't breathe easily until she could see the stars in the night sky.

Brianna led them to cushioned lounge chairs, surrounding the pool. Instead of flopping into one the way Brianna did, Asa paced the side of the pool. She spotted a groggy Liliana coming out through the side door in her pajamas on her second lap. She looked over at Brianna.

"You called her?"

"Umm, yeah, I suck at comforting people." Brianna shrugged.

"Why are you two up so late?" Liliana murmured, laying in the chair next to Brianna.

Asa was a little irritated because she wanted to stew in peace, but her heart was hammering. She needed to get it off her chest. She didn't know these women, not in the grand scheme of things, but she couldn't deny the closeness she felt towards them. Between all the Kokoro business, and them being stuck in Haven, the three of them had formed a sort of kinship.

With that thought, Asa decided to let it all out. "I had another dream about my father."

"How did it go?" Brianna asked.

"He…revealed to me why he hadn't been around, and why he bound my powers."

"And…" Liliana prompted.

"And I'm pissed. My mother had ample opportunity to tell me. She'd left Herman a year ago. At any time, she could've sat me down and told me about her life, my life. Instead, I had to find out from some nasty bitch in the cult she came from."

"Oh, Asa," Brianna whispered.

A tear fell, despite Asa's anger and she gave up pacing, dropping into the lounger on the other side of Brianna. "I just…now I have to fucking decipher clues and read crusty old texts—"

"Hey!" Brianna hit her arm.

"—She could've told me all this. Why didn't she tell me?" She asked softly unable to keep the steam of her anger.

Liliana made a sympathizing sound. "Shame is weird that way. I'm not excusing either of them, because I was once in the same shoes you are. I'm just saying, shame can congeal into this wall between you and the people you love."

Asa wiped her cheeks and sighed. "It's not her fault who she fell in love with."

"She was in love with Azra?" Brianna asked with wide eyes.

"According to my father."

"So they met in dreams?" Brianna threw her legs around to face Asa.

"The same kind of dream I pulled you into."

"Oh shit," Brianna whispered. She pushed her robe off her arm and showed Asa the spot where she'd pinched her days ago. There was a small circular bruise there.

"Whoa," Asa whispered, leaning forward. "It looks like a burn mark. So, anything my parents did in those dreams was real?"

"Wait, catch me up," Liliana demanded.

Brianna explained to her about Asa pulling her into her dream.

"Holy," Liliana whispered. "That's… I've never heard of a power like that."

"We need to visit the Divine library." Brianna insisted.

Liliana snorted "Good luck with that. Your mate's not likely to let you get within a hundred feet of that Esin without him."

Brianna growled, "That's fine. He can go too. I can visit my parents, he won't object to that."

"Oh yeah, we'll see," Liliana snickered.

"I tried to visit my mother's Esin and they wouldn't even let me through the gate."

Brianna winced. "We sort of got into a fight on Esin land last year. They're a little leery about Demi at the moment."

Asa's eyes widened. "What?"

"They tried to kidnap Brianna and take her spell book. Xavier took exception to that. Rugaba got involved, it was ugly." Liliana answered.

"How will you get into the Esin, then?"

"My parents live there. They have a new Oliri, and the relationship is strained, but they can't keep me from seeing my parents."

"Holy, wait," Liliana sat forward. "So you're an actual pure Demi, you're half god and half Divine. That's…wow."

Brianna frowned, "Did your father say how to unlock your powers?"

Asa gripped the necklace resting against her chest. "I have to go to him to get them unlocked. The beacon is supposed to help me find him." She gasped and leaned across Brianna. "I forgot. Did you tell your husband about the nightmares?"

"What nightmares?" Brianna whipped around to Liliana.

"I've been dreaming about what I now know is the beacon. Ofeeree showed me how to program it to find him."

Brianna cursed. "Oh my God, Lily, that's huge. You have to tell Leo."

"I'm going to tell him," Liliana snapped. "I'm telling him in the morning."

Brianna laid back on the lounger and covered her face. "He's going to lock you in your room."

Liliana sighed and laid back as well. "You don't have to tell me. I'll be lucky if he lets me out to work. I can't believe after all this time, Sharine was right."

Brianna snickered. "Please do not tell that woman she was right about anything, she'll be insufferable."

"You're so right," Liliana said, sighing.

Asa frowned. "There has to be a way to end the threat hanging over us. I'm not in the habit of sitting around and waiting for something to happen."

Brianna moved her hands and peeked out. "What do you think we should do?"

"I don't know. You're the researcher."

Brianna sat forward. "I bet we could find something in the book."

"What book?" Asa looked between the two of them.

"*The* book," Liliana answered. "We'll have to go to your apartment, Bri, you can't open it at Haven."

Asa held up her hand to pause their excitement. "Why can't the book be opened at Haven?"

Brianna waved her hand. "Remember the Divine and Demi are still in this sort of Cold War. The Divine don't trust the Demi, especially after the Great War. A spell was cast over the book to keep it out of Demi hands. No one except the Keeper of the Book can read it, and it can't even be opened in or on Demi spaces."

Asa's eyebrows shot up. Now, that was interesting and exactly the kind of story she chased down when searching for artifacts. But, there was no time to ask for more information so she nodded her understanding.

Brianna stood. "Okay, so, let's go. We can take triple the guards."

"Think they'll go for it?" Liliana bit her bottom lip.

Asa shrugged. "I mean, what's the harm in asking?"

The three of them shared a look.

###

Xavier took a deep breath and told himself that tossing his desk at his brothers was not the best thing to do, especially since it would do no good. The two were merely a hologram, hovering in front of his desk from his communicator. Still, it was a hard compulsion to conquer.

"So, I'm to understand that the two of you took our mates to Brianna's apartment. A place where she's already been kidnapped once before. A place where she's been attacked and grievously wounded barely a year ago. Am I getting it right?" He said between his gritted teeth.

"X, we have six soldiers with us, and I have the whole building warded. Brianna said it would only take an hour." Fallon growled.

He knew for a fact that he'd been in his office for at least that, so already they were wrong. He was partially irritated because Asa had not been in their bed this morning, so to find out they left the protection of Haven was too much. His beast rattled around his chest, still agitated from the short note Asa had left on her side of the bed.

Brianna rushed into view, holding up the Book of Divinity, excitement lighting her eyes. "I'm sorry, Xavier. We're on the way back now. We found something and can make a plan."

"Who is we?" He snarled.

"Be there in a sec," Brianna said before the comms went dark.

He cursed and kicked the leg of his desk. Those god damned women. He didn't bother trying to work while he waited. He just paced his office and told himself that cursing as soon as they walked into the door would be counterproductive. He whipped around as Brianna rushed into his office thirty minutes later. He looked behind her, his body tense until he spotted Asa bringing up the rear. He let out the breath he was holding and walked behind his desk.

He sat down and glared at his sister in law. "Explain."

"Well," Brianna looked back at Asa. "We decided that we didn't want to wait around for Ofeeree's goons to kidnap and torture us. I knew that I could probably find a solution in the Book of Divine, so that's where we were."

Xavier swallowed a growl and kept his face passive. Fussing now was of no use. He looked to his mate and she smiled at him before joining him on his side of the desk. He gripped her hand as she stood next to him.

"What did you find?" He asked.

Before Brianna could answer, the alarms he'd set on his comms station beeped. The information he'd been waiting for had finally come in. He dropped Asa's hand and leaned forward.

"Oh shit," he murmured.

"What happened?" Fallon rubbed his mate's shoulders.

"The weapons stolen from the Gu, remember I was searching our databases to find out what they were?" He waved a hand and pushed the information into the air hovering, so his brothers could read it.

"Everything I heard about the weapons said they were old, but not one word about it being from the Great War," Leo stepped forward, his eyes squinted on the information.

"I don't understand," Asa said. "The Gu are the giants, right? The ones who make weapons?"

Xavier nodded and waved a hand again, translating it from the old language to English. "Right, but they didn't make these weapons. These were confiscated from the Divine during the big war. The Gu were hiding them on their realm."

"What's so special about the weapons?" Liliana asked.

Brianna bounced in her seat in unrestrained excitement. "According to the Book of Divine, the weapons were crafted especially to kill the Demi. I knew reading through the wartime passages was the key."

Xavier gave his attention to her. "What else did you find out?"

She whipped her comms pad out of the backpack she carried everywhere. "Well, I'm assuming Lily told you about her nightmares?"

He nodded.

"Well—remembering the purpose of the Kokoro souls—the information needed to free Ofeeree is locked inside us. We've only been focusing on what happens if he's freed. He's been able to communicate with Lily because his prison is loosening. Asa pointed out that the original bearers of our souls were the ones who had initially locked Ofeeree in his prison. It stands to reason, we should be able to tighten the lock currently in place."

Xavier's eyes widened and he waved his hand for her to continue. He gripped Asa's hand again.

"Well, what I've been able to discern about the Kokoro from the little bit of information I've found: One of us is supposed to find him. Lily's dreamt of the spell needed to use the beacon to find his location. Her part is easily done. If what we suspect is true—and some of the things Asa's told me about her father says they are—then he's locked up on Azreal. Which means, only Asa can travel there. Her part is also done."

Xavier's grip tightened on his mate's hand and the urge to take her and run constricted his chest.

"That leaves me. I hold the book, with the spell needed to free him, but also in the book is the original spell. With a few tweaks, I should be able to use it to re-lock his prison and tighten the hold."

"Oh, shit, Bri," he whispered.

The clever woman had figured out what historians had been hiding for centuries.

Chapter 22

"Wait," Asa leaned forward onto the desk. "You said that the Demi and Divine came together to lock him up. You only have the Divine portion."

"Exactly!" Brianna smiled huge, excited.

"The Mina dispute," he hissed, putting the pieces together.

He typed into his comms station, his fingers moving swiftly across the keyboard until he came to a file that he rarely used. It was one that his father set up for him when he first turned over the Amanda to him. Until this very moment he hadn't given it a thought, but he remembered something about the Mina in it that his father had told him to be careful about.

He opened the file and whistled. "The Demi portion of the freeing spell is on Minona."

"Fuck," Fallon said.

"I never knew that," Leo spoke up.

"It's not…it's something that's kept between the Marshals. No one outside of Dad, me, and whoever inhabits the Elder tree on Minona know." He told them.

"And the first thing Ofeeree's followers did was kill the previous occupant," Fallon said grimly.

Xavier wiped a hand down his face. "The previous two. The person occupying the Elder tree now hasn't been there for more than two, three years."

"So they planted someone there," Asa crossed her arms over her chest. "What's the Elder tree? What's Minona?"

Brianna opened her mouth, but he held up his hand. "The Demi realms are in different dimensions stacked one on top of each other, each race with their own realm to keep the peace. The Mina are a precognitive race, we use them for prophecies that determine anything from who is supposed to king or queen, to simple warnings of things to come. The Elder tree is reserved for their oldest, most powerful living Mina, like…a prime minister."

Asa nodded. "What dispute are you talking about?"

He grimaced as he realized how much time he'd wasted trying to resolve the dispute between the Mina and the Benu arguing to get access. "There is only one building on Minona, it's used as a neutral meeting place when there is any conflict where a prophecy could help."

"That building also houses a secret library," Brianna inputted.

"So, say they planted the Elder person, that person would know that the spell is there. What's stopping them from just grabbing it?" Asa asked.

"Not anyone is allowed in the library portion, not even the Elder." Brianna shrugged when they all stared at her. "Remember when I was helping you with the dispute. That's what Penny said. Only Librarians are allowed inside that portion. You can't even use your Marshal authority."

He frowned. "For your plan to work, you'll need to get that portion of the spell so you can change it to match the Divine portion."

Fallon grunted. "Penny is head of all the librarians and I'm her favorite person. Between me and Brianna, I think we can get convince her to get us in."

He nodded and closed his eyes, his mind whirling as he worked to piece a plan together that would work. He had a tentative one forming on the edges, but he needed time to flesh it out.

"Wait," Leo said suddenly. "What would the Benu coup have to do with this?"

Xavier's popped his eyes open. "Why would you assume it did?"

"Well, it's odd that they would want access to Minona for a royal dispute. The Ghekre line has been monarch for centuries. Why a coup on top of the Benu fighting to get access to Minona? How does displacing the current monarchy fit into this?" Leo explained.

They all swiveled their eyes to the door as Adia cleared her throat. She gave them a sheepish look. She'd been eavesdropping.

"I think I know why they're challenging King Herve," Adia said softly.

Xavier growled but nodded for her to continue.

"Prince Regent Julian has control of the Staff of Destiny. It's passed down through the rulers and is as old as the Great War. Only the monarch has access to it."

"It's real," Brianna whispered.

Leo cursed. "That staff kills anything in front of it. It could cut a swath through whatever battlefield it enters. It's one of the main reasons the Ghekres have kept control of their realm for so long. No one wants to be on the other end of that staff."

Asa shivered next to him and he had the urge to pull her into his lap.

"What do you know about it?" Fallon asked his wife.

Brianna shrugged. "It's recorded in the journals in the Esin library. They called it the Harbinger staff. It was laying their asses out by the dozens. Like, dead in a single sweep. No stabbing required."

"Goddess," Liliana muttered.

In light of the new information they were finding out, Asa realized just how thin the line between death and torture she straddled. No wonder Xavier didn't want them out of his sight. She stepped closer to his chair, needing to feel his body heat. They were talking about a war, one where hundreds of people could die, and all of that before they freed the actual evil being. What was she thinking assuming she could easily wade into all this with only her skill for finding artifacts?

Brianna started typing on the fancy tablet she carried around with her everywhere. "So, we need a plan."

Xavier sighed and wiped a hand over his face. He grabbed Asa's waist and pulled her into his lap. He must have known she needed it. Unashamed she curled tighter into his body.

"I thought you guys came up with a plan."

His deep voice rattled his chest against her ear. Brianna gave him a sheepish smile.

"No, I said we decided to come up with a plan, not that we had one."

Asa snorted and shook her head.

Xavier leaned back in his chair and rubbed his hand down her back in soothing strokes. "So, if we want to lock Ofeeree tighter in his prison, the first thing we need to do is work on the spells. How long will that take you, Brianna?"

"If we can get on Minona, then a day, maybe even hours if Fallon helps me translate the language," she said.

"Lily, will the beacon be activated at the end of the spell you've been dreaming about?" Xavier asked his other sister in law.

"Most likely," she answered nervously.

"Then, we'll save that for last." He kissed the top of Asa's head. "*Elewa*, if you can ask your father how to use the beacon once you're in Azreal that will be helpful."

She nodded. "I can take a nap and try to summon him."

"We need to do this fast because if one word of our plan leaves this office, Ofeeree's followers will move that much faster to take out the girls," Xavier said grimly.

Fallon cursed and clutched his wife tighter. "Okay, fuck, let's move."

Xavier walked Asa over to the sofa in his office once everyone left. He instructed his assistant to lock the office behind her and to hold his calls. Her hands were cold, shock, and probably for the first time, fear of consequences hitting her. In all the years of her treasure hunting, she'd never been outright scared. No matter the danger, she'd managed to get out of it. She didn't think a call to Chandra would fix this.

Asa took a deep breath as Xavier kneeled in front of her.

"What do you want to do, *elewa*?" His serious gaze roved her face.

"I can probably sleep in here if you don't have time to go back to the room. I…" She sighed, "I don't know if I'm comfortable being alone right now."

He pulled her head down and devoured her mouth, his fear and desperation broadcasting to her. She couldn't decide if she was relieved that she wasn't the only one scared, or even more scared because he was. He pulled back and climbed onto the sofa behind her, stretching out. He tugged on her arm until she lay next to him, her back to his stomach. He spooned her, cuddled in close, his lips tracing over her shoulder.

"Relax, I got you," he murmured against the skin of her neck.

She chuckled. "I'm not sure I can do that, actually."

"That's understandable. A lot is going on."

"And you deal with it on a regular basis?" She spun around to face him.

He nodded, his hand caressing her cheeks.

"No wonder you're so stressed when you come to me," she murmured, giving him a short kiss.

"You're my peace, *elewa*."

Her heart melted and she sighed, her body relaxing into his. It would've been impossible not to fall in love with this man. The only thing stopping her before was the fact that she didn't think he was real. She leaned forward and kissed him, spearing her tongue into his mouth. His hands moved down her stomach and slid into her jeans. She closed her eyes and sighed into his kiss as he parted the folds of her sex.

"Let me help you relax," he whispered.

She nodded and moved her legs to give him more space. He licked across her lips feathering soft kisses across her face. He pinched her clit and she gasped. He growled and sealed their lips together. He kissed her slow, methodically, his tongue slowly gliding across hers as his fingers gently circled her the entrance of her sex. He pushed in two fingers, the pressure of it sending a streak of heat through her. He used his thumb to press against the bundle of nerves at the top of her sex and she trembled.

He stroked slowly in and out of her as he continued their kisses. She clung to him, whimpering as he caressed her sex. Each touch purposeful and devastating in the effect it was having on her body. He stoked a fire within her, all the while feasting on her mouth. She gripped his arm as he curled his fingers, rubbing against the spot inside of her that was sure to make her explode.

"X," she pulled from their kiss, throwing her head back.

He licked down her neck, gripping her skin in his teeth. "Give it to me, love."

The gruff order pushed her closer to the orgasm hovering just out of reach. He flicked against her clit, his fingers stroking in and out of her, pressing against her g-spot on every stroke. The pressure built until her whimpers became full out moans. Xavier bit her again, pulling her ear into his mouth.

"I love the way you respond to me," he whispered, scissoring his fingers. "The greedy way you grip my fingers."

Her sex clenched, showing the truth of his words. "I want you inside me."

He chuckled, sucking on the skin of her neck. "Later, I promise. For now, I want you to come for me."

"I'm almost there," she hissed out. Tingles started from her toes, extending upward until her body was buzzing, reaching for the finish line.

"Kiss me, *elewa*," he ordered.

She gripped his head, her tongue spearing into his mouth, sucking on his tongue. It was exactly what she needed. With his thumb, he pressed against her clit and held down until the pressure in her womb burst and an orgasm shattered her body. She pulled back and gasped at the power of it. Her sex flexed, squeezing around his fingers even as the rest of her body relaxed. Xavier pulled his fingers from her but kept his hands cupping her center.

"Sleep now, my love," he kissed softly.

She nodded, cuddling into his chest, her hips pressing against his hand, chasing her orgasm to the last drop.

Chapter 23

"Dad!"

Asa clutched the coin at her neck and waited on her father's response. She was back in her childhood bedroom, taking no comfort in the usual scenery. She was relieved that she'd been able to fall asleep though. Azra popped in a second later, his face creased in concern.

"I know what you've come for, *okan mi*." He cleared his face of worry and stood in front of her.

"Then you can help me?"

"Only but so much," he said reluctantly. "There are laws that rule even gods. Especially when it pertains to Ofeeree."

"So it's true, he's there in your hell realm?"

He was silent.

She took it as a yes and paced in front of him. "Liliana has to program the beacon you gave me to take me directly to his hiding place. I need you to unlock my powers."

"You'll need to come to me for that to happen."

She heard the excitement in his voice and couldn't blame him. He'd been barred from seeing her all her life.

"If the beacon is used for Ofeeree, then how will I get to you?" She stopped in front of him.

"Death's Messenger can bring you to me."

"Who is that?"

"Leonalph Tegan."

She nodded, "Oh, okay, Xavier's brother. He can travel to you?"

"His job is to bring souls to me." He stated simply.

She shuddered at the thought. No wonder Leo was a little off, he took souls to hell. Who wouldn't have a streak of looney after that? She studied her father's face, taking in his every feature. She saw her nose, the shape of his face that she saw in the mirror every day. Tears sprang. Would he look any different in person? Despite the circumstances, she was excited to meet him.

"You're worried," she saw his eyes flash.

"What you will be attempting is dangerous, Asa, I won't lie to you."

"What can you tell me that will help? Brianna keeps saying that gods are not very forthcoming with information."

He snorted. "My brother's ward is correct in that. As I said, there is but so much we can do to interfere in the world of humans and demi-gods." He sighed and walked over to her bed, sitting on the end. "The Eshu can open the box that contains the beacon, if what I'm hearing is correct, Ofeeree has already shown her how. You will need to bring the contents to me once she has completed her spell."

"So it is in hell." She whispered.

"That's all I'm able to share with you about it, daughter." His voice was full of regret.

Asa shrugged. "It was more than what I had when I came. I mostly needed to know how to use the beacon once it's activated."

He looked up at her, grabbing her arm to keep her from pacing past him again. "Give me a moment?"

She nodded, gasping when he disappeared.

She sat on the bed and waited for him. He popped back in moments later, his face grim, uneasy.

"Xavier's plan is to reinforce the locks on Ofeeree's prison?"

"Hey, it was kind of me and Brianna's plan, but yes." She protested.

He sighed and gripped her hand. "Pay attention, *okan mi*. What I tell you is the only help I can offer to you."

She swallowed and nodded.

"Your powers will need to be unlocked in order for you to perform the spell. I'm afraid you'll have to learn how to harness them on your own. Once you're in the place where he's located, you need to get as close to him as possible. Your blood will be required to tighten the lock."

She cursed. "How much blood?"

He shrugged.

"Azreal is made of nightmares, Asa, you'll need to prepare yourself for what you could see while you're down there." He sighed. "You'll need to be very careful."

"Thank you, dad. I will," she promised, grateful for his help.

He gave her a bemused smile. "I like that you've so easily taken to calling me that."

"Did you think I wouldn't?" She was curious.

"I wasn't sure what Deena had told you about me. What grudge you may be holding against me. You couldn't have had it easy growing up."

She sighed. "It wasn't great. I'm having a hard time with the fact that mom stayed with Herman, knowing you could help her."

"Some Esins are…"

"Toxic," she filled in.

He nodded. "Deena's, in particular, served Rugaba with a fervor that would beat most religious zealots. I can't speak for your mother, but even as she was kicked from the Esin, I think she thought they'd welcome her back. She had a blind spot for the zealotry there."

"I don't…she'd never even mentioned an Esin when I was growing up, so it's hard for me to imagine it."

"I suspect once you go through her things, you'll find an altar to my brother. He said that she was faithful until the end."

Asa rubbed her arms and plopped down next to him. "I never knew her."

"Humans are complex beings," he said.

She scoffed, "and gods are not."

"That's fair," he admitted.

She turned on the bed and folded her legs. "When this is all done, can we make time to get to know each other?"

"I would love nothing more."

###

Xavier slipped from behind Asa's sleeping body. He conjured a blanket and laid it across her stomach, stretching his body. He was relaxed, having slept for at least an hour. He'd never taken a nap in his life, but then, the way Asa relaxed him was something he'd never experienced. The light on his comms station was blinking indicating he had a message. He walked behind his desk and brought it up.

Penny got us access. Should be back in a few hours.

He cursed, punching in the code for his brother's communicator. Fallon popped on screen a second later.

"Tell me you took guards," he growled at his brother.

"Ten," Fallon answered.

That was slightly relieving. "How is it going?"

"Penny's pretty intimidating when she's in Head Librarian mode, so we were able to get in without a scene. You know the Mina though. Word will spread before we leave the realm."

Xavier cursed, his mind spinning. He needed to get ahead of the gossip that left Minona. "I'll send it down the line that you went to investigate the dispute. The ten soldiers will make sense. Have the guards ask questions about it so that word spreads."

"I should've thought of that," Fallon murmured.

"That's why I get the big bucks," Xavier said, texting his order down through the shift commanders. "Leave at least three men there under the guise of guarding the meeting place," Xavier instructed.

"Okay, will do." Fallon looked over to the side. "Knowing Brianna, it won't take her long to find what she's looking for. Penny gave her a general idea of where the records from the Great War were held. We told her what was going on, so she's helping."

Xavier nodded. "Be careful, brother."

"Always," Fallon said with a salute.

He ended the call and looked up as Asa stretched out on the sofa. Her eyes were drowsy as she looked around. He smiled as her soft gaze caught his eyes. She stood and sauntered over to him. Her walk was everything. Confident, the swing of her hips was hypnotizing.

"My love," she whispered, dropping tiny kisses to his lips.

"Well rested, are you?"

She smiled and nuzzled into his neck. "I think we should make more time for afternoon shenanigans."

He laughed and clutched her tightly to his chest.

"Marshal." Adia's image popped up on his comms station.

"Yeah."

"Asa has visitors at the front entrance," Adia said carefully.

He frowned at Asa, but she shrugged.

"Who is it?"

"Woman named Chandra and her mate?"

Asa stood abruptly. "Chandra's here?"

"Send them to me, Adia." How had they broken through Haven's wards?

"Yes, Marshal."

"Your virtual assistant right?" Xavier asked.

Asa nodded, "Yep, and my best friend." Her anxious gaze was pinned to the door.

Nearly ten minutes later, a wheelchair-bound woman and her mate were escorted into his office. He nodded the guard away and studied the two, his eyebrows raising when he realized that the male was Demi.

Asa rushed forward and grabbed her friend in a hug. "Chandra, Clinton, what are you doing here? How did you find this place?"

Chandra's eyes were taking in his office, not missing any detail he was sure. From half the stories Asa told about the woman, he wouldn't be surprised if she could construct an accurate scale model of his office by the time she left.

"I told you this place existed. You're the one who didn't believe me," Chandra gave her friend a smug smile.

"Your father sent us," Clinton said.

Asa reared back in surprise. "I don't..." She turned and looked at him. "I don't understand."

Chandra's gaze finally landed on him. "Well damn, no wonder you took a vacation."

"Chandra," Asa sputtered.

"My husband was called into duty," Chandra threw her thumb back at her husband. "I, myself, am merely here to be nosy."

"And you will be going back to the safe house with the children once you have assuaged your curiosity," Clinton warned her.

"Called into duty?" Xavier stared at the male.

He nodded. "Lord Azra has called in some of his followers. We were ordered to check in with the Amanda."

Xavier sat back in his chair and frowned. Azra had his own soldiers? That was news to him. "How many are you?"

Clinton looked down at his mate before clearing his throat. "We are many." Was his answer.

"Chandra, how long have you known about this stuff? Your husband is Demi?" Asa looked shocked.

Her friend gave her a sheepish look. "Clinton was assigned to you specifically. Lord Azra called on him to keep an eye out on you."

Asa staggered back. "All these years?"

Chandra nodded. "I was encouraged to apply for the job of your assistant when you posted it. I've had some help over the years keeping you out of trouble."

Asa sat back on his desk, her hand covering her mouth. Xavier could feel her shock through their tie.

"I wanted to tell you," Chandra said softly. "But Lord Azra keeps a tight lid on his servants."

"My God, this whole time." Asa turned to him, her eyes luminous with tears. "He's been taking care of me this whole time."

Xavier stood from his chair and went to her. He pulled her into his arms. Her body shuddered and the spill of her tears wet the front of his shirt. He murmured to her, rubbing her back. She took a deep breath and separated from his chest, wiping her face.

"Is it possible for us to go somewhere and talk?" Asa asked.

Chandra nodded, patting dry her own cheeks. "Yeah, we can finally talk freely."

Asa looked to Xavier. "Is that okay?"

He nodded and watched as the two of them left the office. He turned his focus to the male still standing in front of his desk, putting on his Marshal façade.

"Now, explain to me what you're doing here."

"Lord Azra has ordered me and a hundred more to Haven to prepare for what he thinks is war," Clinton answered.

A sliver of unease slithered down his spine. "You said your family will be at a safe house?"

Clinton nodded and held his hand out to the chair in front of him.

"I'm sorry, yes, sit." Xavier went back around to his own chair.

Clinton sat, his back ramrod straight. "Lord Azra's army has many such places."

"I can make a place for them here."

The man winced and shook his head. "No disrespect to you or the Amanda, but Lord Azra provides."

Xavier nodded. "Will you and the soldiers need to stay at Haven?"

"Were it not for my mate pressuring me to see her friend, we would've only made ourselves known when you needed us."

"That's bold," Xavier growled.

"Again, no disrespect. Azra is careful not to step on his brother's toes. We find it easier to operate without catching the eye of Rugaba."

Xavier grunted because he understood that. Rugaba was possessive with what he claimed as his own and the Amanda absolutely fell under that. If the god got wind that his brother was operating an army of his own, who knew what would happen.

"And how will you know when it's time?"

"Lord Azra will let us know."

"And how will we know who you are? If it came down to war, nothing would stop my men from going through whosoever stood between them."

The male smirked and inclined his head in respect. "We wear Lord Azra's marker."

"The coin?"

"Aye."

Of course, the god's marker would be his own image. Xavier swallowed a sigh. Every minute that passed, it was looking like a war was coming to his door.

Chapter 24

Xavier rubbed a hand down his face as Azra's servant left his office. He pulled up the code for his room and called Asa. He needed to see her. She answered, gasping when her image popped up.

"I have to get used to your image popping up. Are you done with Clinton?"

"He's coming to retrieve his wife."

She pouted for a moment before sighing. "Okay. Do you want me to come back?"

"I'm waiting on Brianna and Fallon to come back first. Order lunch and I'll come to join you once I check my schedule."

Her face brightened. "That sounds good. Maybe I can convince Chandra and her husband to stay for a little longer."

He heard her friend in the back cheering. He smiled, happy that Asa was happy. Haven's proximity alert sounded and he frowned. Was it more of Azra's soldiers? They'd managed to get through without setting it off the first time, so more than likely it was another problem being tossed into his lap. He looked up as Adia came to his door. Her face was worried, her teeth gnawing at her bottom lip.

"Gotta go, elewa, something else just sprung up, so I don't know about lunch."

"Aaaw, ok, take your time." She told him.

He hung up with her and gave his assistant his full attention. "What's wrong?"

"We have more visitors."

"More…" He stood and braced his hands on the desk. "What the fuck?"

"Jin won't let them through the door."

Xavier walked out of his office, stomping down the hall. Who the hell else would show up? Today, it seemed, was the day to drop surprises in his lap. He steps slowed once he reached the club floor. He headed towards the front entrance, his heart thundering once he was outside and got a look at who was there waiting. The men were huge, their leader dark-skinned, his locs pushed back from his forehead with a band. They all wore black, and on the corner of their shirts was a circle with a symbol for wind.

His stomach dropped and worry for his mate and his family threatened to steal his concentration. Oya's soldiers had arrived. The goddess of war was surely warning him that the war he'd been dreading was coming. He took a deep breath and closed the distance between him and the soldiers. There were only six of them, but he didn't know if that was reassurance or not. The back of his neck started tingling, the hair raising. They were being watched. Had Azra's soldiers already set up their post?

"What's going on?" He asked the male clearly in charge, deciding for now to ignore the other soldiers.

The power of the lion surrounded Oya's warrior, his magic strong, stirring Xavier's beast to come forward. He wasn't threatened, but curiosity had the beast rising.

"Our oracle sent us to you."

"For what reason?" Xavier knew, but somehow having the male say it would make it more real.

The male looked around. "Is this something you'd like to discuss out in the opening?"

Xavier sighed and waved the men to follow behind him. He used sign language to signal Jin to keep an eye out for the other soldiers surrounding the property. He'd text his brother so he would alert the rest of the guards that there were other soldiers around. He led Oya's soldiers up to one of the empty VIP rooms. The Aje dispersed through the room taking their posts at the windows that looked down at the dance floor and exit points. Nothing about their energy was menacing, simply alert. Xavier waved off his men who had followed behind.

"Can I offer you any refreshments?" He said, stalling.

"We're fine," the male said. His serious face did take in the opulence of the suite.

"I'm Xavier, Marshal of the Amanda, and you are?"

"I'm Ajani, Mission Commander. Our oracle wanted to come herself, but with the wards over the Haven, her mate wouldn't allow it."

"If it's important, I can ensure her safety."

Ajani cocked his head to the side, but said nothing. One of the warriors behind him snickered and Ajani sighed. Xavier assumed they communicated with their oracle. He'd heard the Aje could speak to each other telepathically. It was somewhat disconcerting.

"Is there a place she can teleport safely inside this building?"

"No, but we no longer allow the Ajo here if she wants to teleport just outside the wards. There will be no one waiting to ambush you, and I'll leave my men there to make sure no one comes up once she's arrived."

He prayed Azra's soldiers would make no moves towards Oya's oracle. He would have to trust that the soldiers knew better than to fuck with Oya or those she marked as hers.

Ajani was silent again before grimacing. "That will work." Ajani turned his head and two men broke off from the group and stood at attention.

"I'll make arrangements," Xavier told them. "If you wait with security at the door, they'll walk you outside the wards."

The two males nodded and left the room. Fallon came in the door as soon as they left, his mate hot on his heels. Xavier raised an eyebrow, not expecting them back for a few hours more. He didn't bother asking how they'd heard about their visitors.

"I'll clear a conference room as well," Xavier told Ajani.

The soldier nodded and the soldiers around him relaxed, some even taking a seat.

Fallon raised a brow. "What are the Aje doing here?"

"I don't know yet. We need to make arrangements for their oracle to arrive."

Fallon whispered, "An oracle."

Brianna whispered. "Who's oracle?"

"Oya's," was Xavier's distracted answer. There were so many chess pieces being added to his board.

"Goddess of Winds. Oh my." Her eyes were lit.

Xavier tucked his communicator in his pocket and wrapped an arm around his brother's mate, leading her from the room. "Brianna, we are not going to ask this female—"

"—lady," she corrected.

"Woman," he conceded, "we're not going to ask this woman a million questions."

Fallon snorted behind him.

"Azra also has soldiers outside of our wards, I've warned Jin, pass it along to the other shift commanders."

His brother nodded and moved from them talking into his communicator.

"I've never heard of the Aje warriors, what do they do?" Brianna asked. "And Azra has soldiers, too?" She was bouncing on her toes, her excitement palpable.

He sighed. "Find us a conference room please," he said instead of answering her question.

She growled but rushed off to do as he asked.

Fallon came back. "Jin and six others are waiting at the gate with the two Aje. They can feel Azra's men, but no one has spotted them yet."

"How the fuck did you and Bri even know the Aje were here? When did you get back?" He asked his brother.

"We just came through the portal. Adia sent us straight here." Fallon answered, shoving his hands into the pocket of his slacks.

Xavier looked up and found Ajani staring down at him from the window. He nodded and the warrior nodded back. His brother stood next to him, silently watching the door. A moment later Jin came over the communicator.

"Package in route, Marshal."

"Thank you, Jin," Xavier said.

He looked up to tell the Aje, but they were coming down the stairs. A massive power entered the front door preceding the Oracle and her mate.

Fallon whispered. "Damn, directly connected to the goddess."

Xavier nodded. Yeah. Oya's oracle was inundated with power.

She smiled when she saw them. "Thank you for meeting me."

"Of course, Oracle." He held out his hand. "I'm Xavier."

The oracle waved away the introductions. "You can call me, Zahra. Ajani filled me in on who you were."

A male he could only assume was her mate stood next to her, his expression forbidding, aggravation, and power intertwined in his aura. His hair was braided back from his face, his expression stern.

"I'm Fynn, Ijoye to the Aje tribe." They shook hands.

"My brother, Fallon, Commander of Haven." Xavier introduced them.

"I got us a conference…holy shit," Brianna whispered coming upon them. "Talk about power."

Fallon gripped his wife at his side. "My mate, Brianna."

The women smiled at each other.

"Follow me if you please," Brianna said.

They were a silent procession, tense and on guard as they walked through the tunnels of Haven. Brianna led them into a conference room that was hidden from the main hallway and he was grateful. Nonetheless, he frosted the wall of windows in case anyone happened to walk by. They all sat, the Aje soldiers, now numbering ten surrounding the room. Xavier waved the Demi soldiers from the room. No need in completely filling the place. Fallon pointed to the hallway and they understood that he was instructing them to stand guard there.

He settled into a chair at the head of the table and waited for the oracle and her mate to be seated.

Fynn sat forward, his forearms on the table. "We were instructed to have soldiers made available to you. Not a lot, mind, but we will lend help wherever you need."

Xavier fisted his hands. "There is to be war."

There was no point in making it a question.

Zahra lifted her brows and gave them a sympathetic look, her eyes glowing, all the answer he needed.

"Why would Oya help us?" Xavier asked, curious about the sudden influx of assistance he was being offered. First by Azra and now the goddess Oya.

"Favors are owed," was the oracle's answer.

"Are you going to be vague about it?" Brianna asked.

Xavier swallowed a growl. That damn woman and her questions.

Instead of taking offense, Zahra laughed, "I'm not about to be cussed out asking for clarification, so…"

Brianna cackled and scribbled in her notebook like always.

"What flavor of magic are you?" Zahra asked Brianna, "Sorry, I'm just curious."

Fynn groaned next to her.

"I'm Divine, first humans, powers from gods and goddesses," Brianna answered, her pen poised over her notebook.

"Interesting," Zahra murmured. "Anyway. I know not this Haven specifically, but a Haven has opened their doors to us before. Your god also helped save my life. It's a debt our goddess will repay. You have maybe a week or two before whatever big thing that is happening goes down." Zahra said her face sobering.

"There's not a lot you can do to prepare that isn't already being done. We can spare at least twenty warriors to you, place them where you will find them most useful." Fynn added.

"I'm happy to know they won't encounter any Ajo while here," Zahra interjected.

"If something were to go down, they would be fighting Demi-gods, can they handle that?" Brianna asked.

Xavier growled and Fallon groaned. Gods help them, only Brianna would piss off a room full of powerful warriors.

"Our magic is different, innate, our lions, fierce fighters, I don't foresee it being a problem," Fynn spoke with no hint of offense.

The men behind him on the other hand…their power flared, their anger pulsing through the room.

"I don't mean offense, just genuinely curious." She hurried to assure them.

Xavier jumped in before Brianna got them into an actual fight with the Aje. "I thank you for the offer of help..."

Xavier paused, unsure how to turn them down without offense. He didn't really want additional lives on his hands. Especially not those loyal to Oya.

Zahra held up her hand. "Please, before you decline, Oya is not inclined to help any other than those that belong to her. That she offered help should tell you how serious she finds this upcoming…skirmish."

Xavier drummed his fingers on the table top and thought through it. "Ok, Brianna, since Liliana is not here, can you find rooms for them."

"I can't stay myself," Zahra looked to her husband and he gave her a warning growl, she sighed, "Right, I can't stay. I'll contact Ajani if I get any other information."

"Can you stay for a little bit? I'd love to take you down to the library and talk to you with our archivist." Brianna chimed in.

"I'd love to! I guess I can let Fynn handle the rest." Zahra said excitedly, standing and rushing out behind Brianna before her mate could object.

Fynn sighed and inclined his head. Four Aje broke ranks and followed the women from the room.

The Ijoye stared at Xavier. "I don't envy you the fighting to come."

"What has the goddess said about it?"

"To me, nothing. From what I gather from Zahra, there is an urgency that worries her." Fynn answered.

"Our gods are not answering a lot of our questions, so I appreciate you doing this," Fallon said.

"We hadn't so much as a timeline before, now we know to prepare," Xavier added, already making those plans in his head.

The oracle had given them a window, and he could work with that. It meant he needed to speed up their plan for the beacon. He'd talk to his family about it once they settled the Aje warriors.

"The only reason I won't allow my mate to stay here is because this will be your battleground," Fynn mentioned.

Xavier's heart thundered and he sat back. "The Oracle didn't say that."

"It's why we're here, specifically. If it were anywhere else, my men could teleport there when the fight was waging. Getting into Haven is not something easily done regularly, I can't imagine how much tighter your wards will be once the fighting starts."

Fallon cursed next to him.

"Anything else?" Xavier asked.

Fynn hesitated and sent his men from the room. Left were just Xavier, Fallon, Ajani, and Fynn. "We have shaman, new in their positions, but strong all the same. Our worlds don't usually collide, but in this, your dead are speaking."

Fallon leaned forward. "Saying what?"

"Already on their end, the war has started, souls choosing sides. Some even preparing to be freed should you not be successful in this war."

"Fuck," Xavier whispered, his thoughts immediately going to his mate.

She would be in the thick of the hell realm, what would she encounter there? Fynn's voice broke into his thoughts.

"When you battle here, it may very well be against your own brothers at arms. My men are here in case it ends up being just your family against the hundreds that will gather to free Ofeeree."

"Shit," Fallon whispered and they shared a look. "Our men are loyal."

Fynn nodded, "all the same, you have back up when you need it."

"A week?" Xavier wanted to confirm the Oracle's words.

"At the soonest, two at the outset," Fynn said.

 Xavier sighed. "I won't forget this favor."

"I wish you and yours good luck. If the tide starts to turn?"

"I will personally make sure your men make it out," Xavier promised.

Fynn nodded. "I would appreciate that."

Chapter 25

Asa smiled as Xavier came into their room. He'd missed lunch, but she knew how busy he got. Her smile dropped as he got closer. His face was a mask of worry.

"What happened?"

He sighed and sat next to her on the sofa. He turned and stretched his body to put his head in her lap. Another sigh and he let his human form slip. She ran her hands through his hair as it grew out. He closed his eyes and crossed his arms over his chest. She let him sit in silence, knowing he'd talk to her as soon as he worked it out in his head. That was one good thing about being in dreams with him for a year, she knew him.

"Your friend's mate is here on behalf of your father." He said after a lengthy silence.

She thought he'd fallen asleep. She scratched his scalp, smiling as he groaned in pleasure.

"Chandra told me."

It was surprising, to say the least, but in the string of things Chandra had told her, it was the least surprising. The most surprising once Asa got over the fact that her father had assigned Chandra and Clinton to watch over her, was learning that Chandra knew about her powers. Azra had protected the married couple's dreams to keep Asa out. It had been done to keep Asa from accidentally finding out about him, so he could keep his promise to her mother.

She got a lump in her throat thinking about it. If she survived this Kokoro stuff, then she would need some serious down time to sort out her emotions. Her mother had left her with a mess, and not knowing whether or not it was on purpose was fucking with her head. Deena had been a great mother to her, making do with the life they'd been served, or so Asa had assumed. Finding out that that was not the case, that her mother had other options…she was battling with the why of it all. Her father had offered to rescue them both. Why had her mother chosen a life harder than it had to be? Had it all been for an Esin who'd abandoned her and her unborn child at the first opportunity?

She had been mad to learn her father was alive. Mad at him, and mad at Deena, but now, to learn from Chandra that Azra had spent all these years looking out for her without making his presence known. Her friend had outlined multiple times where her dad had sent Clinton to help Asa out of the many sticky situations she'd been in. None of it diminished the work Chandra did for her. The woman had been a godsend. She chuckled to herself realizing just how true that was. Her chest tightened and she closed her eyes and took some deep breaths. It was all starting to add up and she knew the hard part hadn't even happened yet.

Xavier turned his body and gripped her waist. "Hey, talk to me, what's wrong?"

Asa shook her head, shocked at how well he read her moods. Now was not the time to break down, though. She needed herself as whole as possible for what was to come.

"We'll have to talk about it after all this," she got out past the clog in her throat.

His eyes studied her, but he nodded and settled back into her lap. "I got a visit from Oya's warriors just now."

"Who are Oya's warriors?" Curiosity was a sure fire way to get her out of her pity party.

"The goddess Oya. I'm finding out that Rugaba isn't the only one with soldiers of his own," he said ruefully.

"What did the warriors want?"

He sighed and grabbed her hand, intertwining their fingers. "To offer their help for the upcoming war."

Her stomach dropped and she gasped. "I thought our plan would stop another war from breaking out."

"To be honest, I'd hoped we could prevent war, but in the back of my mind, even if our plan works, at most, we can keep the war from spilling to the humans." He kissed the tips of her fingers.

"What will you do?" Fear would barely let her get the words out.

"My job, *elewa*. I'm more worried about your end of things."

"Me?" She shook her head. "All I have to do is go to hell and recite a spell. You'll be in the thick of things here."

He sat up and whirled around to face her. "Asa. It's not just a spell. Ofeeree is breaking out of his prison. He's going to throw everything he has at you to stop you."

All at once, all the warnings from Brianna and the last warning she'd received from Chandra crashed down on her. She pulled her hand loose and stood. She needed something to do with her hands. Walking away from him, she went into his bedroom and dug into her bag for her knitting needles. He followed her into the room.

"Love, I thought you said Brianna told you everything."

She ignored him and sat on the edge of the bed and started a slip knot. Chandra could probably use a new lap blanket. She'd loved the last one Asa had knitted for her. Asa had brought her bamboo yarn with her, so while it wasn't what she would've chosen for the blanket, she kept going. The bed dipped as Xavier sat next to her.

"*Elewa?*"

"Give me a second, X. I'm about ten seconds from finally freaking out," she murmured, working the yarn across her needle.

Xavier didn't say anything, for which she was happy. She needed…she needed several moments to digest what had been happening. It probably would've been healthier for her to do all the freaking out when she'd first been kidnapped, but honestly, she'd assumed eventually Chandra would get her out of whatever foolishness she'd fallen into. Chandra had left Xavier's room minutes ago with a warning that she wouldn't be able to help her with what was coming. It was really her own fault. Brianna had not sugar-coated anything she'd told her. From the very beginning, they'd all been honest with her. It had been her who'd been flippant about the whole thing.

She switched her needle to her other hand and started knitting, her hands moving quickly. Her speed wasn't conducive to a neat stitch, more than likely she'd drop a few, but she needed her hands moving.

Fuck, there would be a war.

It was inevitable, according to Xavier, and meanwhile, she'd been in some weird fugue state of horniness and grief. She'd just lost her mother, would she lose Xavier too? Tears finally crested her lids and ran down her face in a trail. Would she lose her own life? It wasn't as though she knew these people other than Xavier, would she really risk her life for strangers? She shook her head and sniffled. She wouldn't just be saving strangers though. If Ofeeree managed to be freed, the entire world was at stake. She dropped her head, and sucked in some air, feeling her heartbeat pick up.

Oh God, she was supposed the save the world.

Xavier pulled her into his arms, kissing the top of her head. Her hands went lax, the needles dropping from her grip. A full-scale panic attack descended and she pushed from him, her chest heaving with her rushed breathing. Xavier moved quickly to lean back against the headboard, before lifting her and putting her in his lap.

"Breathe, *elewa*," he whispered, rubbing her back.

She curled into his chest, and closed her eyes tight, starting her countdown. His heartbeat was strong and steady in her ear as she clutched him. He was murmuring to her, the deep timbre of his voice rumbling his chest and working in tandem with her counting to calm her down. By the time she'd gotten to sixty, she was breathing normal, by twenty-five, her heartbeat matched his in its rhythm.

"Better?" He asked once she'd calmed.

She nodded but didn't release her hold over him. "It's all so overwhelming."

"That's understandable. You're a stranger to this world, I can't imagine being thrown into it the way you have."

"So, this war?"

Xavier kissed the top of her head. "From what Oya's oracle tells us, it will be here at Haven. I'm not too worried, it's our turf, but not knowing who's truly on our side gives me pause."

She shuddered. "If we lock Ofeeree down sooner, will that make a difference?"

He shrugged his shoulders. "Who's to say if, in the process of locking him into his prison, he doesn't send his minions to stop us?"

She hadn't thought about that. Had he escaped his prison enough to influence a war? She sighed, of course, he had. Otherwise, there wouldn't be a steady stream of people coming after her and the other women every time they stepped outside of Haven. She'd had two close calls in just the week she'd been at Haven. How had Brianna and Liliana dealt with it for all the months they'd been going through it? It raised her respect for the two women.

Though she was scared as hell, she wanted it all to be over. "We have to move up our timeline. It could be the difference in the severity of the war."

"Maybe," was his answer, but he didn't sound confident.

###

Asa woke up in the bed alone, her stomach fluttering with butterflies. She rolled over and sighed. She knew what the feeling in her stomach meant. Something was going down and in the past, she'd never questioned that feeling. She would pack her bags and haul ass out of whatever town she was in. The temptation to do so now was great. Her feet tingled with the urge to leave and let Xavier and his family handle whatever war was coming.

She didn't want to leave him though. She couldn't. He was hers and the thought of living life without him, having found him...no, she wasn't leaving. Groaning at the decision, she rolled out of bed and headed to the bathroom. Finishing her morning routine, she went in search of Xavier. She paused at the entrance to the kitchen. His brothers were seated at the table with him, and from their faces, whatever they were discussing was heavy.

"I need coffee before I get into whatever it is y'all got going on," she grumbled.

They were quiet as she fixed a mug, stirring in a ton of cream and sugar. She liked her coffee sweet-sweet. She clutched the cup and turned to face them, leaning against the counter.

"Okay, lay it on me."

Xavier ran a hand over his hair. It was still long even though he was back in his human form. "Brianna worked through the night on the spells. They're ready."

Her stomach turned and she put the mug down on the counter next to her, afraid to hold it in her now shaking hands. She pushed her hands down the sides of the large t-shirt she wore as a nightgown, wiping her sweaty palms.

"What happens now?"

Fallon and Leo studied her, their expression both worried and compassionate, but neither of them spoke.

"Liliana is making arrangements for Kell." Xavier grimaced, fear transforming his face before he got it under control.

She knew how much he cared for his nephew. She couldn't imagine what they were all going through, especially Liliana and Leo.

X cleared his throat. "Once you get dressed, we're going to meet the girls at one of the offices I have next to the main portal station."

Her breath stalled and dizziness swept through her. *Oh shit, it was happening now*. She nodded, her throat dry. They were all looking at her. Were they waiting on her to react or say something reassuring? If so, they were out of luck, she was working on not dry heaving.

"How does one dress to go save the world?"

Leo snickered and turned to hide his head as Xavier glared at him.

"Probably something comfortable," Fallon said, his own smirk behind the teacup he was drinking from.

She nodded and left them, heading to Xavier's closet. She'd wear what she did when she normally went 'treasure hunting'. A comfortable pair of cargo pants stuffed with supplies and a t-shirt tight enough to keep from getting snagged. She blanked her mind as she took a shower, keeping nothing but static there as she got dressed. If she thought too hard on what was going down, she would chicken out. She paused as she slid her shirt over her head. No, she wouldn't chicken out, deities aside, she'd treat this the way she treated every other job she accepted.

She opened the small safe she carried with her and slid a knife into the ankle sheaths she wore on both legs. She reached into the side pocket of her duffel and grabbed the slim bottle of oil her mother insisted she carried everywhere she went. She was down to half of it, and the thought that it was her last bottle had grief trying to push to the forefront.

She stubbornly pushed it down and used the stopper to drop some of the oil into her palm. She set the oil on the dresser and then rubbed it into her hands, the prayer her mother ingrained in her whispering past her lips. She waved both hands one after the other over her head, praying for protection. She waved her hands down her body, asking for strength and finally pressed her fingers into her temples, her last ask for wisdom. She recited the prayer again, this time in a language she could never decipher, but it was second nature. Deena was adamant that it was something passed down through their family. Asa had always scoffed at the prayer, but she'd done it before every adventure.

Finished, she cocked her head at the buzz of electricity that flowed over her skin and heated her body. Her earlier nervousness dissipated, and a sense of ease overtook her. She turned to the oil and squinted. Was there magic in her mother's oil? Or in the ritual? She frowned. She should be terrified for what was to come, and yet, her mind was clear…ready. Was that the work of the oil? Why hadn't she thought about it before? She'd done the prayer for as long as she could remember. Every day before school, twice before important tests and events, Deena had been insistent. Another secret her mother had taken with her to the grave. Asa swallowed down her grief and left the room. She didn't have time for mourning.

Xavier was the only one left in the kitchen by the time she was done. She assumed his brothers went to collect their respective wives.

"You ready?" She whispered.

Xavier shook his head and walked over to her, cupping her cheek. "No. You?"

She was surprised at the laugh that bubbled up within her. "Not in the least."

He kissed her forehead. "Ain't nothing to it but to do it at this point."

She followed him from his room, her body buzzing with a sense of readiness. They passed other Demi rushing through the tunnels, their faces serious.

"Making preparations," Xavier answered her unspoken question.

That's right. They were preparing for war. She squared her shoulders and thought on Xavier's words. Nothing to it but to do it.

Chapter 26

Xavier clutched Asa's hand tighter as they approached the office where he was meeting his family. He wanted to stay strong for her, but between his beast bucking against his control and his worry, he was a mess. . She walked next to him, focused, though he could sense her underlying nervousness. He opened the door for her and stood back to let her enter first. He closed the door behind him and took a deep breath.

The time for waffling was done. Xavier quickly threw a ward over the room, it was important to keep what they were doing a secret for as long as they could. Once the beacon left this room, none of them knew what would happen. He finished the spell and locked the door for good measure.

He turned around and faced the room, spotting the box with the beacon inside sitting on top of the only piece of furniture in the room. The metal desk was beaten to hell and looked like it was tossed into this empty office instead of being disposed of.

He'd given Fallon the chest when he'd left their room after breakfast. Brianna wanted to examine it before Liliana started her spell. He cleared his throat and all eyes swiveled to him.

"We ready?"

Liliana nodded, her eyes red-rimmed, but determined. It couldn't have been easy for her to send Kell to Chuita with his parents. He knew they'd keep the baby safe, and once Liliana had done her part by activating the beacon, she'd be heading there herself. Still, it had to be hard.

Liliana stepped closer to the chest and put her hand on it. Light seeped from the seams of the chest and magic swelled in the room. The chest opened with a quiet snick and they all leaned forward. He frowned at the small black stone inside.

"What is it?" Asa whispered.

"A messenger stone," Liliana said, lifting it from the box. "The gods use it to pass information between them."

"That makes sense," Brianna inputted.

"Finish the spell, Lily," Xavier ordered.

His beast was restless. He wanted this done and the beacon taken from Haven even though it meant his mate would be headed to hell. Liliana did as he ordered, putting the stone back in the box. She waved her hands over it, her mouth moving in silent prayer. A whoosh of magic washed the room and they all staggered back a step. The stone was humming softly, an opaque cloud now swirling inside.

"It's done," Liliana said, sweat dotting her brow.

"Leo," Xavier ordered.

His brother nodded, kissed his wife, and walked over to Asa. Her eyes widened.

"There are three portals we'll need to go through, Asa. It won't be comfortable. I don't…because Azra is your father, it may not hit you as much as those who go for punishment, but to be on the safe side, I need you to wear this." Leo removed the black stone necklace Azra had given him. "We won't be able to talk once we enter the portals."

Asa clutched the necklace, her eyes shooting to him. Xavier gripped her hand, hoping to lend her his strength.

"When we get there, I can't go any further than the gates. It's the point of no return. No one leaves Azreal alive. It's going to be up to you, and you alone." Leo told her.

She swallowed and stared around at his family. He was happy that they'd been so accepting of her. Xavier stared at her, feeling tortured. He clenched his fists but held her gaze.

"I have to do this," she whispered, speaking only to him.

Fallon gripped Xavier's shoulder. "It's the only way."

It wasn't as though he didn't know that, but still, shit, it was hurting.

"Let's give them a few minutes," Leo spoke softly in the tense silence.

"No, you can't leave this office. It's warded. I don't want any hint of the beacon's power to leak out." Xavier said roughly, swallowing down the lump in his throat.

Asa stepped closer. He gripped her arms and pulled her into his chest, turning them away from his family. He had no words of comfort to offer her, not when he was barely holding on himself.

"I don't…"

"I know"

"Elewa—"

"Just…shut up, and let me hold you a minute. I love you," she told him.

His shoulders stiffened and the warm wet of his tears hit her neck. "I love you more than anything in this world, Asa, know that, and understand that if you don't come back to me, I'm nothing."

"I swear I'll do my best. I want this life you've let me have a piece of." Asa realized that even with the chaos, it was true. She enjoyed staying at Haven.

He nodded and stepped back. He wiped the tears from her face and she did the same for him. She cleared her throat and turned back to Leo. Her new family surrounded them.

Brianna ripped a page from her notebook. "Read the spell exactly as it appears. It's a mix of a Demi and Divine spell, but you must read it in order and once you start the spell, you have to finish it, no stopping." She pointed to one line at the top. "Read this first, it activates the rest."

Asa nodded and gripped her new friend in a tight hug.

Lily gave her a stone. "It should lead you directly to his prison. I don't…no one has ever been in the hell realm, I don't know what to expect for you."

Asa pulled Liliana into a hug. "I'll figure it out."

Fallon stepped to her and pulled her into a hug. "Be careful, little sister."

"I will," she whispered, loving that he called her that.

Leo worked his hands until a portal opened in the middle of the office. She only knew it was a portal because the bright light looked exactly like the one Xavier had opened at her mother's house. Leo held his hand out. She looked back at Xavier and he nodded, his stoic face in place. She loved him, and she would do everything in her power to make sure she returned to him.

She cleared her throat of unshed tears and grabbed Leo's hand. She gripped the stone and paper in the other hand. If it reduced the pain of the traveling through the portals as he said, did it mean he would suffer that pain in her place? It was touching, and she was coming to find out, so very Leo. He wouldn't show any outwards signs of his care, but when it mattered, he was there. She took a deep breath and they stepped into the portal.

The light was bright, so much so that she squinted against the glare of nothingness. Leo dropped her hand and moved through another intricate spell. It was warm in this realm, just shy of uncomfortable. Leo finally opened another portal and they stepped through and she felt relief at the cooler temperature. When she looked at Leo, his hands were moving through his spell, but slower. His face was pinched in pain. She felt none. Was it his amulet? She took it off and there was no difference, so she draped it across his head.

He whipped to her, his eyes wide, his mouth dropping open. She shrugged and signaled to him that she was fine. He stared a moment, more. His own body had relaxed and she assumed his necklace was working for him. He worked faster through the final portal. They stepped through and she looked around.

It was dead, all around them. A reddish-orange tinge to everything. There was desert behind them, but in front was a single, daunting gate. Leo touched her shoulder, she turned and recoiled at the sight of the guards. Twelve feet tall at least, onyx skin, stretched tight across their narrow faces. Their sharp cheekbones stood out, ridges raised along the skin of their face. They were bald, their skin shining, a terrifying beauty that made her avert her eyes for a moment. Her heart started hammering. Their fathomless eyes narrowed on her and she felt her head buzz.

Leo turned her to face him and pointed to the ground at his feet. He had to wait there, outside the gate for her. She nodded and stepped forward. The guards put their staffs together, blocking her entrance. Even with Leo's warning that she would be mute in the hell realm, she panicked as she opened her mouth and no sound emitted. She held up her necklace with a shaking hand to show the guards her father's marker. The gates behind them pushed open and out walked Azra.

He strode forward, his steps impatient. "Asa."

His voice was overly loud in the blanketing silence. She stared at her father, taking in his every feature, shook to finally be in his presence. Especially after learning that he'd been taking care of her in his own way for so many years. Tears sprang. He stepped closer and touched her forehead. Heat suffused her body.

"Do you have what you need?"

She nodded.

"You can speak," he said softly, longing covering his face.

"Yes," she cleared the roughness from her voice. She held up the stone and spell Brianna had written down. "I have everything I need."

"The messenger stone." He held out his hand, a relieved expression flitting across his face before it cleared.

She gave it to him and he held up a small piece of parchment and put the stone on it. A curl of smoke went up and letters burned onto the parchment. His lips moved as he read it. Light wavered around him, and she blinked as he went out of focus. She wiped her eyes and he was back to normal. The paper in his hands ignited, quickly burning, the ashes scattering at his feet. She gasped as he crushed the stone in his hand.

He looked up at her. "You won't need the stone. I can send you there, but you'll have to go alone. I can't follow you or help, daughter of mine. That was my price for giving you the information you needed."

"It's okay, you've done a lot. I'd rather face this head-on than to be tortured for the information later." She had to remind herself that the price for failure was torture and a war that could end the world.

He nodded and cupped her cheeks. "You're far more beautiful than I imagined. I'm sorry I couldn't be there for you—"

She put a hand on his arm to stop his words. "I know what you've done for me over the years."

His eyebrows winged high in surprise.

"Not now, but when this is over?" She prayed she'd get out of all of this alive so she could properly thank him.

He nodded and stepped back. "I can give you that which was bound in you." He touched her chest, over her heart.

Her eyes widened as heat filled her body. A rush of power enveloped her and for a moment she panicked, but in a split second, it was over.

"As I said, I can transport you there directly, but nothing more than that. That side of the realm…" he sighed. "I wish I had more time to teach you your powers. Be careful, *okan mi*. Remember what I told you."

She nodded, remembering her father's instruction about her unlocking powers. The magic coursed through her body getting stronger the longer she stood there.

Azra turned to Leo, "you can go."

Leo stepped forward and shook his head, still unable to talk.

Her father held up his hands and Leo's movement halted. "If she cannot find a way out on her own, then she is doomed to stay. Once she enters those gates, she cannot return to this point."

Leo's eyes widened a moment before a portal opened and he was sucked inside.

Azra turned back to Asa. "You must find your own way back, do you understand?"

"How?"

He cupped her cheek. "You are half mine, Asa, you hold power in this realm that no human or demi ever could."

She studied his lavender gaze and nodded after a quiet moment. "Ok."

He kissed her forehead and she felt wind pass her face. She closed her eyes against the strong breeze. When she opened them, she was in a dark spot.

Asa turned in a circle, a chill sliding down her spine. It wasn't pitch dark, but nearly so. She could see no farther than a couple of steps past her nose. Even through the boots she wore on her feet, the heated sand of the desert seeped into her. She bent over and picked up some of the hot sand. The black crystals drifted from her hand, carried on a wind that whipped through it. A pulsing light in the distance caught her eyes and she knew that was her destination.

She set out towards the light.

Chapter 27

Xavier tapped the pen on his desk, his leg bouncing as he fought to stay on task. There were so many little things that needed arranging, but thoughts of Asa crept in, trying to steal his concentration. His gut was churning, but, surprisingly his head was clear. He had his father to thank for that. Ranolph had been with him through every step of Haven's preparation, reinforcing lessons he'd taught Xavier his whole life. They went over battle plans, shored up weak points, and for once in a long time, he and his brothers and father had banded together. They all worked as a single unit, their father's training snapping into place.

Xavier stared at the screens of his comms station, moving around the pieces needed for the upcoming battle. He'd ordered all the doors to Haven sealed. Fallon had already carried that out, using magic that was frankly a little scary but effective. Nothing was getting in or out of the building until he deemed otherwise.

He'd given the Aje warriors weapons that would help them against the Demi and could only pray the spells Brianna built would work the way they were supposed to. His worry for Asa did have him on edge, though. He'd accomplished much through his insomnia. She'd been gone three days with no word and he'd given up trying to get into his human form. Small naps on the sofa in between planning were all he could manage and all of it in his Cagyn form. His beast was restless, and not since he was a kid had he had such a hard time controlling it.

He sighed and pushed his falling hair off his face. His comms rang and he pushed the call onto his computer screen. His brother's face appeared, worry coating his face.

"X, Lily says it's time."

"Kells?"

Leo nodded. "Iya has him secured."

Xavier breathed out a sigh of relief. Fallon and Brianna burst into his office.

"It's time," Brianna exclaimed.

"We'll set up here, take care of your mate," Xavier ordered his brother.

Fallon leaned over so that Leo could see him. "I sent you more guards, they should be showing up shortly."

"Thank you, brothers," Leo said. "See you on the other side of this."

Xavier nodded and ended the call. He looked up at Fallon. "The Aje?"

As if summoned, they entered the office. "Where do you need us?" Ajani asked.

Xavier thought about the strategies he'd been going over. "I want you on the roof, Brianna has to be protected at all costs."

Ajani nodded and stepped back.

Xavier stood. "Let's go."

They marched up to the roof and Brianna spread out the supplies she needed as well as her journal. She opened her comms and Liliana came into focus.

"How will we know when to start?" Lily asked in a worried voice.

Haven shook. Luckily they'd secured all the furniture yesterday, still, the water in the Olympic sized pool sloshed, some of it spilling over the side.

"Fuck," Fallon whispered.

Ajani inclined his head and the Aje warriors dispersed among the roof, making a wall across the whole thing.

Xavier called down to the security room. "What was that?"

"Someone is trying to blow their way into the building, but whatever Commander Tegan put over the building is holding. They're trying to take out the cameras surrounding the building at the moment."

He shook his head. Those cameras were bluffs for humans. The Amanda used the Oras to watch over Haven. Let them waste time trying to hide their identities. He'd find every last one of them if they managed to survive the upcoming skirmish.

Fallon cursed next to him. "I'm getting reports that the portal station at Chuita is under attack."

"Fuck, they know where she is."

"I got it covered," Fallon assured him.

Brianna went down to her knees and clutched her head. "It's starting, Fallon." She hurriedly slid her journal closer.

"I have you, you got this," Fallon kneeled next to his wife. He kissed her forehead and gripped her cheeks. "You got this."

She nodded and took a deep breath. Magic gathered and Xavier felt it press against the air. Brianna started mumbling, and all hell started breaking loose.

Ajani called out, "they're trying to climb up the building!"

Fallon kept a hold of his wife, but yelled to the warriors, "The spells will hold, just make every shot count."

The noise of the battle reached them. A battle cry sounded and Fallon looked at him grimly. "That's Lord Azra's call."

His communicator beeped and Xavier cursed. "They'll hold off the attack from the outside. It buys you a lot more time." He opened his comms.

"Marshal, there are Benu trying to force their way through the portal." The soldier reported.

"How many?"

"A shit ton of them." Was the male's answer.

Xavier looked to his brother. He wanted to be there, helping his brother protect his mate, but… "I have to—"

"—Go, we got this," Fallon prodded him.

He rushed downstairs.

###

The arid air of the surrounding desert made her throat dry and her eyes water, but Asa kept going. The light in the distance was pulsing brighter, lighting more of the landscape around it. Asa set out toward it. The sand in front of her started shifting, dunes lifting and retreating until the light in the distance grew dimmer. Was she losing it? She turned in a circle, the shifting sand confusing her sense of direction.

She sucked in a panicked breath and swung around again, the sands shifting faster, the dunes larger as they lifted from the flat terrain. Asa closed her eyes and took a deep breath, forcing calm throughout her body. Panicking would be the worst thing she could do. She held a fist to her heart and reached for the power moving around inside her body. Her father said she could control his realm. So she would try.

She gasped as magic filled her body, her skin tingling, little electric shocks moving up and down her arms and legs. She opened her eyes and swayed with vertigo as the sand dunes moved faster, seemingly spinning around her. She held out her arms, feeling the buzz coalesce to the tips of her fingers. She made a flattening motion with her hands and surprisingly, the sand obeyed, slamming to the ground.

Asa let out a nervous laugh as everything went still around her. It had worked. She slowly turned in a circle until she found the glow of her destination once again. She growled in frustration. She'd been going the wrong way! She turned in the right direction and started walking.

"Asa!"

She paused, her head tilted in confusion. Had her father come to help?

"Asa!"

No, it was a woman's voice. She turned off to her left where it was coming from. Deena was standing off in the distance, her face battered, her clothes torn.

"Look what you made him do!" Deena rasped getting closer.

Asa shook her head, her throat clogging as memories assailed her. No matter how hard she'd tried to be good, sometimes her temper got the best of her. And every time she'd snapped at Herman, he'd taken it out on her mother. There were many mornings she woke up to Deena in the kitchen, bruises blooming along her arm and neck. Not that Herman had not taken to slapping Asa, but he was more careful with her. The hate he felt for her, never quite spilling over as she'd expected. Now that she knew who her father was, the pieces were coming together. The hasty, urgent whispering between Herman and Deena, about consequences, made more sense.

Her mother being hurt for her words was effective in the end. It hadn't taken long for Asa to retreat into herself, some days never saying more than ten words when she was home. It had taken years after leaving college before she could afford therapy and even more years after that before she'd felt safe enough to open up to people.

Asa sucked in air as the vision of her mother moved closer. She knew it had to be a vision because no matter what Deena had done in life, it hadn't been enough to earn hell. Asa swiped the tears from her face and kept moving forward. She kept her face straight ahead, refusing to acknowledge the specter of her mother.

"I should have never had you! How much easier would my life had been without you?" Deena hissed.

Asa knew then that the ghost was throwing her every insecurity at her. Every guilt-ridden thought she'd had about their situation was spewed from Deena's mouth as she pushed forward. It hurt, but Asa kept her feet moving. Images of their fights played in her peripheral at a volume that drowned out the wind rising as she got closer to Ofeeree. Her chest seized as the image of her mother, lying dead in the morgue, flickered to life at her side. It seemed to fill the sky, and where the air was heated before, Asa shivered as she remembered the chill of the city morgue.

A sob escaped her, loosening the hold she had over her tears. Asa paused, going to her knees in grief, her body shaking as she cried. The urge to stay there in that spot and wallow overwhelmed her. She cried out for her mother, all the rage and unprocessed grief stealing her breath until her chest tightened. She slammed her hand into the hot sand, tears burning a track down her cheeks. All at once, all the points where she'd dabbed her mother's oil started to warm. The heavy feeling in her chest started to lighten and Asa took a huge, grateful breath. She looked down at her hands and gasped as they started glowing. She started chanting her mother's prayer, the glow getting brighter until the ghostlike images around her dissipated.

She jumped to her feet cursing the time she lost. She had to push on. Gathering strength, she marched towards the light getting brighter in the distance.

Asa stopped right next to the pulsing light emanating from the sand. There were tears still coming down her face, and her hands shook. She reminded herself that her father had promised her Deena was in a peaceful place. She wouldn't let the visions stop her from her task. She unfolded the sheet of paper, and with a shaky voice, started reading a line of spell Brianna had written at the top, separate from the binding spell.

A light flashed off to Asa's left and she tensed in dread expecting more horror images of her life. Instead, it was a vision of Brianna on the rooftop of Haven in the center of a circle and next to that, one of Liliana at a black beach that they'd told Asa was the family home on Chuita. All three of them were in place, bringing the Earth, the Demi realm, and now Hell together. Each of them clutched their portion of the binding spell.

Both women looked up, locking eyes onto Asa, waiting on her to start. She knew that once she started the chant she couldn't stop, so she turned her eyes to her own paper and took a deep breath.

It was time.

Asa started off slow, stumbling over the unfamiliar words until all at once they felt natural. In response the wind got harder, whipping around her, the sand pelting into her face and arms. At first, she couldn't feel it, the protective spell from her mother holding. But soon, the sheer power and persistence of the malevolent wind pushed through it. It left behind a trail of scratches, some deeper than others, burning across her skin. Before long, blood started a slow trickle down her arms from the wounds, but she spared it no glance. Everything was riding on her completing her task.

She raised her voice, and the other women's voices joined hers. As they chanted, a dark hand reached from a hole in the ground, ghostly images swirling the entrance. Fear had Asa's heart beating hard in her chest, but she kept going, bolstered by the feeling of the women she was coming to admire as sisters. The ground shook beneath her and she stumbled, landing hard on her knees but she didn't stop reading. The sand beat harder, blood flowing down her arms and neck faster than before, but Asa kept going.

Her breath caught as Deena's voice sounded over the wind, pleading with Asa to stop. Asa's voice was hoarse as she shouted the spell louder, rage and pain coalescing within, strengthening her determination to lock away the evil of Ofeeree. She could hear the strain in both Liliana and Brianna's voice as they continued to chant, knowing the women were also battling something on their end.

Asa was getting closer to the end of the spell. She had to dig her hand into the sand, to brace herself as the wind picked up, strong enough to push her around. Her blood flowed down into the dirt from her cuts and the sand lit up like crystals, brightening the landscape around her. Her father told her that her blood was needed to strengthen the binding of the spell and from the power raising around her, he was right. Her power filled her chest, and the world around her shook, a keening cry sounding out from Ofeeree's prison.

Chapter 28

Xavier ran into the portal room, sliding to a stop at the chaos in front of him. There were demons, flying Benu, and Gu, the iron giants, pushing their way through the portal despite the spell Fallon had put over it. His men were rushing into formation. The noise of it all swept over him and his heart picked up its rhythm. Panic never had time to set in though, because immediately his training snapped into place.

He moved forward, yelling over the din. "Amanda! Fall back formation."

The males followed direction, throwing off their human forms, a rush of magic filling the cavernous space. The Benu were the first to break through the portal, their wings keeping them above the fray of soldiers. The Benu in the Amanda launched high to reach the threat. The demons were next, the Abiku rushing his men. They came in, the magic in their scales fully activated. His men were trained to ignore the beguilement built into the demons, so he wasn't too worried. His soldiers fought to get into position, cutting down the Demi who'd managed to get in front of them.

Xavier manifested his sword and pushed his power into it, making it glow. He swung at the demon in front of him, slicing through its neck, kicking it from him as he made his way to his point position. He jumped over bodies, throwing up a shield as a giant punched down at him with its mace. Xavier shook from the power of that swing as it clashed against his shield. He pointed his sword towards it, shooting power at the Gu, growling in victory when it hit its mark. The giant barely made a sound as it fell backwards, taking some Ofeeree's followers with him.

Xavier hissed as a Benu broke through their line, slicing a cut across his thigh. An arrow whizzed by his head, before he could lift his sword, thunking into the Benu's neck, taking her down. The room was hazy from the magic being thrown around, but muscle memory had X moving into position, his sword moving almost of its own accord.

He cursed as he heard the whine of the portal before a flash and a whooping battle cry sounded. How many were coming? Would they over power his men? The first one out of the portal was the Benu Crown Prince, Harbinger staff in hand.

Fuck.

Friend or foe?

The prince looked out over the crush of bodies, found Xavier's eye, and nodded. Friend then. All the better. He rushed to the front of his men and he yelled out another order, snapping them to attention. They flanked the intruders at his next order, pushing the enemy between them and the forward pushing Benu led by the Crown Prince coming through the portal.

"Archers aside," he yelled, thanking the gods that he'd thought to pair an archer with a Benu. They would know who to aim at.

He'd already had Fallon put spells over the arrows. Every nock of their bows would mean death to whoever their arrow hit. He prayed their aim would be true and waded into battle. For a moment, even amid battle, his mind strayed to his mate. What would she be facing? That she would have to do it alone unsettled him.

That momentary lapse of concentration cost him as a demon clawed across his chest, splitting his shield and leaving a stripe of bloodied skin. It burned and he cursed before removing the Abiku's head from its shoulder. He needed to focus or Asa would be truly left alone.

He growled and kicked out at the Demi racing towards him. Sweat soaked his hair, the strands sticking to his face and neck as he fought. The room was muggy, the scent of blood and beast filling his senses and riling his battle lust. Power saturated his body and he funneled it into his sword. He would not be defeated, not in his house.

Asa kept chanting, her voice hoarse, her chest hurting with the effort it was taking to speak through the wind pelting her. Her hand was trembling, the paper shaking in her grasp, but she held tight. Sand crawled up her arms, seeming to feed off the blood of the cuts there. Power filled her body to the point of bursting and she screamed out the final words of the spell.

"Foolish child!" A raspy voice boomed throughout the dark.

Asa shivered at the power behind the voice, her skin crawling. Malice filled the air, taunting magic that had her stomach roiling, and fear seizing her body. The world swayed as Ofeeree tried one last time to push against the prison in which they were binding him. Urgency had Liliana's voice high, and something akin to panic filled Brianna's but neither of the women stopped their chant. Asa gripped the sand tighter, trying to brace against the wave of magic shaking the ground beneath her feet.

Color exploded around her, the cuts on her body burning, her muscles aching as she strained against the wind. As the last word was uttered, a fierce some cry rent the air, a noise Asa knew she'd hear in her nightmares for the rest of her life. But it was too late. The prison was set, the magic combined with her blood, cutting the last tie Ofeeree had to the world. The connection between the three women closed soon after and the image of Brianna and Liliana disappeared.

Asa bowed her head and closed her eyes in relief from the silence, her chest heaving as she sucked in the dry air. Her heavy breathing was the only thing audible in the night. She dropped to her butt, spreading her legs in front of her as all the energy seemed to leave her body. She needed to leave, but for now, she could barely move, never mind find the magic to poof out of this place. She laid onto her back and sucked in desperate breaths, fighting to slow her racing heart. She just needed a minute…

She swallowed past her parched throat and opened her eyes after what felt like hours, but she had no way of telling how long. She hadn't meant to fall asleep, but her body had had different plans. She needed to find a way out. She gasped at the crystallized sand under her palm, marveling at the glowing grains. She lifted her hand and it went dark. She stood and looked around, unsure of what to do. Her father had warned her that he wouldn't be able to help her get out of the hell realm. So she was on her own.

She put her hands on her hips, her mind frantically going through solutions. But, there was only one: she had to figure out her powers. She wiped a hand across her brow, groaning when it came back bloody. She wiped her bloody palm on her pants and took some deep breaths. Xavier made using his power look easy. He and Leo had opened a portal right in front of her, surely she could try and do it herself.

Asa waved her hands in front of her and thought hard about a way back to haven. She pushed out an irritated breath when nothing happened. Having no other solutions, she tried it again, this time closing her eyes and envisioning Xavier's office. She opened her eyes a few moments later and nothing had happened. She growled and kicked the sand beneath her feet.

Her father was a god for heaven's sake, she had power, it was swirling in her chest, sending electricity up and down her skin, she just had to figure out how to use it. She looked down at her hands and sighed. She didn't even know where to start. She paced the sand, her arms crossed over her chest. She blinked as blood slid down her face from who knew how many cuts and scrapes. She used her forearm to wipe it, steadily pacing. She gripped the coin on the end of her necklace and chewed her lip.

How to use magic…

She stopped and gasped. She used magic to pull Xavier into her dreams every night for a year. Could she reverse that same magic? She closed her eyes and thought of him. She'd thought thinking of his office would help, but what if he wasn't there? How long had she been gone, a few hours? She was anxious to see him and knew he'd feel the same way. He'd called her his soulmate, and now that all of this was over, they'd have time to explore that. No way would she get stuck in hell when that was in her future.

With every thought of him, her chest started to tighten, and the magic that had filled her when she fought to close Ofeeree's prison returned. She closed her eyes and brought up her memory of Xavier's face, the tender way he looked at her when he thought she couldn't see him. The bemused look on his face when she did something unexpected. She smiled and light turned her vision behind her eyelids red.

She was going home to him.

Wind whipped past her and her body seemed to spin until she lurched to a hard stop. She stumbled to her knees and opened her eyes. It was pitch dark outside and it was disorienting, but there was still sand beneath her palm. She was still in Hell. Growling, she closed her eyes and tried again. Tears of defeat clogged her throat by the sixth or seventh try, but she refused to give up. This time instead of only thinking of Xavier, she thought of how at home she felt in Haven. His family had accepted Asa, folding her into their shenanigans as though she belonged. The sense of family she felt around them was something she'd never felt outside of her mother and Damn it, she refused to lose that. She thought about the closeness she felt with Liliana and Brianna over the days they'd spent together, the three women would be forever tied by their experience. As the thought of the two came to her mind, Asa's chest warmed.

She frowned and put her palm over her heart. There was a weight there, an almost nagging presence that she wasn't quite alone in her body. Was it her magic? She closed her eyes and tried to concentrate on that feeling. As she did, images of Brianna in the library and Liliana tending to Kell popped up. Asa gasped, opening her eyes, and the wildest theories started playing through her mind. Panic started to overwhelm her, the implications staggering.

She needed to get back to Haven before she got trapped in the hell realm!

That sense of urgency spiked her power and Asa closed her eyes, focusing on Xavier the way she did in her dreams. Behind her eyelids, she saw a pinpoint of light pulsing, same as she did with Ofeeree, but this, she recognized as Xavier. Relief coursed through her, and instead of pulling that light towards her the way she did in dreams, she willed her body closer to it.

Same as before, her body spun, jarring to a hard stop moments later. She opened her eyes and this time there was no darkness. Instead, it was the last twinkling of city lights in the distance as they fought the beautiful streak of pinks and light blues transforming night into morning. Asa sucked in a great full lung full of moist, southern air.

She'd left Haven during the morning, and while she understood that time would pass, it was jarring seeing it. At least a day had passed while she battled in the hell realm. Her head spun and all at once, the cuts and bruises on her body bloomed, stealing her breath. Her chest tightened and her breathing shortened as her body fought to acclimate to its new surroundings. She dropped down to the soft grass beneath her and laid back. She'd just sit there for a few minutes until she got her equilibrium back.

She heard footsteps a moment before a guard stood over her, leaning down, his eyes widening.

"Asa?"

"That's me," she murmured, giving him a tired smile.

He stood and started speaking softly into a fancy device. He kneeled next to her when he was done, lifting her shoulders and bracing her against him.

"Let me help you down to the infirmary."

She waved him off. "Just give me a few moments please."

She closed her eyes and laid back down. Just a few minutes and she could get up on her own.

Chapter 29

Xavier sipped at the coffee in his mug, his eyes burning, and his hands shaking. He'd not slept in weeks and if this cup of coffee didn't work to get him out of his apartment, then nothing would. He closed his eyes and tried to work up the energy to get out of the chair. All around him was proof that his mother had been in his apartment, trying to help. There were pastry trays on the counter, fruit in baskets he knew he'd never owned, and flowers.

Flowers every damn where.

He was pretty sure she'd make an appearance at any moment to check on him like she'd been doing for the past three weeks. He could admit to loving the attention his mother was lavishing on him. Sharine was finally leaving the bitterness she'd been living with for so many centuries behind. He looked across his dining room table and spotted the box Asa had left there so many weeks ago. It sent piercing pain through him. He remembered her putting it there when they came back from her mother's house. Sharine had tried to move it as she went through his apartment cleaning up after him, but he'd barked at her to leave it.

It felt like the last normal thing they'd done, and he wanted the reminder.

Asa had been in Azreal for fifteen, no, today made sixteen days, and though he wouldn't say he was giving up hope, he was reaching the part in the waiting game where every hour felt like a whole day. But, he knew his mate was alive, he could feel her deep in the part of him where his instincts ruled. He'd sent his brother down to the hell realm, but Azra had refused to give him an audience. His mate was lost in the darkness of hell and he could do nothing to help her. He slapped the coffee cup down on the table fed up, hissing as the hot liquid splashed onto his hand.

He sighed when his front door beeped. He already knew who it would be.

"Iya, I'm not in the mood," he said as his mother rounded the corner.

"You're not in the mood for your mother to check on you? Well, too damn bad," she snapped, leaning down and kissing his forehead. "I don't know if you know this, but I could've lost my entire family in the war that was waged in this damned place, so you'll forgive me for hovering."

His mother was right, so he snapped his mouth shut. Not that he hadn't had confidence in his men, but it had been harrowing there for an hour or so. He stretched his legs out in front of him and drank more coffee.

"As you can see, I am alive and well this morning."

"Sarcasm is common," she grumbled.

He chuckled because if that wasn't the pot calling the kettle black. "What's on your mind this morning, *Iya*, you look like you're back up to your old tricks."

"I didn't come to start trouble," she said defensively. "I just wanted to know what you were going to do about your *di êjê*, now that this nastiness is over."

He growled. "My mate hasn't returned yet, so this 'nastiness' is not over."

"Of course, I understand that, Xavier. I just...we have to stay positive."

"Fuck positive," he hissed.

Sharine rolled her eyes. They both looked towards the door as it beeped again. This time it was his father. He groaned. Gods, he was not in the mood to hear the two of them arguing.

Ranolph paused at the entrance to Xavier's kitchen and cleared his throat. "I didn't know you had company, I can come back later."

"Goddess, this is ridiculous. Just come in, I'm not likely to curse you out while our son is suffering," Sharine snapped.

"That would be new," Xavier said into his mug as he took a fortifying sip.

His mother glared at him and sucked her teeth. She turned back to his father. "Would you like a cup of coffee?"

"Will you spit in it?" Ranolph asked deadpan.

"You should be so lucky," Sharine said with a saccharine smile.

"Gods above," Xavier whispered and closed his eyes.

He should've taken his ass to work. He could've maybe avoided his parents. "Did you want something, baba?"

Ranolph settled into the chair across from him and crossed his arms over his chest. "I wanted to know how you were handling the fallout from the skirmish."

"Skirmish? That was a bloody battle." Sharine placed a steaming coffee mug in front of Ranolph.

"All the same, how are the realms taking it?"

Xavier sighed, forcing his mind into work mode. "So far we've had most of the realms distancing themselves from Ofeeree's followers. The Benu are claiming that we're lying on their fallen kin. Prince Julian reported that they were having a hard time with his involvement."

"Are they demanding proof?" Ranolph took a wary sip of his coffee.

"I've sent surveillance footage where I could. Some of the magic around the battle was chaotic, but so far, the Eminzu are reviewing it and will get back each individual family complaining." He told his parents.

"What will the Eminzu do?"

Xavier shrugged. The ancestors were reluctant to get involved but with the number of prayers coming from the families for answers, they had to step in.

"We were lucky in that most of the followers killed were already banished from their realms. The ones we were able to capture are down below, awaiting trials."

"I'm sure that's a whole other set of problems," Ranolph commented.

Xavier nodded. Some of the families were in deep denial about the involvement of their family members. No one wanted to believe that they'd be a part of an uprising. He had their security room working around the clock to secure footage as proof. Once the trials started, he wanted the Amanda cleared of any claims of wrongful death.

"You're going to be busy for a while then." Sharine sighed.

His communicator rang, startling the three of them. His brother's face popped up, worry, elation all showing on his face.

"It's Asa, she's here," Fallon announced.

His heart beat a rapid tattoo as he jumped from his chair. "Where is she?"

"Down here in the infirmary," Fallon answered.

"I'm on my way." He ended the call, rushing from his room and through the halls.

The Demis still cleaning up from the battle moved from his path. He rushed into the room and paused at the door. His mate was there, her chest moving imperceptibly, but moving all the same. Her hair was a mass of kinky curls, spread along the pillow, much longer than it had been when she'd left. Her skin was a burnished onyx, and the tips of her ears were pointed. His eyes took in the tiny minute changes to her appearance as he realized something. She was in a Demi form, but more importantly, she was alive.

His knees hit the ground as relief overwhelmed him. Tahir was sweeping her body, his face a mask of concentration. Xavier sat on the floor, his heart pounding. Fallon slid onto the floor behind him as he came through the door.

"Brother," he whispered, putting his arms around Xavier's shoulder. "She's alive."

Xavier nodded, tears streaming down his face. He took a minute to compose himself and stood, Fallon helping him. He walked towards her, careful not to interrupt the Kira. When Tahir was finished, he stepped back.

"She's just sleeping as far as I can tell. I've helped her wounds along, though they were healing on their own." Tahir reported.

"Thank you for looking over her. I know you didn't have to," he said around the lump in his throat.

Tahir nodded. "I just so happen to be here visiting Fallon and Bri."

Xavier tuned the male out, taking his first good look at Asa. Her face was covered in scratches, her arms more so.

"Commander Tegan…Leo has said before that traveling to Azreal is particularly hard on the body. She'll wake soon." Tahir told him.

"Can I…will it be okay if I joined her in the bed?" He whispered.

"Of course, your touch will probably help."

"I'll go tell the others," Fallon said before turning to leave.

"Wait. Tahir, can I move her to our room?"

Tahir shared a look with Fallon. "I wouldn't advise it just yet."

Xavier gently crawled into the bed with her, clutching her in his arms. He took his first real breath in what felt like forever. He buried his face into the crook of her neck and wept. Fuck, his mate was safe, she was in his arms. He kissed the skin underneath her ear and breathed in her scent. He said her name over and over, a prayer of thanks that she was alive. She was different, even besides her Demi form. Her scent had changed, deepened. There was a dark smoky essence to her that was sensuous, even as she lay sleeping. Her father had marked her as his and it was all throughout her aura. Power surrounded her, the heat of it brushing against Xavier's own.

It gave him a moment of pause. How else would she have changed? What could she have faced in Azreal, and how would it reflect on her person? Would she still be the same Asa? He prayed so. He would take her however she allowed him to be in her life, but worry had him tightening his hold over her. He knew praying that she would be unscarred by the experience was naïve, but he prayed he could help her through whatever happened.

Her body stiffened, catching his attention. She opened her eyes and hissed before closing them back.

He cupped her cheeks. "Baby, say something."

"Something," she whispered. "Now can I go back to sleep?"

"Oh Gods." He pulled her into his arms.

"Let me get a look at her, X." Tahir rushed to her bedside and pried her from Xavier's arms. "Hello, Asa, remember me?"

She blinked and nodded. Tahir put his palm against her forehead. The warm flow of the Kira's magic filled the room. Asa's body relaxed and she breathed easier. She smiled and gave Tahir a sleepy thank you before going back to sleep. Xavier's eyes whipped to the Kira.

Tahir smiled. "She's just sleeping. You can take her to your room, now."

Xavier pulled her into his arms and gave himself just a few more minutes holding her.

###

Asa turned in a circle, her face bunched in confusion. She was just on the rooftop of Haven. Where was she now? The room was all white until it looked blank. Oh God was she dead?

"No, *okan mi*," her father answered behind her.

In front of her eyes, the room changed into a comfortable sitting room. She frowned recognizing it, but not sure why.

"Where is this place?"

"Your mother used to live in a place like this. It's where she first started visiting me."

She nodded, now remembering the pictures she'd seen of her mother younger.

Azra stopped in front of her, his eyes raking her. "You're alive."

"I am, though, my body is paying for it." She winced, remembering all the cuts and scratches her body had. She held her arms up. The wounds were there, but the pain was missing.

Azra looked relieved, pulling her into a tight hug. "You did well, daughter."

Pride suffused his face and in turn, filled her. Her father was proud of her. She got misty-eyed. At least until she remembered the revelations she'd had while she fought to get home. She stepped back from her father, narrowing her eyes.

"You broke the tether," she accused. "How?" Even though she suspected how she wanted to hear it from his own mouth.

"The Eshu did it for me."

"Liliana?" She frowned as her mind spun through the possibilities.

He'd burned the parchment with the beacon spell on it, it had seemed strange at the time, but she didn't understand how he could twist a location spell.

"The spell she put over the beacon, you…oh God." She turned and paced away. "You knew about her dreams of Ofeeree. They weren't only Ofeeree, though, were they? Brianna said you worked and visited people in dreams," she mumbled more to herself as she worked through it. "You went to Liliana in those dreams and planted the spell?"

Her father pulled up a chair and sat, crossing his leg over his knee. "The Eshu are messengers for the gods. Their power allows them to control gateways. It was her power, weaved with you and the human that allowed the gateway separating Ofeeree from the world to tighten. It couldn't have been done without her."

Asa sucked her teeth, trying to work out how that applied to her question. "But you sent me directly to Ofeeree, we didn't need the beacon to find him."

His lips lifted in a small smile, "no, but her spell over the beacon opened the gateway to my own prison."

She growled, grudgingly understanding what he'd done. Had she been trapped in a place for a millennium, would she have not done something to escape? Short answer: she would've done whatever it took.

"If you're free, what's tethering Ofeeree to his prison?" That was the question causing dread to pool in her belly. What had her father done to her in his quest to free himself?

He raised an eyebrow but said nothing. Her mind flitted through the whole process that she and the others had gone through.

"My blood," she whispered as it came to her. "You were insistent that I use my blood to bind the spell."

"You are of me," he said. "My flesh and blood."

"Mother fucker," she hissed, all at once understanding that his reputation was well earned.

If even his own daughter wasn't exempt from his trickery… then her mother had probably made the right decision in not trusting Azra. He was a trickster god, everyone had said so, and to see the evidence of it gave her another perspective on her mother. Had Deena seen it and known her father would always put himself first? A woman with a child making her way in an unfamiliar world, Azra wouldn't have been someone to count on. For Deena, Asa imagined Herman, for all his faults, felt stable. She took a deep breath and released some of the anger she was carrying for her mother. The images on the hell realm had shaken her, but uncovering her father's trickery…yeah, those options she'd thought her mother had had, perhaps were not there.

"So technically, your blood still binds him."

"Bingo," he smiled.

Her heart lurched and the remembered panic of her being unable to get out of the hell realm staggered her. "Will I be stuck in hell?" She whispered.

"Not at all, *okan mi*. But you are the living embodiment of his prison. All you have to do is live."

Her heart thumped with his implications. "The three of us, the spell we used tied the three of us to Ofeeree?"

He looked sheepish.

"Oh cut it out, you're in no way ashamed of yourself," she snapped.

She paced the room, her mind spinning with all the implications. She thought binding Ofeeree would make the three of them free, but they were in a more dangerous position than ever. Now, the only thing standing between an evil entity being free was their death.

He fixed his face, "Asa, I've kept you safe your whole life, I've done everything in my power to ensure your survival, I wouldn't stop now just because I'm free."

Yes, he'd kept her safe over the years, but how much of that was because he needed her to free himself. Damn, that hurt a little bit. It probably would've hurt more had she not grown up the way she had. Compartmentalizing her feelings was a skill she had, unfortunately, perfected.

"What will happen if the rest of the Demi find out that we three are the only things stopping Ofeeree from being free?"

He changed his form, going between he, she, they, short, tall, black, white, settling back into his original form. "It never needs to go any further than those involved."

She cursed. "How did you know Brianna would do the spell correctly?"

"How did I know the spell I planted on Minona would bind Ofeeree and thus the three of you?" He raised an eyebrow. "You forget her mate is one of mine, I have the same access to her dreams that I have to you and the Eshu."

She growled and threw her hands up. "You were fucking playing us all along."

She wanted to be super mad, but damn if the whole thing wasn't clever.

"I am self-serving in all things, but you are still very important to me, daughter. Weaved within Brianna's spell is a lifespan and protections that make the three of you damn hard to kill if that puts your mind at ease. I know it will put your mate's mind at ease once you finally tell him."

He seemed to know it was a given that she would tell Xavier. She put her hand over her face. Oh god, she had to tell Xavier what they'd done.

"He's going to hate you," she whispered.

He shrugged, "there is no shortage of creatures who do." he was unrepentant.

"I should be pissed at you."

"And had you been any other's daughter but my own, you probably would be. But as I said, we're disgustingly practical."

She sighed knowing he was right. Luckily for him, they were new enough in their relationship that he felt like a stranger still. The sting of his actions didn't quite penetrate the shell she'd built around her heart, despite the softening it had undergone from Xavier. She saw Azra for what he was and would move forward in their relationship with that in mind. There would be no romanticizing the father and daughter dynamics between the two of them. Azra was who he was and the honesty of that felt oddly freeing.

Damn.

She *was* disgustingly practical.

But, it had served her well all her life. She shook her head deciding to deal with her father's antics when she was more rested.

"Will your anger stop us from having a relationship, *okan mi*?"

She shook her head. "For better or for worse, you're my father, and I want to know you."

He looked relieved, standing and closing the distance between them. She accepted his hug.

"I just came to tell you that I made it home."

"And I am very proud of you. I'm sure your mate misses you after the weeks you've been off-realm."

Weeks?!

She jumped from the dream in panic, sitting straight up, breathing hard.

"Xavier," she whispered. Forcing her body awake. "Xavier," she whispered again, happy to feel him next to her.

"Here, love." He murmured, gathering her into his arms.

She reached around and felt the sheets of his bed. "Where am I, what happened?"

"You been gone a month. I thought we'd lost you." Xavier's sigh of relief brushed across the skin of her neck.

"I told you our girl was stronger than that," Leo said from the door.

Asa turned to him. "What happened?" She hurriedly touched her ring finger, exhaling in relief when she encountered her ring.

Leo came and sat on the edge of their bed. "Well, you in all your badassness, saved the world."

"Hey, she had some help." Liliana came to the door, their son on her hip.

Asa pushed out of her mate's arms and rushed to engulf his sister in law. That extra feeling in her heart rejoiced at their closeness. They were literally tied together now, and Asa could feel the other woman's relief. "We did it!"

"I have to admit, we were worried a little bit." Liliana gripped her tight.

"Only you," Brianna said smugly, coming around the corner.

She had a scar on her neck that hadn't been there when Asa had left but otherwise looked unharmed. It was when they locked eyes that Asa knew Brianna could also feel the binding tethering them together. They shared a look that communicated their new shared closeness, but also promised that they would wait until the three of them were alone before they discussed it.

"Why are all of you still here?" Xavier growled.

"It's called sitting vigil, brother," Fallon said, putting his arm around his wife's shoulder, nuzzling into her neck.

"What's up with the scar?" She asked Brianna, pulling her from Fallon's arms and hugging her.

"She won't let me heal it," Fallon complained.

"Hey, I earned this shit," Brianna answered with a smile.

Asa went back to Xavier in bed, cuddling under his arm. "Tell me everything."

"Later," Xavier interjected. "I want time with my mate."

"You're such a grump," Brianna tsked.

"Don't worry, Bri, we get her for the *di êjê* planning and there's nothing he can do about it." Liliana linked her arms with Brianna.

"Ugh, no thanks on wedding planning," Brianna said as the two of them left the room.

"Wedding planning?" Asa raised an eyebrow and looked at Xavier.

"That's our cue to leave," Leo said. He tugged Asa's feet. "Happy you're alive."

Fallon gave her a salute. "Welcome home, little sis."

Asa warmed, her eyes stinging. A few weeks ago, her only family had died, leaving her alone in the world. Now, she'd found the man of her dreams and a new family that welcomed her as though she was one of their own.

Xavier laid her back onto the bed, his eyes tracing her face. "How are you feeling, *elewa*?"

She wrapped her arms around his neck and brought his weight down on her. "Happy to be home."

He smiled and kissed her chin, nuzzling into her neck. "I was so worried."

"I didn't realize time moved differently there. A heads up would've been nice."

Xavier snorted against her skin. "Well, now that you know that, handle your visits with your father accordingly."

Her eyes widened as she realized that she could really visit her father, and not just in dreams. Even in the hell realm, she'd be able to go see him. She needed to ask Brianna about that, along with the other stuff. She had so much to learn about her new life. She turned her focus away from her father and back to her mate.

"Let's talk about this wedding business."

Epilogue

Asa rubbed her hands down her pants, nervous energy buzzing through her body. Her father flashed into her dream, looking around at the construct of her dream world.

"You're getting better," he commented.

She smiled. "You like?"

She'd built a new room for them to meet in. Even though her father was free, until she got better at her magic, and until she better understood him, as a god, she thought it safer to still visit in dreams. The space she'd constructed was white with wall to ceiling windows on one side, looking out into a desert landscape. The décor was a mix of southwestern hues of orange and browns with large green plants breaking up the color. Everything she'd seen of his realm was desert, so she thought it fitting.

He smiled. "I like that you want a place that's just ours."

Asa sighed in relief and walked to him, hugging him. His grip on her tightened.

"Today is your *di êjê*. Are you happy?"

"I am. I wish you could be there."

He pushed her hair behind her ear. "I wouldn't want to tempt fate."

She nodded, understanding. She stepped back from his embrace and twirled for him. She wanted her father to see the change that was all him. She was still getting used to the fact that she had a Demi form she could transform into. Her skin matched his, the ebony color darker than her normal skin tone, and shining with iridescence. It was beautiful, and she tried to spend a lot of time in it. Especially since she was in Chuita and not Earth. It was hard to keep the form in place though, but she was able to do so for longer periods with practice.

Her body defaulted to human when she wasn't paying attention, but she was getting there.

"I only had a few minutes before the *di êjê*, but I wanted to see you today and let you know I was thinking of you."

He swallowed, his eyes softening. "Oh, Asa, you are a miracle. Good luck on your very special day."

"Thank you, dad. I'll be back to see you soon." She promised.

His smiling face was the last image she saw before she woke. She opened her eyes to find her soon to be sisters-in-law and Chandra staring down at her in bed,

"Seriously, girl," Brianna sucked her teeth and put her hands on her hips.

Asa snorted and threw her feet over the edge of the bed. "What, I wanted to visit my father before the ceremony."

"I can't believe you're not mad as hell," Brianna grumbled. "If he wasn't so scary, I'd love to give him a piece of my mind."

Asa hid her smirk. Understandably, Brianna and Liliana hadn't taken the news of being tethered to Ofeeree quite as easily as she had. The guys even less so. They'd all been pissed and rightfully so. Fallon had apologized to them all, taking it on himself because he'd made a deal with Azra without considering the full impact on his family. It had taken her weeks to get them to understand that Azra would've carried out his plan with or without their permission or consent. It was a part of who her father was. Still, Brianna was 'holding onto her petty', she'd said.

"Well, there's not much time for you to play around. Hurry and get into your gown," Chandra fussed, turning her wheelchair towards Asa's robe laid over a chair in the corner of the room.

"Always bossing me around," Asa joked with her friend.

"It's the only way to get you to do anything," Chandra parried back.

Liliana clapped her hands. "Let's go ladies. We gotta get you down to the beach, Asa."

Asa shed her clothes in front of them and wrapped the robe around her body.

"So, no modesty. The ceremony should be easy enough for you," Brianna mumbled under her breath.

Liliana snorted. "We've seen her soul, you cannot possibly be bothered by a pair of tits."

Asa snickered and tied the belt around her waist. "Lily, are you going to use your magic to do my hair?"

"With pleasure," Liliana said, cracking her knuckles.

Brianna stepped closer to her and pulled Asa's robe to the side, sighing at the three triangles nestled together in a tri-force on her chest. It looked scorched into Asa's skin matching the marks on both Liliana and Brianna. It was the only outward sign of the tethering that bonded the three women.

Asa gripped Brianna's arms. "It's fine, Bri. We're badass, remember?"

"It's all worth it in the end," Liliana whispered.

###

Xavier adjusted his robe and tried to control his heartbeat. It was damn near galloping from his chest. The Shaman was already in the water and now he waited for his mate to take the path down from their family's home. The women had outdone themselves. The path was lit with twinkling lights, and flower petals scattered the beach sand.

His beast roiled beneath his skin and his magic spiked, raising the hair on his neck. It announced the presence of his mate. He straightened his spine and let out a breath of relief as Asa marched down the beach towards him. She was in her Demi form, her skin reflecting the moonlight, and mesmerizing him. She smiled and his heart melted. She stopped in front of him, water lapping at their toes.

"You ready, elewa?" He whispered.

"More than, Mr. X," was her answer as she dropped her robe.

The full moon bathed her skin, making the onyx glow in the light. His mouth started watering, and all the blood in his body rushed south, fueling his erection. He dropped his robe and took pleasure in the way her eyes widened. He grabbed her hand and guided her into the water.

Her grip tightened on his hand as they got waist-deep into the water. Her breath hitched when it reached her chest. Her body was tense as they reached the shaman.

"I got you, elewa," he murmured into her ear, holding her tight until she relaxed.

She nodded and he waved for the shaman to start.

The shaman started and magic filled the air around them. Asa's skin started to glow as the first cord wound around their wrists. The second moved around their heads, the warmth of the shaman's magic heating as the binding spell progressed. He threw his head back in elation when the heart cord activated, displaying a solid gold cord between her chest and his. His teeth grew and his beast moved forward hungrily, his power raising.

He leaned forward and Asa moved her head to the side, allowing his bite. He took his time, kissing her skin first, licking over the spot where he wanted to bite. She shuddered, her eyes dropping to half-mast. He finally bit down, moaning as her blood filled his mouth. He swallowed it down, her power filling him, melding with his own. It felt like he'd waited his whole life for this moment with her. He reveled in it, sucking at her neck, even after he closed the wound.

He moved back, drunk off the magic. He was in awe, the full weight of her power humbled him. After all, she was the daughter of a god. He knew anyone who mated him would have had to be strong. The fates more than delivered in Asa.

Asa's eyes lit, the lavender color bright. She smiled, showing off her two pointy incisors. She bent over his chest and bit down, right over his heart. He went up in flames. They'd tried to warn him about how the di êjê would affect him, but there was no way to prepare for this moment. The moment he could feel his mate moving through his soul. Her presence was in the back of his mind, a warm buzz of contentment. She licked across his chest to close her bite and it took everything in him to stand still while the shaman finished the ceremony.

The chanting ended moments later, the gold of the magic tying them together dispersing into small embers before it disappeared. The shaman moved around them, leaving the water. He held his mate's gaze, warning her with his eyes of what was to come.

Heat, as she'd never felt, was flowing through Asa's body. She was having a hard time standing still in the water. Every wave lapped across her skin, a caress that heightened her lust until her body was shaking with it. Once the magic ropes wrapped around their body disappeared, the shaman left them in the water. Xavier was staring down at her and her clit was throbbing with need. A growl rattled his chest and he tilted his head, listening. She didn't hear the shaman leave the water, but he must have because he lifted her, wrapping her legs around his waist.

"Need you," he growled before devouring her mouth.

She reached down with desperate hands, guiding his shaft to her sex. They moaned together as he pushed inside, pushing through her clenching channel. She gripped his hair, her nails scoring his scalp as he moved his hips, seating in to the hilt. His fingertips pressed into her skin as he lifted her and pulled her back down. She arched her back, relishing every stroke. Her feet pressed into his ass, fighting for purchase on his slippery body. She wanted him deeper, harder.

Xavier growled, and lifted her hips, slamming down again and again. They were fighting against the water, his movements slow and methodical. Pleasure rocked through her. Her increasingly loud cries sounded in the still night. She leaned forward and scraped her teeth along his neck. His response was a harder stroke, water splashing around them. The sex was frantic, a carnal joining that she would never forget. Her stomach clenched, and her legs tightened as an orgasm exploded through her. She bit down on his shoulder to stop her cry. He threw his head back and with one final deep stroke, came inside her.

"Fuck, fuck, fuck," he murmured, kissing her neck, holding her tight against his chest.

They stayed in the ocean, the water lapping against them until they came down from their high.

"You okay?" he whispered.

She licked against his skin, tasting the salty air. "More than."

He hummed and walked them towards the shore. He was still inside her, his shaft getting thicker, going hard again with his every step. By the time his feet hit the sand, she was wiggling her hips in anticipation. He walked her further onto the beach and laid her down on a blanket. This time, he took his time. His strokes, slow, torturous. Brianna and Liliana told her that the period after her ceremony would be amazing, but she didn't think their words did it justice. Xavier was insatiable, and she equally ravenous. Their second time was slower, their gazes joined as they enjoyed the closeness of their new bond.

Xavier closed his eyes as Asa squeezed around him, a sign her climax was nearing. He wanted to stretch it out and wallow in the feeling of being inside her. But every clench of her sex around his dick was sending him closer coming himself. He lifted her leg higher, putting her ankle onto his shoulder, pushing in as deep as he could go. She moaned and arched, grabbing her breasts, fondling the nipples.

That touch did it, and she exploded around his erection. He pulled out and slammed home one final time, his orgasm sending chills down his spine. He collapsed on top of her, his hips jerking in ecstasy. She wrapped her arms around him and sighed. Her soft kisses clenched his heart and he floated, content and happier than he'd ever been in his life.

She was finally his. His fantasy come to life. To think it all started with a dream.

Now that they were bonded he also felt the tether on her soul, and the tie the three women shared. It brought home just how close he'd come to losing Asa. He gripped her tighter, grateful for the safety measures her father had put in the spell. Yes, Azra had used them, but he was as practical as his new mate, and knowing her father had made her stronger than before was worth it to him. He was glad Asa felt the same. It was reassuring how alike they thought. It also meant that Asa would treat his father's machinations in the same way, seeing through Ranolph's own games he played with his children's lives. They would hopefully have centuries together, and it was a point of pride for him that his mate could maneuver with the best of them.

He heard the whistle in the distance and knew that signaled that his brothers were coming to interrupt. Xavier growled and pulled out. He conjured a robe on them both and lay next to his mate, debating how he'd sneak past his mother. If he could get past Sharine—who he knew was waiting at the top of the only entrance into the house from the beach— he could lock him and Asa in his room and skip the rest of the party.

Asa smiled and wrapped her arms around his waist. "Don't you worry. The girls clued me in. I have a plan. Close your eyes with me."

He kissed her, realizing his mate would always have an escape plan. The woman was brave, and damn near fearless, and had survived a trip to hell, of course, a wedding party wouldn't faze her.

About the Author

I am a full time photographer, and a mom of two. I've been writing my whole life, and after the birth of my first kid, I decided I couldn't very well bring up a fearless human without first trying the things that scared me. So, I wrote my first book, and then subsequently more.

I try to write stories I love to read: love stories that feature brown girls like me. Some of my stories feature gods and goddesses, and creatures I derived from old, African folk tales remixed and thrust into a modern world. Visit my website, www.driaandersen.com for more information on my other novels.

Other titles by Dria Andersen

Chasing Savannah

Hers to Call

Novellas

The Friend Contract

Destiny Series

A Destiny Awakened

A Destiny Revealed

Haven Series

Haven

Soul Bonded